Obscure Felicity

CHARLOTTE WOODLAND

Print ISBN: 978-1-66781-591-6
eBook ISBN: 978-1-66781-592-3

For John, my Assistant Muse

&

For Skip, forever and always in my heart

PROLOGUE

"May I have a closer look at your tattoos? They're fascinating," Brenda asks with a smile. She hopes she's not being too forward, but figures that given the way the young woman is dressed, plus the fact that she spent a fortune on her inked skin, she'll be quite happy to allow a closer look.

The young woman brightens, and points to the intricate tangled vines interlaced with flowers circling her arm. "These I just had done a few months ago."

"They're magnificent, almost three-dimensional. How do you choose what to get tattooed and where? Does everything mean something?" Brenda asks, while continuing to closely look at each visible tattoo with an artist's eye.

"Oh, it just comes to me, or they have this huge book that has every ink imaginable. It's kind of addictive. When I'm feeling sad or need a change, I end up at *Skin Deep* getting needled with tears rolling down my face, and I love it. They're really awesome about helping you figure out what would look good and where. Some places hurt more than others, but I feel like my body is becoming a work of art. I dream about tattoos, think about them all the time. I'm obsessed."

"Quite impressive. The person who did these is a talented artist," Brenda says as she starts to peruse the young woman's tattoos to the point where the girl wants to pull away, feeling a little embarrassed to have a stranger touching and examining her so intimately. Brenda senses this and steps back, saying, "Sorry, got carried away. Just never really thought about tattoos as art like this before. Interesting. Well, thank you for the closer look."

"No worries; glad you like them. My parents hate them, so it's nice that someone older— not that you're *that* old—likes them," the girl smiles again, and turns to leave.

The barista and his coworker behind the counter share a covert glance and eye-roll knowingly. Brenda's in the little coffee shop several times a week. They like her, most everyone likes her, but at times they find her somewhat eccentric. They can tell that she perceives things differently than most people, as though she knows something, sees something that they don't. People find it strange when she gets that distant look in her eyes, knowing something they can't imagine is going on inside her head. She'll suddenly stop talking, cock her head as though listening for something, and then come back to herself with a strange expression on her face. It takes a few seconds, an almost indiscernible shake of her head, and she's back as if there were no interlude, or fugue, or whatever it was.

They find her interesting; and the servers in the coffee shop, as well as the regular patrons, know a lot about Brenda's life, as she's a talker. They think she's embellishing, or more like exaggerating, some of the time, and she often speaks at a level they don't always understand. Some think she's brilliant, and others find her too airy-fairy for their tastes. When she talks about her life, she gets carried away; they can't help but wonder if maybe she's leaving out a few even more unbelievable details of what happened. Brenda makes you want to know more, yet you're not even sure what you should ask. She's a mystery, not yet willing to divulge the real Brenda, only throwing out bits and pieces and leaving you wondering who she really is.

Maybe her stories are closely based on something that really did happen, but with some fantasy elements mixed in. Or maybe she just wants to keep you interested. What they don't know is that on the days when Brenda doesn't make her rounds to the coffee shop, she's closed off in her studio painting like a madwoman, the inspiration pouring through her as if her creative genius has an abundance that she doesn't know what to do with.

Today's a good day, and she's still feeling the aftereffects of a recent creative high— satisfied, peaceful, and reflective. She looks around the shop to see if there's anyone else interesting she might strike up a conversation with. The bell above the door jingles, and a scraggly looking young man in a faded T-shirt and jeans comes in. He looks around after getting his coffee, and catches Brenda's eye. She pats the seat next to her and says, "You can share my table if you want."

He's surprised by this, thinks about saying *no thanks*, shrugs, and comes over and sits down.

"Are you in school here?" she asks to break the silence.

"Yeah, one more year to go."

"What's your major?"

"I'm studying to be a geologist. I love the Earth; I'm really interested in the processes that shaped the Earth. Besides rocks and minerals there are earthquakes, volcanos, other things that can be studied to prepare people for natural disasters. There are many areas I can focus on, and I can be out in the field conducting research in some of the most geologically amazing places on the planet. I love that part."

"Hmm, yes, that sounds wonderful; seems you've found your passion. Have you ever spent the night in the desert?" Brenda asks with a raised eyebrow.

"Uh, no. Can't say that I have yet. But I'd definitely like to. I love the desert and what all its formations can tell us about the processes that shaped it, the beauty of what our planet is made of. How it's changed throughout geological time."

The young man goes on and on about rocks, earth, and minerals, but Brenda's stopped listening. She's no longer in the coffee shop; she's looking up at the stars in the inky black sky of the desert, so abundant and close she can reach out and touch them. So close, she can feel them move with a sweep of her hand. So bright and full. The desert at night: stunning, terrifying, alive.

He stops talking and watches her for a few seconds, realizing she's drifted off to another place only she can see. She looks past him to that faraway place, and as he looks at her, he gets an odd feeling he can't identify that makes him squirm. He blinks and breaks the thing that's pulling him in. He gets a slight sense of that fight-or-flight phenomenon, and his heart is racing. He feels like he was almost in the place she was for a few seconds.

Brenda shakes her head a little and asks slowly, "Have you ever had a memory so strong, so real, you see it in your mind exactly as it was, and feel it in your heart exactly as you felt?"

The young man's eyes dart back and forth as he thinks about it, not knowing what to say.

"Yes, you *should* spend the night in the desert. It will show you everything's different than what you think you know. It will take your soul, and will give it back to you fuller than it was. In the morning, the sun will send its wavelengths of light into your eyes and you'll question what you saw, but know you've been changed." Brenda sighs and leans back in her chair, suddenly feeling very tired.

The young man still doesn't know what to think, and finally he says, "Okay, I'll definitely spend the night in the desert, but you make it sound a little scary or something."

"Not scary, just enlightening," she says as she gets to her feet, shakes out her long skirt, and reaches down to pick up her well-worn red leather satchel. With a wave of her hand, she starts towards the door and says what she always says when she's leaving, "See you soon, it's been real." They all laugh, but the young man still looks a little puzzled.

"Don't forget your sunglasses, Brenda," the barista calls to her. "If you keep leaving them here, I'm going to keep them."

"Oh no, can't forget them! These glasses are my new favorite pair, one of a kind—hand-painted the frames myself," Brenda says as she puts them on.

"Well then, stop forgetting them. See these?" he asks as he picks up a pair behind the counter and puts them on. "Some guy left these a couple weeks ago and never came back for them. I feel kind of bad about it since they're really good quality, but I'm going to keep them if he's not back to claim them soon."

Brenda looks back at the barista, then stills completely as she focuses on the sunglasses. Listening to the thumping of her heart, she has a very unsettling feeling come over her. She suddenly gets a vivid vision of Vincent with his eyes so clear, his smile so bright. She almost asks if she can have a closer look at the glasses, but something tells her to leave well enough alone. *Nah, it can't be,* she thinks as she shakes her head, *it just can't be.*

Instead, she asks, "Did I ever tell you about my Vincent and the designer sunglasses we used to make?" The coworkers nod, even though they don't really recall much about the sunglasses. Looking away, they both pretend they have cups to wash, coffee to make. They've had enough conversation with Brenda for one day, knowing there will be many more to come.

After the door closes behind her, the young man looks up and says to no one in particular, "Wow, that was interesting. Do you know her? Who is she?"

The barista looks up and thinks for a few seconds before answering. "That's Brenda. She's our famous local artist. Her work is incredible, and she really is quite famous. A bit strange, definitely different. We're still trying to decide if she's brilliant, or a little nuts. From the way she talks, if her stories are true, she's had quite a life. She knows a lot, and has certainly seen a lot. A mystery, though."

CHAPTER 1

He's really glad his roommate has that early class this morning; now he can have the apartment all to himself. Opening the window, he looks out to see it's going to be a nice weather day for a change. He watches the few cars along the road and is surprised it's still so quiet. Lighting up a joint, he takes a deep hit, then watches the smoke swirl as he blows it out the window. The weed is soon doing its job, and everything starts to look brighter and funnier. Finishing the entire joint, he finds himself contemplating life, enjoying for the time being the humorous side of things. He doesn't allow himself to think about any of his worries, and mentally pulls himself away from going down that rabbit hole. For some reason, whenever he's high, Vincent starts reminiscing about his childhood, and the sad parts take center stage.

After eating and showering, he looks at the clock and realizes he still has an hour before he has to head to class. Time really does seem to slow down this morning, and he feels really good for a change, glad the weed is the *up* kind, and not the depressing shit the stoners are always trying to sell him. Vincent gathers up his books and heads towards the door, figuring he'll hang out on campus before class since it's such a nice day. *Damn, I feel good today. Maybe it'll be a fine day, one of those stellar kinds where things line up and you can do no wrong.*

The picture of his parents on the table by the door catches his eye, and he feels the familiar tightening in his stomach. The photo is about eight years old, and from better days. From when his Mom was still alive, his parents not divorced. They look so happy, and his Mom looks so pretty with her big smile and cool sunglasses. Those were better days for sure. *I miss having days where I have nothing to worry about, no loneliness.*

On campus, he wanders through the quads towards where his next class is and decides to sit on a side lawn and soak in some sun. Seeing a guy he knows, he walks over and plops down. "Hey, Mark."

"Hey, Vince, what's happening?"

"Nada," he says while he lies back and closes his eyes. "Just digging the day, you know?"

Mark doesn't answer, just nods and gazes out at the people walking about. He suddenly sits up straight and asks, "Hey, who's that? Who's that girl with all the brown curly hair and sexy walk?"

"Who, where?"

"Over there, by the water fountain talking to that guy."

Vincent looks over to where Mark's pointing and sees the prettiest girl he's ever seen in his life. As he looks her over, he gets a flash of his mother, and thinks the girl kind of looks like his Mom did when she was young. She has the same smile. *Interesting; wonder who she is.* He gets an overwhelming feeling that he must meet her, almost feeling like he knows her from somewhere. He sits up, then jumps to his feet and starts walking towards her.

"Hey, where are you going?" Mark calls from behind him.

Vincent turns around and says, "Have to find out who she is."

"Wait, I'll come with you."

Vincent doesn't wait, walking quickly towards where the girl's standing, chatting to a guy who seems very interested in what she's saying. As he gets closer, he tries to think of a good opening line, but nothing comes to mind. He feels kind of hot, and hopes his face isn't red and his nervousness doesn't show. He's usually confident with women, but now he feels anxious and different.

As he approaches, they both look over and he walks past, going to the drinking fountain as though that was his intention all along. He takes a drink and looks up to see the pretty girl looking at him. He wipes his mouth and suavely says, "Hi."

Duh, he thinks, *how creative*. She keeps looking at him and says, "Hi," back to him and they have eye contact—long enough for him to notice her pupils dilate. *Ah, that's a good sign for sure. The eyes are a giveaway, the mirror of one's soul and emotions*, he thinks, as he feels his heart beating faster.

The guy she's talking to looks back and forth between them and shifts his feet a bit, noticing the long look they're sharing. "I've got to go, Brenda," he says as he holds his books closer to his chest. "I'll catch up with you later."

"Bye, Josh," she says, quickly glancing over to him and flashing him a smile.

With Josh out of the way, Vincent approaches and says, "So you're Brenda. Nice name. I'm Vincent. I have a class in about twenty minutes. Do you have time to talk a little?"

"Sure, we can even talk a lot if you want." She laughs self-consciously. "I'm taking a short break from the piece I'm working on. Been having some difficulty bringing it alive the way I want it to look. It's not conveying the motion I need. Kind of frustrating," she says as she points to the art portfolio case she has propped against her leg. "I thought getting away from it for a while would give me a new perspective. You know how you can get so involved with making something work that it gets away from you?"

"Yeah, I get it. I'm not an artist, though. I can barely draw a stick figure. But when I'm working on a project, I get so involved I forget to eat or even sleep sometimes. It's like I get too involved, and realize once I do take a break, I feel that I'm missing something. My Mom used to say 'Don't forget to breathe' when I was a kid working on one of my chemistry experiments. I would realize when she said that I actually was holding my breath, like that was going to help anything. No wonder I felt lightheaded all the time."

Brenda laughs and then asks, "What kind of experiments? I hope you didn't blow up your house or anything."

"Ha, not quite! But I was known to create some really stinky stuff that got me in trouble. I had a little lab set up in the basement, and my Mom would yell down for me to open the window, and stop whatever it was I was doing, I was stinking up the whole house. She was really patient, though, and always encouraged me to do what I found interesting."

Now they're both laughing, but Vincent finds he has tears in his eyes from the memory. Brenda notices and thinks he must be a sensitive guy. Looking away for a few seconds so as not to embarrass him, she tries to think of something else to say. Looking up again, she finds him searching her face. They just keep looking at each other, and the connection is so obvious they keep looking, and eventually smile, then break eye contact.

"Well, I do need to head to class. It's probably my favorite course this semester—Optical Metrology. I don't want to be late; the professor is a real stickler about being on time."

Brenda's curious to know more, and is about to ask some questions when Vincent says, "Sorry for talking so much about myself. I really meant to learn more about you. Can we meet up later for coffee?"

"I'd like that, but I'm pretty much tied up for the rest of today. Tomorrow, maybe? Can we meet for an early breakfast in the dining hall? The pancakes are decent. Around 7:30?"

"That works. I'll look forward to it. See you then." He turns to leave, looks back, and sees she's still looking at him. With a smile, he walks away, and has to keep himself from turning around to see if she's still looking. *Damn, I knew it was going to be a good day. I knew it,* he thinks as he starts humming softly to himself and increases his pace.

He makes it to his class in plenty of time, gets his notebook ready, and looks around. He makes a conscious effort to stop thinking about Brenda and looks to the front of the room, where Professor Krauss is writing today's topics on the board. As he looks over the questions, he finds himself drawn into the subjects at hand, and starts thinking about whether the lines in the spectrum of a continuous-wave laser are exactly equidistant.

#

She watches Vincent walk away for just a second or two, then turns quickly, so as not to be caught staring. *Oh my God! Did that just happen? I can feel my heart beating like a drum and my face hurts a little from smiling. Vincent, Vincent, Vincent. What kind of name is that? I'm so excited I can't think. That dark thick hair and those hazel eyes, I could get lost in those eyes. What should I wear tomorrow, will he even notice? He likes me, I can tell. This type of thing never happens to me, I can't believe it!* These thoughts are swirling around in her head as she walks back to her dorm room. She slows her pace and looks around, and finds that everything looks a little better. The grass is greener, the clouds are fluffier, her body feels lighter, and she feels like running, jumping, laughing.

"What's up with you, goofball?" her roommate Sarah asks, as Brenda flings the door open. "You look like the cat that just ate the proverbial canary."

"Oh, I just met the most amazing guy. It was weird how we clicked in such a short time. It was like we fell into each other's eyes. I could see inside of him."

"Whoa, that sounds so corny, like a movie script. Nobody says stuff like that."

Brenda laughs, "Well that's how I feel. I can't help it. I'm going to have breakfast with him tomorrow morning. We met by the water fountain. He seems brainy but also cool, kind of sensitive, and actually didn't complain about going to class. He was almost anxious to get there, something called Optical Metrology or Optical Mythology."

"What? It can't be mythology, I don't think. Whatever, you're acting goofy. I think that's a good thing. How's that last piece you were working on? Any progress? I know you were stressed about it."

"I feel more inspired now. Ha, I wonder why. Actually, I'm going to work on it now."

"Okay, I'll leave you be. Wish me luck on my psych exam."

Brenda gives Sarah a thumbs-up as she closes the door, and goes back to daydreaming about Vincent. With a slight shake of her head, she starts focusing on the drawing she needs to work on, and pulls it out of her portfolio case. Eyeing the sketch critically, she thinks about what Professor Jane said about her work during their last one-on-one. *She said I have talent, a lot of talent, but I'm holding back. Afraid of criticism, afraid to show through my work who I really am, what I can really do. I think she's right, in a way. It's like I feel I'm a fraud, not good enough to pass as an artist, not talented enough to really think I can go anywhere with it.*

I hate feeling this way at times, and the real me knows it's not true. I am *worthy, I* am *talented, I am beautiful! Well not sure about that last one.* "Ha," she says out loud, and chuckles. *I can do this; my last piece practically bled out of me, and everyone in class raved about it. I did feel kind of funny about it, but also felt like a gate opened from somewhere, and the muse I keep locked up got out and was finally free. I wish I could feel like that more often. I'm feeling like that now, though,* she thinks as she starts drawing in earnest, working her way around the sketch and bringing it to life. Before long, it comes alive even better than she'd envisioned. Her mind's eye flows onto and into the sketch with ease. Without realizing it, she's drawn a very small figure in the grass, barely visible, almost indiscernible unless you're looking for it. *That's my muse, right there. Come out, come out, I like having you around.* She smiles to herself. With just the finishing touches left, Brenda stands back, viewing her work as the door opens and Sarah bursts in and throws herself on the bed.

"I aced it. I think. All that studying paid off. I'm pretty sure I aced it. But now I feel so tired after taxing my poor brain so much," Sarah says as she closes her eyes. "I need a nap."

"Good for you! But before you go off to La-La Land, I want you to take a look at this and give me your honest opinion, please."

Sarah pulls herself up off the bed and comes over to see the sketch. "Holy shit, that's awesome. I mean it, wow! Wait, give me a minute to really look at it. I see so much here, it's beautiful… I'm having trouble finding the words to describe how it makes me feel. It's as though you poured your heart and soul into this. It may be the best piece you've ever done."

"Thanks! Do you really think so? Do you see anything special?"

"It's all special the way it flows from one thing to the next, like the cycle of life but without being obvious, you know what I mean? You need to think about what you're seeing, and yet it keeps changing. How do you do that?"

"Yes, yes, exactly! I'm so glad you can see it, the way I felt it, when I was drawing it. I feel like I'm on this incredible high; the energy is coming from somewhere different, a different place. Hard to explain. I think I need a nap too, before I completely drain myself."

"Don't you have that meeting thing in a little while?" Sarah asks.

"Yes, but not for another hour, so I have time for a quick nap. I'll set an alarm for forty- five minutes. Sound good?"

"Sounds like a plan," Sarah says as she lays back down, sighs deeply, and closes her eyes.

Brenda closes the shade and snuggles into her blanket, but can't stop her churning thoughts. She hasn't told anyone about seeing the school counselor once a week since the beginning of last semester. Dr. Cherry has helped her so much, and she's grateful to know she's not crazy, suffering from depression, or anything weird like that. She's a victim of toxic parents, and fortunately, according to Dr. Cherry, able to overcome a lot of the negative stuff they subjected her to. Brenda remembers Dr. Cherry telling her most people live their entire lives not necessarily realizing the fault is not with them, but with their parents, or other negative influencers at an early age. She still doesn't want to tell anyone she's seeing Dr. Cherry, because she's afraid they'll see it as a weakness. She wonders if Sarah is onto her, and knows about her weekly *meetings. Things are looking up, though; maybe I'll tell Sarah about Dr. Cherry after my next session.*

As she starts to doze off, her thoughts return to Vincent, and she can't wait until tomorrow morning to see him again. Maybe she'll bring her latest sketch. That will give him some insight into who she is, how she thinks, what she can do. She wonders if she should tell Dr. Cherry about him… or is it too soon? The image of her little muse from the drawing comes to mind, and for some reason right before she tips into sleep, she pictures the muse with a tiny pair of sunglasses on.

CHAPTER 2

Brenda feels rested after her nap, and is in high spirits when she gets to Dr. Cherry's office a few minutes before her appointment. On the way over, she thinks about what they discussed last week, and what she wants to talk about today. Her foremost thought is wanting to tell her about meeting Vincent, even though she hardly knows him at all. *It's the type of thing I would want to tell my mother, if she even cared enough to hear about it,* she thinks. This thought leads to thinking about Sarah and *her* mother, and how she's really jealous of their relationship. Sarah's on the phone with her all the time, and they always have so much to talk about. Sarah tells her everything. Well, almost everything, but at least she can tell her mother how she's feeling, how she's doing. *Her mother knows who she is; mine doesn't have a clue.* Brenda's thoughts flit around, and she makes a conscious effort to bringing herself back to the good thoughts about Vincent and her latest work.

"Hi, Brenda, come on in. Good to see you," Dr. Cherry says, as she closes the door behind them.

Brenda goes to her familiar spot at the end of the comfy couch and grabs one of the soft pillows strewn about, hugging it to her chest. Her favorite security pillow is soft and velvety, and makes her feel good holding it. Her hands are a little sweaty, and she wipes them off on the pillow surreptitiously, hoping Dr. Cherry doesn't notice.

“Tell me how you’re doing. Tell me anything—how you’re feeling,” Dr. Cherry begins, looking fondly and expectantly at Brenda.

“I’m doing really well, Dr. Cherry. It’s like all of a sudden, things are going my way. I’m almost afraid to think about how good it is. Like someone flicked a switch and said ‘Okay, now it’s Brenda’s turn.’ I have a sketch that was kind of giving me some trouble; I felt blocked trying to pull it together. Then I felt truly special when I met Vincent, and something opened up inside me, this rush of something—inspiration maybe—took over, and the sketch came out amazing.”

“Whoa, let’s back up a little. Who’s Vincent?” Dr. Cherry asks, leaning forward.

“I don’t know yet, really. He’s some guy I met this morning, and we only talked for like fifteen minutes, but we really clicked. I felt super-happy all of a sudden. I got this feeling that I was walking into something meant for me, that it was important, and to just go with the flow and everything would be better than ever. Then I went back to my room and finished my drawing as if my hand were being guided by something greater than me. Hard to describe. Like something was missing for the longest time, and I’m getting it back. But then, I also feel like maybe I shouldn’t think anything can come of a relationship with Vincent. Maybe it’s just lust or something. Hard to believe he would really like me. But he did ask to see me again. I’m having breakfast with him tomorrow morning, and now I’m really nervous about it.” Brenda takes a breath and smiles to herself, feeling self-conscious for being so chatty.

Dr Cherry nods and has a slight smile on her usually expressionless face. “We’ve talked a lot about your narcissistic mother, and how being raised by her has influenced so many facets of your adult life. The beliefs you have, that’ve been programmed into you throughout your childhood, are harmful and based on false premises. Unless those beliefs are changed, un-programmed if you will, they’ll stay the same, so the behavior will stay the same. Not being loved enough, neglected and shamed, brings you to the conclusion that you’re not lovable, not worth looking after, shameful.

As a child, you need to believe your parents are good, that they're right in everything, so it must be your fault for why you are aren't loved, that you're unlovable. This belief gets programmed into your brain. You must learn to believe the reason you feel you weren't loved is *not* because you're unlovable, but because your mother, as a narcissist, is incapable of love."

"I know it in my head, Dr. Cherry, but I always seem to forget to really try and feel it. It still hurts, and I still have trouble accepting it at times. I try to remember it when it's time for me to call her, but as soon as I hear her voice, I feel like I'm eight years old again and doing something wrong. I try to remember what you told me about how she doesn't really have a clue as to how her behavior affects me. How she has no real compassion or empathy. It's hard for me to understand and accept, and why is it okay for her to be that way?" Brenda squirms a little, remembering the last time they spoke.

Dr. Cherry seems to read her mind and asks, "Did you speak with her this week? What happened?"

"Well, I didn't talk with her for more than a minute and a half, I think," she says, feeling somewhat embarrassed as her voice cracks. "She sounded all out of breath and annoyed, like I was disturbing some monumental thing, only to tell me she had to run upstairs from the dryer, and now all her clothes were getting wrinkled. She doesn't ask how I am. It's more like what do you want. The more I try to be independent, the more she treats me like this. I felt like crying when I hung up."

"That's understandable, and it's going to take some time to work through this. You fortunately know enough as a young adult to understand your childhood wasn't normal, that it's affecting your emotional growth and self-confidence. Some people live their entire lives believing it's their fault, unaware of the abuse they suffered, because they bury the pain in order to survive. They even may think their childhood was great, and that their mother was wonderful, making excuses for her behavior, thinking their mother loved them selflessly. Even now, after all we've talked about, you're thinking maybe you're being disloyal, that she isn't really that bad. Am I right?"

"Oh, Dr. Cherry. Yes, you're right. Once again, I understand what you're saying on a logical level, but I need to work on the deprogramming you talked about." As Brenda says this, she again has the feeling that today's a turning point, a triple-crown kind of tipping point, where the understanding finally feels real and she can embrace it. "It *is* sinking in, though, and I'm feeling like a few layers of hurt are being washed away. I haven't felt this positive in a long time."

They continue talking until their time is up, but most of it feels repetitive to Brenda, and she's tired of overthinking it. There are just a few things that stick in her mind from the rest of the session, as she's only half-participating, half-listening. Once she'd embraced the deprogramming idea, she mostly lost interest, and half-hoped the session was over. One thing she knows for sure is that it's an excellent sign that she's getting tired of talking about her mother, and wants to move on.

One of the last things Dr. Cherry says to her before their time is up is, "Brenda, you're one of the most refreshingly normal people I've ever had the pleasure to work with. Now go and enjoy getting to know that young man, and remember: you *are* lovable. You deserve to have any kind of relationship you want."

"Thank you, Dr. Cherry. I think that will become my new mantra. I *am* normal, I *am* lovable, I deserve a good relationship! I like it a lot. Thank you, see you next week."

CHAPTER 3

Vincent wants to get there before she does, and is kicking himself for not getting up earlier. He's still ahead of schedule, but doesn't want to be all sweaty and disheveled looking. Not a good first impression… second impression, really. One last hit on the joint and he's good to go.

Amazingly. he gets a close parking space, then sprints to the cafeteria. He hangs around by the entrance, off to the side, so he can watch for her and hopefully get to look at her without her seeing him first. Is that her? Yes, and he's getting twitchy just watching her walk, And, those sunglasses, they look vintage—*like the ones my Mom used to wear,* he thinks. Oh. My. God! *She's beautiful, and doesn't seem to know it. It's not like she's shy, more like vulnerable the way she looks around almost self-consciously.*

"There you are," she says as she lifts her sunglasses off her face and puts them on top of her head, pulling her hair back in the process.

This simple gesture makes Vincent gulp, and he smiles as he takes her arm, leading her to the door. "You look great," he gushes. "And those sunglasses, where did you get them? My Mom used to wear a pair like them, except they didn't have the tiny flowers painted on them."

"Oh, thanks," she says as she ducks her head a little shyly and touches the sunglasses. "I got them at the thrift store and painted the flowers myself."

"Incredible! You could sell them."

"You think so? My roommate Sarah said the same thing. It would be nice to make a little money doing something artistic."

"I see you brought your artwork—I hope you'll show it to me. Let's get a table over by the window. I've never been here this early, I don't think. I've lived off campus for a couple years now, but I do remember the smell of the cafeteria. *Aroma de yuck*, I think they call it."

They both laugh and put their stuff down. "I like the pancakes—it's hard to mess up pancakes, especially if you drown them in something. Let's get some food, then we can eat and talk. Surprisingly, the coffee is decent too. Maybe they stepped things up a notch since you've last eaten here. I like to eat breakfast here rather than lunch or dinner—it's the lesser of three evils. Next year I hope to live off campus. My roommate Sarah said she would room with me, and we could share expenses on something close by. My parents want me to stay on campus, but senior year, no way." Brenda takes a breath and realizes she's talking a lot, and that Vincent likes listening to her.

She's really cute, he thinks, and *I feel comfortable with her*. Right now, he feels he could talk with her all day, and is glad he has over an hour before his first class. This is a great way to start the day, and the pancakes actually do look pretty good.

Once they're settled and eating, Brenda reaches down and pulls out a sketch from her portfolio. "What do you think?" she asks quietly, like she's almost afraid of what he'll say.

Vincent puts his fork down and holds the sketch in front of him. The drawing takes his breath away and he closes his eyes for a second, then opens them again to really focus. Maybe because he's still a little stoned, he sees figures and shadows within each other, turning into something else that goes through a symbolic cycle of life.

"I've never seen anything like this," he says, his eyes still on the sketch.

"I'm thinking of incorporating some color. What do you think?"

"I'm speechless. I don't know. It seems perfect without color, but now that you mention it, that might be awesome." He feels Brenda watching him carefully as he continues to stare at the sketch and then suddenly she says, "Are you stoned?"

"Huh, what?"

"You heard me. Your eyes are kind of red, and you have that dreamy, stoned look," she says with a half-amused smile.

"Yikes! Guess I'm busted. Are you mad?"

"No, not at all. Especially if you tell me how amazing my sketch is, and that you can't wait to be *straight* to really appreciate it." She sees him trying to process this and his raised eyebrows, and bursts out laughing.

"Wait, isn't it supposed to be the other way around?" he asks guiltily.

That was the turning point, and they spent the next hour talking and laughing so much that others around them were moving away because they were being too loud. Neither of them cared or even noticed anything but each other, and it was probably the best breakfast they ever had. Vincent told Brenda about his parents divorcing when he was ten, and about his Mom getting sick when he was twelve, and how his Dad was never around. How his aunt, his Mom's sister, took him in after his Mom died and raised him along with her two daughters, his cousins, who were older than him. He told her how he got a full paid scholarship that everyone was amazed about, because he ran pretty wild in high school.

"What can I say?" he says with a grin. "I'm a smart guy, and a lot of things come naturally, so I don't have to study as much as some people do to get good grades. I'm no genius, but I've been told I have a really quick mind, especially when it comes to math and science. I was also a member of the Chess Club, and we were undefeated my senior year."

He goes on to tell her that the only black mark he has was getting caught smoking a joint along with a couple other guys on his senior class trip in Washington, D.C. Their guidance counselor threatened to throw him out of the National Honor Society, and he says he didn't really care about that, except for how it would affect his scholarship. In the end, Mr. Naylor took pity on him, and just gave him a severe reprimand and three-day suspension. Mr. Naylor later took him aside and said he gave Vincent a break because he'd had a rough childhood with his Mom dying and an MIA Dad, and hoped he got his shit together and made something of himself. He assured Mr. Naylor he would, and thanked him profusely for having faith in him. He confides in Brenda that what people don't understand is that he's had to keep his emotions under control for most of his life, hold his sadness and grief in check, and a welcome distraction in the way of a recreational drug was actually helping him, not hurting him.

Brenda listens attentively, nodding or furrowing her brow occasionally. She then starts telling Vincent about her childhood, and that she also has an MIA father. Her two brothers, one older and one younger, get the lion's share of attention from her father, and he basically lives his life through them. Fortunately for her older brother, he's good at sports, and gets a lot of approval from their father for it. The younger brother is really brainy and also good at sports, so he's the next golden child. Brenda explains that her father just isn't interested in her, and doesn't know what to do with her or how to relate to her. He doesn't know what to say to her, so he pretty much avoids her. He's critical of her appearance and often mentions it's too bad she doesn't look more like her mother, who happens to be beautiful.

Both of her parents expect her to excel in school, yet neither is especially interested in her art or other pursuits. She explains about her narcissistic mother, and educates Vincent as to what she's learned about narcissism that he didn't know. She also tells him about her dream to have her artwork shown in galleries all over the country, maybe even the world, and be known for her different technique, like Monet or Van Gogh. He jokingly tells her she may have to be dead first for that to happen.

When it's time to break away and get back to the reality of school, Vincent reaches across the table and takes her hand. She doesn't flinch or look away, just smiles and puts her other hand on top of his. “Now what?” she asks with a big, beautiful smile.

“Now everything,” he says with a shrug. “Now is the beginning of everything.”

CHAPTER 4

Brenda floats on Cloud Nine through the rest of her day, and can't stop going over everything from breakfast. Every word, every look, every feeling. Her heart seems to be beating double-time, and she can hardly focus on anything else. Oh, when he took her hand and said *this is the start of everything*, she almost felt like crying, like every emotion welling up at once was too much.

It seems she's been waiting for something like this forever. In high school, she only sort of had a boyfriend once, but only for a month, and he told all his asshole friends that he felt her boobs. That was the end of that. She couldn't stand those immature idiots. Then they all thought she was weird and stuck up, because she didn't belong to any group and kept to herself. She had a couple of friends and her art. She was happiest painting and drawing in her room. Her mother would tell her friends she was talented, but to Brenda she would say, "Stop moping around in your room trying to be an artist." But Brenda feels this is a turning point for her; she feels it with her whole being.

Vincent is so funny, and yet there's a sadness underneath his smiling face, like he has to pretend all the time, so people don't see his vulnerabilities. *That must be so hard*, she thinks. He was making her laugh like crazy, and she can't believe he was stoned! She wonders if she should have been a little mad that he came to their first real time together stoned. She was surprised when he asked if she was. Even more surprised with her comeback. *Don't know where that came from, but have to admit it was pretty witty*, she chuckles to herself. She imagines her hand still tingling from his touch, and knows it won't be long until they… until they, um, make love. Her hand isn't the only thing tingling, ha!

For a fleeting moment, she thinks about calling her mother and telling her she met an amazing guy. But the thought passes, as she knows she'll be disappointed. She never gives up, does she? Einstein comes to mind when she thinks of wanting to do the same thing over and over again and expecting a different result. According to him, that's the definition of insanity. She's proud of herself for not giving in to wanting her approval this time, or even caring, and setting herself up for disappointment.

Brenda's hoping Sarah will be there as she makes her way back to their room. She's thrilled when she sees she's there, and rushes into the room, throwing herself into her friend for a hug, almost knocking her over.

"Breakfast went well, I take it," Sarah laughs, hugging her back.

"Oh, it was all right, nothing great," Brenda says deadpan.

"You are so full of shit, you know that?" Sarah replies, pushing her back to get a look at her.

"Okay, so it was amazing and I think I'm in love. Or at least in lust. But I'm feeling a little queasy in a way, with lots of mixed emotions. Almost scared."

"Of what?" Sarah asks, shaking her head

"Of everything. Of getting hurt, of being fooled because he's the first guy I really like who's paid attention to me in a while. Of not being good enough."

"Brenda!" Sarah says loudly. "I thought you were doing better about being insecure. You're so pretty and smart and talented and funny. Should I go on? Any guy would be lucky to have you. Do you really not know that?"

"Yeah, that's what Dr. Cherry says, that I have to believe in myself more, that I'm worthy, that I have to stop thinking about the negative influence of my parents." As these words leave her mouth, the expression on Sarah's face tells her she just said more than she intended to.

"Who is Dr. Cherry?" Sarah asks, although Brenda somehow feels she has an idea.

"Oh, well, uh," Brenda stammers, takes a deep breath, and says, "Dr. Cherry is, like, my shrink. She's the school counselor. I've been seeing her for over a year." She watches Sarah's face process this, and then sighs with relief when Sarah smiles and gives her another hug.

"Brenda, my friend, I had a feeling something was going on, because you seemed to blossom this year more than any time since I first met you. You also hardly ever mention your mother anymore, and that's something you used to do all the time."

"I did?"

"Yes, but not for a while now. The last we talked about it, you said you would trade her in for my mother in a heartbeat!" Sarah laughs.

"I would, for sure!" Brenda is relieved that Sarah's not making a big deal out of it.

"Well, good for you then. I mean it, it's nothing to be ashamed of. I think it's great you sought help, and now you're getting into a relationship with someone who actually seems worthy of you," Sarah says, truly meaning it. "So, tell me more about this guy. What did you talk about?"

"Oh, everything! And he gets my art, too. When I showed him my latest masterpiece, in one sentence he expressed the essence of it. Plus, he made me laugh until I thought I was going to pee my pants. He also told me about his family, and when he did, he got sad. His Mom died a few years ago, and his father is pretty much a no-show. So we have dysfunctional family in common. Maybe not such a good thing, though." She stops to take a breath and thinks for a few seconds about the look on his face when he talked about his mom. "Another thing—he was stoned! Is that kind of weird? To show up for a sort of first date stoned? I called him out on it and he asked if I was mad, which I wasn't, I don't think. He said getting stoned helped him to handle some of his sadness and troubles. He's gone through a lot, and it's amazing that he seems almost normal," she laughs, but she's not sure that's really how she feels about it.

"I've only smoked a few times," Sarah admits. "I liked it when I was with people I trusted and cared about. I don't think I could do it just any old time, definitely not before class. There's a guy in my Psych class that reeks of it all the time. Funny thing is, he doesn't seem to act any differently, although he does smile a lot." She laughs as she thinks about this. "Have you smoked much? We should do it sometime together. We're always so busy with class and me going home most weekends, it really just never came up. I can ask the guy from my class for some; I'm sure he'd give it to me if I smile back at him."

"Sure," Brenda tells Sarah. "That would be fun. I could even ask Vincent, but I don't want to yet. We didn't really talk about whether I also liked getting stoned, and it's something we can work up to. I feel I need to know him better, but I'm sure he would love to get high with me."

"Absolutely. From what you tell me, he's already thinking about it. Well, I'm not heading home until early Saturday morning, so maybe we can get high and then eat an entire extra-large pizza. I know smoking makes me really hungry. I become the Munchie Queen, and need to eat everything in sight. Just us, it'll be fun!"

CHAPTER 5

Thankfully, Vincent's roommate doesn't seem to mind that Brenda's practically living there, since he's hardly ever there himself. After graduation, he'll be going to the big city for an intern job he already has lined up; then Brenda can officially move in. Vincent feels so fortunate he got a job with Wave & Light Industries right in town, as a Junior Optical Engineer, so they can stay in the apartment while Brenda finishes her senior year. He can make some money, get hands-on experience, and work on getting that grant to continue his degree. Then he'll be sure to get his dream job of working on Hubble technology, or other high-end technologies down the road.

Vincent heaves a big sigh, feeling more content than he ever has in his life. Everything's coming together. Brenda doesn't start her fulltime job at the art gallery until a week after he graduates, and they have a few dozen designer sunglasses yet to sell at the flea market. She's done an amazing job buying up lots of vintage sunglasses and then painting intricate designs on them. Not just flowers but geometric designs, even miniature landscapes running over the top and onto the temples. It was his idea to sell them, ever since he saw the pair she was wearing when they first met. She even signs them with her name and a tiny logo of a creature wearing sunglasses. When he asked who the little blob creature thing was, she just laughed and said it was her muse.

When the phone rings, it startles him for a second before he breaks out of his thoughts to answer it.

"Hi, Vincent, it's Aunt Carol."

"Hi, you, how are you? Can't wait to see you in a couple days, and Brenda's so looking forward to meeting you."

"Oh, honey, that's why I'm calling. We aren't going to be able to come to your graduation; I'm so sorry. Uncle Joe is in the hospital!"

"What? Oh *no*! What happened?"

"He fell off the ladder when he was coming down from the roof. I told him not to go up there, and he said he wouldn't. He lied to me—as soon as I wasn't looking, he was up there trying to find the source of a leak we have in the attic. He broke his leg in two places, bruised a couple ribs, and has a slight concussion. He's lucky he didn't kill himself."

"Oh my God! That's terrible, is he going to be all right?"

"Yes, but it's going to take a while. I'm really mad at him, but he's so beat up, I can't bring myself to say *I told you so*. He's so impetuous, and look where it got him."

"Yikes! So sorry to hear it, and that you'll be missing graduation. It's not that big of a deal, though, so don't worry. I know Brenda will be disappointed, but we'll come for a visit as soon as we can. Stay with Uncle Joe and send him our love, the idiot!"

"It *is* a big deal, Vincent, and we're so proud of you. Really, we are. When do you start your new job?"

"I start a week after graduation, and Brenda starts her job at the same time, so I don't think we'll be able to come see you right away." He feels a little guilty not telling her about the three-day camping getaway they have planned, that they could cancel if they had to.

"That's wonderful, Vincent. Amazing you both have jobs lined up."

"I have Professor Strauss to thank for telling me about the company and the job opening they had. He knows people at the company, and he even wrote me a glowing recommendation letter I sent with my resumé. He's given me an incredible amount of support, and really believes in me. I interviewed with several people there, and every single person I met with was super-intelligent and someone I want to work with."

"Wow, that's great. It's really something special when people believe in you, isn't it? So, what does your job entail? I'm sorry I'm not more technical, but I'm not even sure what you studied, or what you'll be doing. Can you tell me a little about it?"

"Sure, do you have a couple hours?" Vincent laughs.

"Is it that complicated?"

"Nah, I'm teasing. In simple terms, I deal with light and how to manipulate it to do specific things. Sometimes we just bend it, or change the color, and sometimes we make it carry information for us. We make use of optics to solve problems, and to design and build devices that make light do something useful. The results are all around you, from simple things like reading glasses, to the subtle tinting in your windshield. Optics is used in telescopes, fiber optics, and even the price scanning device they use at the grocery store. I could go on and on, but I think you can see that there are lots of opportunities for me with this degree."

"Ah, I see. I actually made a few notes so I can tell your Uncle Joe when I see him later at the hospital. I have to say again, we're so proud of you—you've overcome so much to be where you are now. I think I'm going to cry. You'll go so far in this world, and do so much good! Oh, honey, I'm so sorry we can't be at your graduation," she snuffles, blowing her nose.

"Aww, don't cry, Aunt Carol. I haven't saved humanity yet," he jokes. "I have a long way to go, and am just happy I got this job so quickly. It'll be a great learning ground, a steppingstone, and still allow me to stay here until Brenda graduates. Plus, I can work on getting that grant, but we'll talk about that later."

After they say their goodbyes, Vincent decides he needs to celebrate a little, and he takes a couple of hits before Brenda walks in the door saying,

"Honey, I'm home!" She loves saying that, because she really does feel like she's home. This feeling of belonging is what she craves, and what she feels she's always been missing. Brenda is happy, and it makes all the difference in everything she does. She feels loved. What a simple thing, and yet it changes *everything*. The world has a special glow now. Everything is brighter, cooler, easier. Nothing's impossible.

"Guess what happened today," she gushes. "You'll never guess!"

"Hi honey, how are you? I'm fine, thanks for asking. Okay, tell me what happened," he laughs as she gives him her wide-eyed look.

"Guess who came into the gallery today? George Connelly, the actor! It was the most amazing thing. I showed him around, and we talked for almost an hour! And he bought the Hammond abstract for $25,000! I can't believe Robert, the owner, let me handle the whole thing. What a stroke of luck that he came in on a Wednesday, the only day of the week I'm there this week! I still can't believe it. Mr. Connelly wrote out a check for $25,000, just like that, and I carefully wrapped the painting and he carried it out the door himself. And get this… just before he left, he saw a pair of my sunglasses, the ones with geometric lines, on the desk and asked where I got them. When I told him I make them, he gave me his card—his card!—and said he wanted to get a pair for his wife. I told him I had several, and about the flea market, and he said he wanted to see what I had and to maybe have a pair custom-made. Wow, can you believe it? And that's not all, Robert said he would give me a commission since he could tell that Mr. Connelly liked me, and said he would be back. Oh my God, what a day!"

"Incredible, Brenda. Come here and give me a hug. I love you so much."

Vincent hugs Brenda closely, then grabs the small pipe that still has a few hits left in it and lights it for her. "This is cause for a celebration. Indulge, my dear, while I make us something to eat. At dinner, we can talk about our incredible good fortune, our perfect timing, and upcoming trip. Just when you think things can't possibly get better, they do!"

As he walks towards the kitchen, Brenda draws in a hit and has a funny feeling come over her. *I wish he hadn't said that; it's like a jinx. How long can all this good stuff keep happening? It's so perfect. God, part of me feels I don't deserve this. Dr. Cherry would have a field day with it.* She shakes her head and vows to stay positive as she silently recites her feel- good mantra over and over.

CHAPTER 6

They leave early in the morning for the three-plus hour drive to the desert camp they have reservations for. Much of the area had been sacred Indian lands from years past, and is known to be stunningly beautiful. There are many legends about the area, and the small campground where they're staying is relatively unknown, with lots of open space and trails to discover.

Once on the road, they're like two chatterboxes, fueled with caffeine from their several cups of coffee and their excitement to finally be getting away. Vincent officially has his graduation behind him, and they now have so much to look forward to. They talk about everything under the sun, like they always do, and the conversation turns to their new jobs. Brenda had gotten a nice commission from the Gallery for her sale to George Connelly, and when they get back, he's promised to come by the flea market to look at her designer sunglasses. She's especially excited by this, and Vincent has to admit to himself he's a bit jealous of all the attention this guy is giving her.

The topic then changes to his new job and the types of projects he hopes to be working on. During his interviews, he met with several people from various departments, all focusing on different areas of optics. Vincent has always dreamed of working on Hubble type technology, but after meeting with these diverse folks, he found his interest getting drawn into other areas. Everyone he met with had so much enthusiasm for what they were doing at the company, and that added to his excitement and curiosity of what he'd be learning.

"During one part of my interview, I talked with a woman who was a scientist, *not* an engineer. She's the department head for an area that's sort of like a liaison for the science in engineering. The way she explained it is, 'Scientists want to know how the universe works. Engineers try to use the facts of science and math to do things that are useful to people'. It's a simple concept, but I never really thought about how much crossover there is. She talked about one project they're working on that involves the psychological impact of light and color. I know various kinds of light and colors have a psychological impact, but I didn't know that wavelengths can be greatly altered by the type of optics they're filtering through, and that each wavelength can have different effects on each individual. We're not just looking at output sources like telescopes, cameras, projectors, etc. but also input sources, and how the input source of the light can affect the individual."

"Hmm, interesting," Brenda says as she takes off her sunglasses to look at them. "I kind of get that. Not all the sunglasses we get have the same lenses or filter color. Some are darker, like these, and I can't see as well out of them unless I'm in really bright sunlight. I actually feel more tired when I wear them for a while, and I don't like wearing them if I'm driving. I have a different pair for that. I'm thinking maybe we should be more selective in buying up the lots of sunglasses, and try to find some higher-quality ones, now that we'll both be making money. Plus, if we get more customers like George Connelly, they'll have to be better quality."

"Makes sense," Vincent replies distractedly, as his mind wanders around the effects of selectively filtering light through optics.

They switch drivers at about the halfway mark, and Vincent dozes off while Brenda drives the remaining miles. He starts dreaming and finds himself at some sort of convention where a huge banquet is in progress. As he approaches a table laden with food, a chef with a tall white toque calls out his name, and starts putting what looks like asparagus on a plate for him. It *is* asparagus; he starts eating it, and it's delicious. But then the plate is taken away before he's done, and he's told it's time for his speech. He's worried that he hasn't prepared a speech, but decides to go through with it anyway. He's led down several long hallways before he finally comes to an open room filled with an auditorium of empty seats. The person who led him to this room is gone, and Vincent figures the conference must be over. He's wandering through long hallways again when he wakes up.

"Whew, that was weird. I just had the strangest dream," he says, rubbing his face and shaking his head to clear it.

"It must have been a doozy the way you were mumbling and smacking your lips in between the snoring," Brenda laughs.

"Oh God, was I snoring too?"

"Yep, and you look cute when you drool," she teases.

"Ugh, my biggest fear. Getting caught snoring and drooling."

"No worries, I've seen it before," she laughs, as he gives her shoulder an embarrassed nudge.

The tent is easy to set up, and they climb in to arrange their sleeping bags. "Mmm, this is cozy," Vincent says as he grabs Brenda and pulls her down to him. "This is perfect. I like it here, and if we need anything we forgot to bring, there's a small store and common area just around the bend next to the bathhouse."

They decide to open the rain fly just enough to let some of the sunlight in overhead, while still blocking most of it. Curiously, even though it's still the middle of the day, the desert has a coolness in the air that makes the bake of the sun on their skin tingle between that cool/warm feeling that can't decide which to be. Lying down next to each other, they listen for the sounds of the desert, and it's silent. There are no voices or car sounds, only the slight breeze as it rustles over the dry, crackly grasses. They lie there for a while until they think they can hear the sand moving a little from the wind, a bird calling from far away. They start to kiss slowly.

Their lovemaking is unhurried, and they feel they have all the time the universe has to offer to explore every sensation. Slowly, slowly they fall into the feeling of nothing else but each other, every caress, touch, liquid unfolding. There's nothing else but this right now, because time has stopped; there's no time here, only now. In and out the feelings unfurl, rise, and spill all around them. It's an eternity before they come back from where they went with each other, letting their in-sync breathing slow, and their heartbeats whisper instead of drum. They lazily become aware of the sunbeam still shining overhead, adding to the glow of their smooth skin.

Vincent rolls onto his side, and they lie facing each other with the band of light between them. "This is magic, another world, supernatural. Do you feel the magic of it? Do you think we're in an alternate reality? Have we crossed over to another world?"

"Yes, yes, and yes. Definitely another world, an enchanting place I've never been before. I was even thinking that when we were driving in. I kept thinking how stark and craggy and rough it all looks. Hardly any green, lots of sand and rock, yet so alive. It shimmers and moves. A beautiful paradox."

Vincent takes Brenda's hand and kisses her palm. "I have a surprise for you," he says as he reaches over to find his pants, digging around in the pocket until he finds what he's looking for.

"What's that?" Brenda asks as he shows her a small plastic bag with something that looks like dried spices in it. "Is that weed?"

"No, it's something better, something special. And now is the perfect time and place for it. It's dried psilocybin mushrooms." He sees her eyes go wide and her expression change. "Have you heard of it? Have you ever tried it?"

"Yes, I've heard of it. I read *The Teachings of Don Juan* for a class I had last year. It was a little difficult to get through, but interesting. I've never tried mushrooms; I hardly even smoked weed until I met you. You're a bad influence on me," she laughs. "Seriously though, I think I'm kind of afraid to try it."

"I knew you'd feel that way. But this is special, and the perfect place for it. We may never get the chance to be here again, in this surreal, mystical desert. The time is perfect too, for both of us. We have the perfect readiness of embarking on new journeys together, as we expand on our own directions of realizing our dreams. Just think, right here could have been a sacred ceremonial place from thousands of years ago, and now it's our turn to experience it."

His enthusiasm is contagious, and Brenda feels so content she's almost ready to agree when she asks, "What if something goes wrong, and I get scared or something?"

"I'll be right here with you the whole time. I promise, it'll be something we both never forget. Something beautiful and transcendent. Have I ever steered you wrong? Ever?"

Brenda nods her head in silent acquiescence. They hug tightly, each with their own thoughts. Vincent moves away to open the plastic bag and prepare the mushrooms for them to take.

CHAPTER 7

Brenda has a little trouble swallowing the dried mushrooms, and takes several swigs from the water bottle. She's asked a lot of questions and Vincent's given a lot of reassuring answers. Her dosage is smaller than his, as he's taken shrooms before, and has a better idea of what to expect. He assures Brenda over and over that all she has to do is relax and accept the experience. He tells her if she starts to feel weird, to just accept the feeling and surrender to it, knowing it will pass.

"So now what?" Brenda asks. "Should we just sit here and wait for it to take effect?"

"Nope, what we should do is fill this pack with some water, our jackets, a blanket, a flashlight, and a couple of other things. Then we're going to take that path around that big rock formation we saw by the entrance. Remember it?"

"How could I forget? It reminded me of a huge cluster of different people, all squished together into a giant mound. I was thinking I should draw it when we drove by it."

"Funny, I was thinking the same thing. You *should* draw it. Should I put your sketch pad in the pack? I'm going to bring my camera. We might not use either, but it'll be good to have them, just in case."

After a few minutes, they're ready. It's a short walk to the trailhead, and they hold hands as they walk and talked about the beauty of their surroundings. Neither of them has seen all the different cactus varieties before, and they stop frequently to get a closer look. They talked about time, and how long it took in geological time to form what they were seeing now. Then they talk more about time, looking up at the still-bright sun, wondering about the moon that's just starting to be visible. Every thought they share starts to seem quite profound, and they can't believe how wonderful it is to see something in a way they never have before.

"Look at the color of this sand," Brenda says, pointing to the gently sloping dune up ahead. "It's coral pink. I have to remember this color, and how it changes with the light. See how it now has a more pinkish color where it's bright, and more coral in the shade? Oh, look! There's a rabbit with really big ears, and his ears are pink too and translucent! And there's black on the tips, and he's so cute. Oh God, I feel like Alice in Wonderland."

Vincent starts laughing so hard he falls over into the sand. "Brenda, you are so funny! Do you feel different? Do things look different?"

Brenda sighs deeply and says, "Let's look at the big rock with all the squishy people in it. I don't think they're all people, though. I think some are creatures."

Vincent gets up, and they walk back to the rock formation Brenda's talking about. "Let's count all the faces and see who they are, and give me my sketch pad," she says. "I'll draw them. I see a priest with a robe, and a gremlin, and there's an old man with a big nose."

"I see a naked woman with long hair, and a dragon," Vincent says as he squints and looks for more shapes. The longer he stares, the more it seems that each figure is moving and looking at him. As he makes what feels like eye contact, he hears messages in his head, and sees visions of what each is showing him. He gets lost in the wisdom each figure is imparting, and realizes each is from a different time and place. He starts to feel that he's floating, and has to look down periodically to see if his feet are still on the ground. He's being shown mathematical formulas, suddenly understanding light and matter in ways he never knew before. They're telling him everything he needs to know, pouring into him the sacred secrets that define life from the highest level.

Brenda's lost in her sketching, and feels she's drawing the meaning of life itself. As the figures come alive on the page, she's reminded she's already drawn this piece. It was what she was working on when she first met Vincent. But now, it's all flowing into itself and creating something she can't define, but knows is important. She starts to sing, and realizes the figures in the rocks are telling her the words, in a language never sung before.

Her singing brings Vincent over, and they sing together their new-found knowledge. But it's not known words they're singing. It's flowing sounds they harmonize together, that perfectly define the feeling of dusk gently settling on them, like a light breeze.

They start walking again, and Vincent wraps the blanket around Brenda's shoulders as it gets darker and cooler. They find a large, smooth rock, lay out the blanket, and lie down together. "I feel a little sick," Brenda says, and is surprised her voice sounds so far away. "I feel kind of nauseous and a little achy."

"Me too, but just a little. This is normal; I remember it from before. It will pass. Here, have some water, and then we'll just lay here and close our eyes for a bit. Hold my hand and focus on how our hands feel together, and just breathe."

They close their eyes and hold hands. Brenda focuses on her breathing and feels like she's floating, tethered to the earth only by Vincent's hand. She can feel the blood pulsing through his veins, and imagines being the blood flowing on the pathway to his heart and back. The images change to those of rocks so large and tall, they're like skyscrapers lumped together, reaching for the sky; and at the tops are tiny lights, barely visible. Brenda realizes the tiny lights are stars, and she watches them move like an intricate dance, changing color and brightness.

Her nausea has gone, but she starts to feel a little afraid, and like she can't move. She doesn't try hard to make any movements, she just feels like she wouldn't be able to move if she wanted to. The images change to a garden so green and bright; she wishes she had her sunglasses. The smell of flowers is so strong, and she tries to identify which flowers she's smelling. At a turn in the garden, her mother pops out of one of the bushes and gives Brenda a disapproving look. Brenda recognizes that look and wonders what she's done wrong. No words are spoken as her mother turns her back and leaves. The image changes again into a long tunnel, and she tries to see how far it goes, but it swallows her up and is starting to constrict, so she can't get out. She gasps loudly and cries, "Help!"

Vincent sits up and pulls his hand from hers and says, "Open your eyes. Brenda, open your eyes!"

"Oh, oh, oh!" Brenda exclaims as she opens her eyes and looks around wildly.

Taking her hand again, Vincent says reassuringly, "I'm right here. Look at me, I'm *right* here." He brings her hand to his lips and kisses her palm as she watches the gesture with interest. "You're safe with me, you're fine."

"I'm so glad you're right here. I was afraid. I was in a tunnel and it was closing in. Right before that, I saw my mother in a beautiful garden, the most beautiful garden I've ever seen, and she turned her back on me. Before she turned away, she looked at me with such disdain and even though her mouth wasn't moving, I could hear her say, 'I don't love you.'"

"*I* love you, Brenda. So, so much. More than you can imagine. More than I can explain. I grow so huge just thinking about how much I love you." Vincent feels himself choking up, and his eyes start to water. "You know this, right?"

Brenda nods solemnly and kisses him. They both feel sparks like tiny shocks on their lips. They hold their lips together for what feels like an eternity, each seeing different waves of color behind their closed eyelids. As they finally move apart, Vincent says, "Let's go for a walk. It's starting to get dark and a little chilly. Get the blanket and we'll wrap it around us as we walk."

They only get a short distance before stopping to listen to the sounds of the desert as dusk turns to darkness. Leaning on a rock, they look up at the stars and can't believe the abundance and brightness. "There are a billion, gazillion stars right here, and I feel like I can touch them," Brenda says as she reaches her hand up. "They're moving and leaving trails, and it's the first time I've really seen shooting stars. Do you see them too?"

"Oh yes," Vincent replies slowly, with riveted attention. "I see them in formations, and they're showing me formulas I need to consider. It's like a formula for happiness, and a formula for enlightenment or something, or maybe both. And there's more, they're all over the sky. I need to write them down. Please, where's a pencil and paper?" He fumbles around in the pack they brought with them, and pulls out Brenda's pad and pencil. He starts writing furiously, not looking at the paper, but looking up as if watching the most amazing spectacle in the world.

"Do you need a flashlight to see what you're writing?" Brenda asks.

"No, no. No light, I can see, I'm feeling what I'm writing." This goes on for what seems like an eternity, and they both start to have sore necks and shoulders from looking up for so long. "I think I have enough. I don't think I can absorb anymore," Vincent says as he lowers his head and rubs his neck.

They start shuffling back to their tent, and Vincent finally takes the flashlight out so they can see the path more clearly. They follow the light slowly and listen to the desert come alive with sounds they hadn't heard before. Every sound is amplified, every scuttle of desert creature sounds like giant's footsteps, and they pick up their pace as they get closer to the tent. Throwing themselves inside the tent, Vincent zippers up the entry, and they both climb into their sleeping bags. Cocooning like caterpillars, they hunker down and move about until they're both settled and comfortable. Several hours have passed, and they both feel like the effects of the magic mushrooms are starting to wane. But Vincent knows from past experience that the effects come in waves, and there may be more to come.

"How're you doing?" he asks Brenda. "You okay?"

"Hmm," she says. "I'm good. After I saw my mother, I started to freak out a little, but I remember you telling me to accept the experience, and just kind of surrender to how it feels. So, I told myself this is just going to roll over me, like a tumbleweed. That's what I thought, a tumbleweed, and felt like she was going to roll away with the weed. Kind of funny, know what I mean?"

"Yeah," he replies distractedly. "I think I saw the meaning of life in the stars. We're all one, all part of this monstrous thing, and the formulas show the secrets."

"Wow. Oh, do we have music? Can you put on something good, please? Something with a lot of guitar but not heavy, more like the masterful stuff."

"Got it," Vincent says as they hear the first notes.

They settle back and spend the rest of the night listening to music in a way they've never listened before. Brenda sees every note in a stream of color across her vision. Vincent hears and sees the music as waves of light and sound. Both of them feel moved to tears, with such a feeling of elation that's bursting with a significance yet to be defined; mystical in its profundity, challenging in its exposure of the unresolved self.

CHAPTER 8

Things are different after what they refer to as their *Mystical Desert Adventure,* as though the experience had a life of its own, its own personality as a separate entity, its own name. It was a new tangible thing that came into their lives. Sometimes one of them will shorten it to MDA and say things like, "During our MDA, did you feel like you were one of the stars in the universe?" Or "After our MDA, do you feel like you know more now?"

The MDA is brought up often as they remember and think about different pieces of the experience, and feel the need to talk about it with the only other person they shared it with. One piece they constantly revisit, especially Brenda, is the flowing paradox of feelings she felt between somberness and exhilaration. For her, it was like a river flowing back and forth between the two feelings, sometimes quickly, in a flash, and other times like a slow trickle. Vincent understands this, and also felt the rollercoaster of emotions, but most of the time his were of elation, discovery, and lucidity, with a feeling of being on the edge of something amazing. Although they discuss how they felt during their MDA frequently, neither fully discloses the true intensity of *what* they felt. It seems beyond explaining, and if they're truly honest, there's a feeling of vulnerability in revealing all, and how it affected them.

They find it interesting how the depth of their respective MDA experience was similar in its clarity defining ways, but so different in its distinctiveness to the individual. One feeling they share, though, is that the mushrooms seemed to know what they needed to feel and see in that moment. For Brenda it wasn't always comfortable, but in retrospect she feels it was helpful in providing insight into some deep-rooted issues her feelings couldn't pin down. Vincent never experienced the level of discomfort that Brenda had, only a minor frustration in not being able to absorb all the information he was being given by what he perceived to be the *Universal Mind* as quickly as it was being offered.

He thinks a lot about the *Universal Mind* while he's in the lab at work, trying out the new software they've installed. Being a Saturday morning, he has the lab to himself; he was thrilled when his supervisor told him he could come in on weekends and evenings whenever he wanted to. So far, they're very satisfied with how quickly he's integrated himself into the work and the company's culture. Vincent loves the nature of the work, and oftentimes has trouble dragging himself away from it.

He's supposed to be helping Brenda at the flea market today, since they haven't been there the past couple of weeks, but he felt compelled to come in to work and quickly immersed himself in playing with the new software. When he takes a break to get some coffee, he starts thinking about the formulas he'd written down during his altered state in the desert, and wonders if he really was receiving the information and inspiration from what he could only describe as otherworldly means. Did the mushrooms really allow him to tap into the *Universal Mind*, altering his vibration to the perfect wavelength? He made copies of the writing he'd done in the desert while looking up at the stars, and had a little trouble deciphering everything he'd written down, partly because he'd written on top of Brenda's sketch. It actually made for an amazing drawing, the combination of her sketch of the desert rocks and his formulas. That in itself made it a supernatural work of art.

While Vincent is contemplating the *Universal Mind*, Brenda is busy setting up her table at the flea market. She got there early to ensure she had everything ready by the time the early birds starting coming through. So far, she's seen only a handful of people wandering around, when a couple coming towards her catches her eye. He has a baseball cap and sunglasses on, and the woman has her hair wrapped up in a head scarf and sunglasses also. As they get closer, Brenda realizes it's George Connelly, and the woman must be his wife. Her heart rate goes up and she finds herself blushing as they approach.

"Good morning, Brenda," George calls out with a wave. "We're so glad you're here early. We're trying to stay incognito for as long as we can, and figured now would be a good time."

"Great! So nice to see you again!" Brenda says a bit too loudly, giving her excitement away.

"This is my wife, Caroline," George says as his wife approaches with outstretched hand.

"Nice to meet you," both Brenda and Caroline say at the same time as they clasp hands, and then step back laughing.

As Caroline starts to peruse the sunglasses Brenda has on display, George makes small talk. "I'm glad we caught you. I'll be overseas doing a shoot for a new movie and will be in Australia for at least a month or two if all goes according to plan. Caroline will be joining me a little later, but has her own work to focus on."

"Oh, what does your work involve, Mrs. Connelly?" Brenda asks.

"Please call me Caroline. I'm in the fashion industry. I design clothes and accessories for a few different labels, and this time of year is quite busy. We're already working on fall, and I have several more designs to submit before I take off to the land Down Under."

"Sounds wonderful! You sure are a creative couple."

"You're quite creative yourself. I love these sunglasses, especially this pair with the desert scene. It's impressive the way you can paint on such a small space so beautifully," Caroline says as she continues to admire the glasses. "These are really wonderful, but…" she trails off, looking up at her husband.

"What Caroline is thinking, and I already mentioned this to her when I first told her about your glasses, is that the quality of the frames and lenses don't do justice to your artwork. We feel you need to use better quality materials to go along with your beautiful creations. I don't think you realize how special these are," he continues, sweeping his arm across the table. "They're truly magnificent. That's one of the reasons I wanted Caroline to see them too. She knows fashion; she knows quality and originality. You're very talented, and these sunglasses can become a big fashion statement."

"Wow!" Brenda exclaims, taking it all in. "Well, we buy the sunglasses in bulk, and since I'm really just starting out, I didn't think I could make back what we laid out if we spent more for the base sunglasses. I felt no one would buy them if they were priced too high. It takes some time to do the paintings on them, and I'm barely making a profit as it is if you figure my time in. I was hoping to make enough here at the flea market over the summer to start investing in glasses with better frames and lenses."

George and Caroline look at each other and exchange a smile. "I have a proposition for you, Brenda," George says, still smiling. He reaches into his pocket and brings out a check for $2,000 and hands it to her. She takes it, and looks questioningly at both of them.

"This is for my first order. I want four pairs, each one different, and each one of high quality. You can work with Caroline on colors and designs, and she can also help you find sources for the quality sunglasses at wholesale prices. Your artwork is extraordinary and extremely valuable, so don't sell yourself short. In addition, I'd like to invest in helping you get started, so we'll pay for your first order of one dozen quality glasses. This way you'll have good base sunglasses to work with. How does that sound?" he asks with a smile he shares with both of them.

Brenda's speechless and looks at the check in her hand, then looks at both of them, then clears her throat. "Uh, I'm overwhelmed. I don't know what to say. How will I pay you back? It may take a while. How will I sell them at the higher prices? How will I..."

George cuts in, saying, "We'll work all of that out, not to worry. Next week you can sit down with Caroline to work out what she wants for the first four pairs, and work on procuring the additional dozen for you to customize." Then he laughs and says, "I think you may have forgotten I'm kind of famous, and know a lot of people who have money." He chuckles at his own joke.

Caroline laughs with him and says, "Brenda, George has spoken so highly of you and really liked the way you handled the sale of the painting he bought at the Gallery. He understands a lot about my business, what I do, and who my clientele and contacts are. He has an excellent feel for good art, and knowing talent when he sees it. What you have here, what you are creating, is remarkable, and we want to help you with it. Once I have the first four pairs, I'll show them around to the right people, and I'm sure we'll find that you'll have more orders than you can fill. We'll work out the details next week. I have to check my calendar, but I think I can meet with you early next Wednesday morning for a couple of hours. Will that work? I'll call you with the details," she says as she hands Brenda her card.

"I work at the Gallery on Wednesdays, but I can let them know I might be in a little later, and I can meet as early as you want. I'm so overwhelmed right now, and need to process all of this. It's like a dream come true. All I ever wanted to do was to be an artist, and I can't believe I can actually make money doing something I love! The timing couldn't be better, either, since I'm not in school for the summer, and I'm only working at the Gallery three days a week, so I'll have time to devote to this.

"Wow, thank you so much! It's starting to sink in. Do you have my number?"

"Yes, George has it from the Gallery when he purchased the painting."

A young woman approaches the table, and George moves aside so she can get a closer look. While she's engrossed in looking over the sunglasses, George and Caroline say their goodbyes and hurry off before they're recognized. Brenda's still holding the check with a somewhat bewildered look on her face, when the young woman looks up holding a pair of sunglasses and asks how much they are.

"That pair is $25," Brenda says. "They're handprinted, by yours truly."

"Hmmm, they're nice, but out of my price range," the woman says as she puts them back on the table. "Any chance for a discount?"

Before this morning's events Brenda would have said *yes*, and would probably have been talked down more than she wanted. Instead, she says, "No, the price is firm."

The woman nods and walks away. Brenda smiles to herself, thinking the woman has made a big mistake. If anything, she's going to raise the prices on the ones she has left.

The rest of the morning Brenda's walking on air, working on autopilot as her mind goes over and over again her encounter with George and Caroline. She wants so badly to just pack up and go, and find Vincent to tell him all about it. *Unbelievable*, she keeps thinking, *incredible, too good to be true*. Finally, it's time to pack up, and she looks in her little box she keeps the sale money in, and realizes she's sold three pairs today. That's better than average, and that alone would have been considered a good day at the flea market. She rushes home, hoping Vincent's there, but he's not. She has his work number and has never used it so far, but decides this morning's events warrant a call to disturb him.

"Hi! Are you really busy, am I disturbing anything?" she asks before he even has a chance to say hello.

"No, I'm just finishing up here—kind of hit a roadblock on something I've been working on. Everything okay?"

"You're not going to believe what happened. George Connelly and his wife Caroline came to the flea market early this morning, and they want to buy custom sunglasses, four pairs! He gave me a check for $2,000."

"What? Oh my God, really? For four pairs?"

"That's not all. They want to help me get started in business, and get me high-paying customers who want quality, like them. I'm so excited I'm shaking, and I've been going around in circles since I got home. There's more, but I'll wait until you get home and tell you all at once, and you can tell me what you think."

"You know, Brenda, I've always known you're exceptionally talented, and I knew your break would come, I just didn't know it would be this soon," he laughs. "Let's go out to dinner and you can tell me everything. I'll be home in about twenty minutes."

CHAPTER 9

Brenda stands back, scrutinizing the painting she's working on, but her mind is elsewhere. She'd had trouble sleeping after her long talk with Vincent, which had lasted well into the night. Churning what was discussed over and over in her mind, she still isn't sure if what Vincent was telling her is wonderful and leading-edge, or perhaps dabbling in something he isn't meant to—almost too manipulative, or maybe tempting fate. She can't pin it down, but it somehow seems like it's going into unchartered waters with no clear direction, without concern of the consequences, or what might be encountered. She can't shake her sense of foreboding.

Bringing her attention back to the painting she was commissioned to do, she adds more color, remembering what the client had asked for. As she thinks of color, she considers the part of the conversation they had when Vincent talked about the formulas he'd written down during their mind-altering night in the desert. He self-consciously referred to it as their MDA, using the old acronym, probably because they hadn't talked about it for quite a while. What started the conversation was that Brenda had started a painting using her old sketch from that night in the desert, without mentioning it to him. It was inspirational on her part, and not like she was trying to hide anything. When Vincent happened to see it in her studio, he freaked out because she had incorporated a few of the formulas exactly as Vincent had written them, almost illegibly on top of the giant rock formations.

When Brenda asked why he was so upset about it, he said they had to sit down and have a long talk. He asked that she keep an open mind and hear him out. At first, she thought it might be something terrible, and couldn't imagine what he had to divulge. He started out explaining about how his work at Wave & Light Industries had evolved after being there for almost five years. He had initially thought it would be a stepping-stone, and that he would only be there for a year or so, or just until Brenda graduated. But with Brenda's art taking off the way it did, and his work at the company taking directions he hadn't known would be as compelling as they were, they'd ended staying where they were.

Vincent admitted to Brenda that their night in the desert had been much more life-altering than he let on. He said he wasn't sure why he held back, and thought maybe it was because he thought she wouldn't understand, or she would think differently of him and stop loving him. Although she was surprised by this, she had to admit to herself that she might have been put off a bit, and thought maybe they were just too different to make a lasting relationship work. She knew all couples held back things from each other for those very reasons. She herself was guilty of not revealing how deep her insecurities ran, and her fears of mental illness being hereditary.

Vincent opened up completely about what he thought had happened to him in the desert that night. He felt that the mushrooms, by putting him in an altered state of consciousness, had allowed him to receive inspiration by otherworldly means, like accessing knowledge outside of the brain. He felt his brain became a receptor of cosmic intelligence, explaining that our minds are already part of what is known as the *Universal Mind*. Not everyone can tap into this *Universal Mind*, he said, but the mushrooms enabled him to, because the vibrations and wavelengths to this pathway were exactly right. He asked Brenda if she remembered when they talked about how the mushrooms seemed to know exactly what they needed to see and feel. She did remember, except her experience was much more emotional, while Vincent was tapping into something beyond transcendental.

He also spoke of how he hadn't expected to be so involved in the type of projects he was doing at work, and found them so engrossing he often lost track of everything else. Brenda obviously knew this, but had saved the discussion on how this was affecting their relationship for another time. Vincent was working closely with one of his colleagues, who happened to be the scientist who was part of his interview process, and they'd ended up working together on the psychological impact of light and color. Vincent's part was to take the study a step further by creating different lenses to be used in researching the effects on the individual, based on input or output of various light and color combinations. Since light and color creates more than just visual effects, they delved into what could be learned about the biological and psychological effects using different lenses, along with different light sources as another variable.

Vincent went on to explain how it was already known how light and color can improve or disrupt sleep, affect our moods, and even our emotional processing. In the past, though, they'd left out of consideration how different lenses and the filtering of various light sources through these lenses could affect a person on many different levels. The current study he was involved in would use the findings to possibly help to influence emotional brain processing, and eventually even help reduce or possibly cure anxiety, depression, and other mental disorders.

This all seemed interesting to Brenda, but when watching Vincent explain all this, she saw a wild-eyed gleam in his eyes that was overzealous and somewhat disconcerting. He went on to explain that he'd been working more and more to decipher the formulas that were shown to him that night in the desert, so he'd be able to create a lens that would selectively control how much light came in while effecting the wavelengths. By doing this, using varied light and color, it would create a biological and psychological effect that allowed a person to tap into the part of the brain that effected their higher reasoning, and become a receptor of the *Universal Mind*. When Brenda looked somewhat uneasily at him, trying to take it all in, he said, 'Don't you see? With the right lens, I'll be able to recreate the same effect the mushrooms did at will, under the right conditions. The lens I create will do what the mushrooms did! Can you imagine the monumental impact and effect of something like that?'

Brenda is brought out of her ruminations by a knock on the door of her studio, followed by a voice calling out, "Hello, anybody here?"

"Oh my God!" Brenda exclaims when her friend and old college roommate Sarah walks in. "It's you! I was just thinking about you yesterday. How are you?" she asks as they reach in for a warm, lasting hug. "I've missed you!"

"I've missed you, too! Geez, how long has it been?"

"Too long!" Brenda exclaims. "What brings you here? You didn't come just to see me, did you?"

"No, I wish that was the case. My grandmother died, and I'm on my way to my parent's house. I told them I was coming in tonight so I would have time to visit with you. My Mom is a wreck—she was really close to my grandmother, and is having trouble accepting she's gone, even though she'd been sick for a while."

"Oh, I'm so sorry to hear it. How are you feeling? Are you okay?"

"Yeah, I'm okay. I loved my Nana, but she was in a lot of pain for too long, and it was horrible not being able to do anything about it. So now I have to believe she's on the other side and pain-free," Sarah says, choking up and trying to control her tears.

"Aww, Sarah, here, give me another hug. I'm so sorry; I know it's hard. Can I get you some coffee, water, anything?" Brenda asks. "I think I'll make some coffee; will you have some?"

"Sure," Sarah says as she starts to wander around the studio. "You know, it's funny, but I always knew you would become a famous painter. Your work is extraordinary. I honestly don't know a lot about art, but your work gives me feelings that the other stuff I see doesn't, certainly not in the same way. Except for maybe Monet and some of the other greats," she laughs.

"Well, I'm not famous yet, that's for sure. But I *am* getting known for the designer sunglasses, and that's really where I'm making my money. My *real art,* as I like to call it, is hit or miss. My paintings can hang in a gallery forever and not sell. I've actually had to take some out and get them into other galleries so they could use the space to give other artists some exposure. The sunglasses, on the other hand, are more than I can handle, thanks to George and Caroline. I owe everything to them for getting me started and believing in me.

"I'm pretty sure I told you how close we've become. At first, I was somewhat intimidated by their celebrity, especially George's. Then, after I got to know Caroline better, and realized how intelligent and grounded she is, and how genuinely she believed the sunglasses were deserving of the high price and collector value, I relaxed and just got into creating the best I could. The business took off, and Vincent helps, too. Did you know he's been making some of the lenses for the sunglasses, depending on the client, and if they need prescription lenses, whatever extras like unique polarization, color, etc.? It's really raised the quality and value of the glasses, and absolutely adds to the customization we're able to provide.

"Enough about me, though, what about you?" Brenda asks as she brings in the coffee. "Tell me about your new job. Are you seeing anyone? I want you to *spill,* tell me everything."

For the next couple of hours, the old friends talk and talk, like all good friends who haven't seen each other for a while. Sarah talks about getting her master's degree, her job, the next job she hopes to get, and the amazing guy she met who unfortunately lives in another state. She talks about how she's worried about her mom, whom she's close to, and hopes she'll be able to eventually accept her Nana's death.

This leads to a conversation about Brenda's mother, and how she's so jealous of Brenda's relationship with Caroline and George Connelly. About how her mother tells all her friends how close she is to the celebrities, and downplays Brenda's relationship with them. How Brenda once heard her mother bragging to her neighbors about Brenda's designer sunglasses and how wonderful they were, and yet to Brenda's face she once said, "The glasses are *interesting*, but I have to say, I'm surprised anyone would pay the prices you're asking for them." In the meantime, she's always hinting around for a new pair to go with her favorite outfits.

They reminisce about Dr. Cherry, and how helpful she was to Brenda in overcoming some of the deep-rooted affects her childhood had on her, and that leads to talking about the field of psychology Sarah is focusing on, and how thrilled she is to feel she's making a difference.

Fueled with caffeine and the excitement of seeing each other again, the conversation starts to become more intimate, and Sarah asks Brenda how things were going with Vincent; is she happy? Brenda's hesitation in answering speaks volumes, as she confesses to feeling somewhat neglected, with Vincent being so involved in his work all the time. It often feels like they're just crossing paths with each other. She also admits she sometimes feels depressed, even though so many things were going well. Brenda doesn't want to say anything too negative about Vincent or reveal too much to Sarah, but what she says is enough for her friend to understand they have some issues to work out. Sarah is tempted to offer more help as a psychologist, but she knows it's too close to home, and if anything, the asking for help will have to come from Brenda.

As they start to wind down and the stretches of silence become a little too long, Sarah is ready to continue on to her parent's house. "I'm so glad I stopped by. It was wonderful to catch up with you, and it made me feel better about my Nana and the funeral tomorrow. I love you, Brenda—if you need anything, you know where to find me," Sarah says as she gathers her purse and takes one last look around.

"It was wonderful to see you, too. It was perfect to just talk and talk; it was what I needed. Let's not make it so long next time, if we can help it,"

Brenda says as she reaches out for her goodbye hug. "I love you, too! I'll be thinking of you tomorrow, and please give my love and condolences to your family, especially your mom. I hope someday you'll tell her I wish I had a mom like her, if you haven't already," she laughs as she walks Sarah to the door.

"Later, my friend," she says as she closes the door.

After Sarah leaves, Brenda walks around her studio and stands in front of the *Night in the Desert* painting. She looks closely at the formulas, and wonders if these are the key that opens a lock that shouldn't be opened—the lock that controls higher forces that shouldn't be dabbled in or trifled with.

CHAPTER 10

After they have the initial talk when Vincent bared his soul about the night in the desert, giving full disclosure on what he experienced and how it affected him, there's a shift in the dynamic between them. When he's home, Vincent tends to be distracted, even though he makes a concerted effort to be more present. He tries to pay more attention to Brenda and what she's involved in with her work, although he really isn't all that interested, except when it comes to the sunglasses. He enjoys making the custom lenses for the glasses, and is glad he can contribute to the making of them; plus, they're bringing in so much money. He's grateful for this one thing they can create and share together, so he gives it his all. For him, it's the recreational part of his work, and since he mostly makes the lenses after hours, he occasionally smokes a joint while doing so, convincing himself the finished product is even better that way. *If only they knew,* he chuckles to himself.

His work at Wave & Light Industries is mostly all consuming, and he sometimes thinks about how great it would be if he could just live there and work 24/7. It isn't that he doesn't love Brenda, it's more an obsession with his goals he has trouble keeping in check. He feels he's found his purpose in life and knows his innovations are making a difference in so many lives. His work on creating a light filtration system that was effective in treating anxiety and depression has earned him the National Engineers Innovation award. The company is ecstatic about this for multiple reasons, which results in them giving Vincent his own lab and whatever resources he needs to continue his ingenious inventions.

Not to sell himself short, but Vincent knows that a lot of his inspiration came from the formulas he was shown in the desert that night. He's sure he'd tapped into the *Universal Mind* with the help of the mushrooms, and he wants more of that, not knowing how long the residual effects will last. There are times the ideas come to him suddenly and without conscious thought, easily implemented, and other times when he feels that his brainwaves are blocked and he can only access the mundane. Those times are the most frustrating, because he's becoming accustomed to higher thinking, and wants to be able to do it at will.

One evening while working in his lab making prescription lenses for a pair of Brenda's sunglasses, he decides to experiment using the lenses to see how newly innovative filters, under various lighting, will enhance or otherwise effect the vision of the user. He himself doesn't need glasses, but he's intrigued by the nature of this particular prescription, since it's unlike any he's previously worked with. For several hours, he tries various combinations of filters and light conditions, and is quite taken in with the results. He becomes convinced the experimental filters are affecting the wavelengths of light coming into the lenses. This greatly alters the clarity of what he's seeing, especially under what would be described as simulated bright sunlight. One particular filter he uses looks rather dark to the naked eye, but has a minuscule embedded geometric pattern that allows direct light wavelengths in through different filtering techniques. The interesting inconsistency is that the brightest sunlight he experiments with, along with darkest filters using geometric technology, provides the greatest distinctness of vision.

There's a thunderstorm brewing outside, and Vincent becomes more aware of it as the last lightning bolt and thunder cause the lighting in the lab to dim. He put the lenses on and goes to the window in hopes of seeing another lightning bolt. There are several over a brief period of time, but none of them have any kind of effect on what he's seeing. He's disappointed as he closes the shades when the storm starts to move on, then chuckles to himself, thinking, *Okay, Dr. Frankenstein, back to work.*

The next three nights, Vincent tries different combinations of light and filters on the lenses until he's certain he has the right filters; now he needs to pin down the exact light source. He's getting frustrated, as he feels he's so close, but has tried every type imaginable and is stuck. He decides to get some air and goes outside for a short walk to the back of the building, where they have a few picnic tables set up as an eating area. Even though it's after 8:00pm, it's still light out, being the middle of summer, and he looks over to where the setting sun is leaving a beautiful glow of light on the trees and mountains in the distance. The light is stunning; *a photographer's dream,* he thinks as he pulls the lenses out of his pocket and put them on, turning his head to the beautiful light.

Oh. My. God. That's the last thing he remembers consciously thinking until he becomes aware of an uncomfortable tingling on the inside of his left arm. He realizes he still has the lenses on and takes them off, carefully putting them in his shirt pocket. By now it's civil twilight, but looking around, he can still see his surroundings. He glances down at his arm, and is shocked to see it's covered in almost illegible writing done in black ink. Feeling a little lightheaded, he stands up and starts walking back towards the entrance of the building to his lab. The light is bright inside and hurts his eyes briefly, until he adjusted the lights to a dimmer setting.

He sits there staring at his arm until he begins to recognize that he's seeing new formulas. These formulas are unlike anything he's ever seen before. He keeps staring, trying to absorb and accept that he has indeed tapped into the *Universal Mind* once again. He spends the rest of the evening transcribing the formulas into the software he's using, and making sure he saves everything in a private folder to access later. He carefully and painstakingly makes sure he copies every single thing he's written on his arm, double checking to make certain he didn't miss anything. He then carefully inserts the lenses securely in a sturdy frame, and encloses them in the least breakable case he has. While recording every detail about the lenses, filters, light source and conditions surrounding the light source, he realizes he's sweating and breathing heavily. He stops to take a deep breath and wipe his brow; then, laying his head down on his desk, he closes his eyes and immediately falls into a deep sleep.

It seems like moments, although it's more than an hour later when he opens his eyes, feeling slightly disoriented. Sitting up, he becomes aware of his arm again and the evening's events all came rushing back to him. *This is a discovery that would have a monumental effect on mankind, and I'm sitting here with an arm covered in writing, like a toddler let loose with a magic marker and no paper.* He suddenly can't stop laughing as he goes to find his camera, to photograph from every angle the life-altering evidence of harnessing the ability to control tapping into the *Universal Mind. Okay, Dr Frankenstein, time to clean up,* he tells himself as he heads to the restroom, hoping it wasn't permanent ink in that pen.

On his short drive home, he's trying to decide if he should share his discovery with Brenda yet. He knows he has to tell her eventually, but when he pictures her reaction, he decides it might be best to experiment with the sunglasses more first. He knows she'll be excited and happy for him, but he also knows she feels like it's opening Pandora's box. If he can prove to her how wonderfully beneficial his discovery is, he feels sure he can allay at least some of her fears.

As he slips into bed, trying not to disturb her, she stirs and reaches out to cuddle with him. "I made an amazing discovery today," he whispers into her hair as he holds her tightly.

"Hmmm, good," she mumbles, settling into his arms. A couple of minutes later, just as he's falling asleep, he hears her mumble, "You smell like soap."

CHAPTER 11

Vincent feels several huge internal changes, as well as countless subtler effects after his second encounter with what he perceives as the *Universal Mind*. He wonders if he was chosen by some higher force to be the one to use this formerly unknown information for the greater good of mankind. Or is he just getting carried away with the spiritual aspect, and should he be looking at it in a scientific way, as an engineer? *The information is out there, I tapped into it unconsciously, then created a way to do it consciously, therefore…what?* He doesn't know, isn't sure, and uses that as an excuse to not divulge to Brenda what happened, until he has a chance to sort it all out.

Vincent carefully documents his work with the formulas, studying and experimenting with each one, resulting in everything from new innovations in wavelength theory to creating software that helps enhance optics used in surgery. He's making tremendous discoveries more quickly than seems achievable by one person, and his colleagues start to view him with an even higher respect. Some of them are baffled by this somewhat sudden increased burst of genius, and even ask him about it. He's tempted to tell someone he can trust, but feels he needs to be able to have more control and understanding of the method of accessing and receiving from the *Universal Mind* before he can divulge anything to anyone. He understands that this is not something to get carried away with, and sometimes feels a sense of trepidation in trying to access something he now believes is sacred.

In documenting every after-effect as it occurs, Vincent is intrigued by the sometimes overwhelming emotional side effects he's experiencing. Brenda often teases him about thinking like an engineer, and he teases her about thinking like an artist, and they'll laugh, saying opposites attract. There are times they both wonder what the heck they're doing together, but more often than not they feel like they belong. Recently, he's started feeling more sentimental and loving towards Brenda. There are even times he feels tears in his eyes when he thinks about how fortunate he is to have Brenda as a partner. Their lovemaking is infused with new life, and even though he's immersed in his work, whenever they're together, he can't stop himself from wanting to touch her and be physically close to her.

The disturbing part about all the residual effects is their inconsistency. He experiences periods of elation, where the direction and nature of his work is guided by something outside of himself, and other times by something inside that he didn't know he had in him. Vincent can never be sure if he will be feeling overly sentimental or completely engrossed in life-altering discoveries. He knows receiving the formulas was only part of what happened. The *Universal Mind* is not one- two-, or three-dimensional; it's of a dimension unable to be perceived, described, or explained. It's a puzzle that he embraces, and feels attached to from his very core as a human being. He feels it's beyond simple or complex humanity, but rather belonging to an all-encompassing Creator. He wonders if the after-effects are long-lasting or quickly fading, and vows to appreciate every effect, not knowing how long- or short-lived it may be.

In addition to trying to stay balanced while juggling so many facets of life and work, Vincent feels he must devote time to creating another pair of sunglasses in exactly the same way to achieve the same effects. Imagine being able to share this ability to tap into the *Universal Mind* via technology. Is that messing with universal things that should be left alone, or shared with all of humanity? How can he be sure it will be used for the greater good? How can he harness just the best aspects, and alleviate the greed that's sure to arise if he's able to create another pair?

So far, Vincent's kept the sunglasses in his possession at all times during work, and hidden them in his closet when he's at home. He struggles with not putting them on again, at least for now, but at times finds he's almost on the verge of giving in. After much deliberation, he decides to show Brenda the glasses, and asks her to do a painting on them of a triangular prism with laser light reflecting through to banded colors. He'll tell her he made this pair for himself and that the custom lenses, a special prescription, give him real clarity of vision in all kinds of light. Once he's decided, he pats the jacket pocket he keeps the sunglasses in and decides to go home at a reasonable hour to spend time with Brenda, and make his request at dinner.

"You're home early," Brenda exclaims as he walks through the front door. "I was just putting some chicken in the oven and going to make a salad. Are you hungry?"

"Hi, honey. Yes, I'm hungry. That sounds good," he says as he walks towards her for a hug.

"Is everything okay?" she asks, still hugging him. "You're hardly ever home this early."

"I was getting a little headache," he says, rubbing his temples. "And I felt like I needed a break, kind of getting burnt-out."

"Geez, I never hear you say that—you *must* be worn out. Come sit down and relax. Do you want something to drink? I was going to have a glass of wine."

"Ah," Vincent sighs as he sinks into his chair, putting his feet up. "Come sit with me for a little while. I have something to show you."

Brenda brings the wine, they clink glasses, and just sit back for a minute enjoying the restful feeling of being with each other. "What do you have to show me?" she asks. "Is it a present?"

"Actually, yes, but unfortunately not for you. It's a present for me," Vincent laughs as he takes the sunglasses out of the pocket of the jacket he'd thrown on the back of his chair. They spend the next half hour talking about the *special* sunglasses Vincent made for himself, and what design he would like Brenda to paint on them. She likes the idea a lot, and feels it's the perfect design for him, envisioning the colors and how she'll make it flow. It's Vincent's idea to have both of their initials on this particular pair, as a symbol of their collaborative effort for his own personal use. Interestingly, Vincent had previously been happy with whatever pair of sunglasses Brenda gave him to wear, so this is kind of a big deal to her that he's specifically asking for his own design. She wishes she'd thought of it herself, to have done as a gift for him. She also likes the idea of both their initials to designate a personal pair, and thinks about a special design she can create for herself.

The following morning, after Vincent has gone to work, Brenda takes the sunglasses into her studio and first draws a sketch to scale, to see how it will play out on the glasses. She surprises herself sometimes with how skilled she's gotten painting in miniature, and wonders if people realize how difficult it is. Satisfied with the sketch, she organizes the brushes and paints she'll use, and picks up the sunglasses to really scrutinize where the best spot will be to paint both of their initials. On impulse, she puts them on and looks around. Her studio gets a lot of natural light, but today is somewhat cloudy, so the light keeps changing. She can see that the lenses are of excellent quality, and likes the medium darkness of the shading, but honestly doesn't see anything special about them. She takes them off and gets to work.

Once finished, Brenda puts them on the windowsill to dry, feeling quite satisfied with the way they turned out. As she starts working on another pair for a customer, she thinks about how fantastic her relationship with Vincent has been these past couple of months. However, she's no dummy, and knows something is up. She likes the changes in Vincent, but at times feels he's running on automatic, like a robot, fluctuating between being an emotional softy and a distracted engineer. She tries not to dwell on this as she goes about her work throughout the day.

In the late afternoon, she takes a break and checks to see if the paint on Vincent's glasses has dried. She really likes the way they turned out, and puts them on to see how they look in the mirror. As she's admiring them and thinking they may be the best ones yet, the light from behind her shines through the window and bounces off the mirror, directly into her eyes. For a few seconds she can't see, so she turns from the mirror and looks out the window. Taking the glasses off, she puts them aside, because suddenly she feels inspired to start a new painting.

After what seemed like only minutes, but is actually three hours, Brenda puts her brush down and steps back from the painting she was so engrossed in. The strongest emotion she feels is confusion. Part of her feels euphoric, as though she's taken the worst negative energy out of herself, put it on the canvas, and left it there. Another part of her feels sad inside when she looks at it, like she's wrapped in a shroud. The painting is so emotionally dark, emitting a lifetime of hurt. Now she feels lighter, as though the painting were the cathartic cleansing she needed.

When Vincent comes home, she's still in her studio, now with the lights on, standing in front of the painting. She doesn't acknowledge him or even seem to notice him, so he comes over to see what has her so mesmerized. He gasps when he looks at the painting, and literally takes a few steps back. "What the hell is that?" he asks, holding his hand over his heart.

"I don't know," she says quietly, finally looking at him, then adds, "I put your sunglasses on this afternoon."

"Oh," is all Vincent says as he sighs deeply.

Brenda too sighs deeply and says, "We need to talk."

CHAPTER 12

They can only talk about the sunglasses in very small segments and never specifics, only generally. But the *general* part is so huge, gigantic in concept, that they tend to ask more questions rather than make concrete conclusions. The whole concept is too much for words. However, when each of them is alone, their internal conversation becomes much more specific and subjective, using their inner selves as the sounding board.

Vincent has had more experience tapping into the *Universal Mind*, and his experiences have been more positive and productive than Brenda's, up until now. Her first and only experience with what the sunglasses allowed her to tap into was more painful and cathartic than Vincent's. This has them wondering how and if the *Universal Mind* knows, just like the mushrooms did in the desert, exactly what the individual needs on a higher level than can be explained. They use words like *metaphysical* and *spiritual,* maybe *otherworldly* when trying to flesh out the experiences they've had, as well as what's continuing to happen. They've learned this may not be a one-time burst of amazingness. They're both undergoing residual effects they never thought of as something they needed, yet proving time again to be exactly that. In some ways, it scares them, because they don't feel in control, and in other ways they're euphoric, because they have never perceived such a sense of knowing or felicity.

The morning following Brenda's painting of what she now thinks of as the *darkest hurt on canvas*, she wraps the painting in an old sheet and stuffs it in the deepest part of a closet they hardly ever use. Vincent notices it's gone and he doesn't ask about it. The painting speaks volumes, more than hours of discussion could explain in words, and that's enough for him. He had felt such discomfort looking at it that it shocked him, yet it also helped him to understand more about Brenda's internal battles. Those demons now live on the canvas, and in a sense, she has been exorcised.

Brenda views herself as a skilled artist, and like most true artists, believes she could be better. At times she feels that there are elements missing, keeping her from creating masterpieces rather than just good paintings. She takes criticism to heart and compliments with doubt, wishing she could make that leap to what she views as a *great* artist. Even though she doesn't realize it, the *darkest hurt on canvas* painting *is* a masterpiece. That painting is her first masterpiece, but will probably never be shown or recognized as such. Gathering dust, hidden away in the closet is probably best for it, and she forgets about it.

Knowing what Vincent has told her about the *Universal Mind* and what she has accessed, Brenda recognizes this unique infusion of energy and creativity. With renewed ability, she allows her muse to dance upon the canvas, realizing her barely conceptualized ideas are flowing from her brush into magnificent creations. She's using techniques she always felt she was on the verge of discovering, seeing the intangible become visible in form and emotion. Each painting brings her the greatest satisfaction, and she relishes every stroke. She wonders if the greatest painters felt this way, and where they got their inspiration and expertise from. Did they still have doubts about their work? Always, in the back of her mind, she wonders if this feeling and skill will last. Is this ability beyond her wildest dreams really her? So much hurt has been left behind, yet the human apprehension still remains.

Vincent sees the enrichment in Brenda's work; some of it is subtle, some of it breathtaking. He also sees the change in Brenda herself, and enjoys the lightness and contentment she seems to be experiencing. He finds it interesting that she's pulled back from her family, and limits any time with them to a minimum. In the past she would have felt guilty doing this, and now it's something she hardly gives a second thought to. He doesn't ask her about it, but feels sure they both know where her sense of peace is coming from.

Vincent hasn't told Brenda that he's been experimenting with his *special* sunglasses; attempting to tap into the *Universal Mind* again, as he feels she would not approve. Admittedly, he has some apprehension, but his desire for more information is stronger than his fears. Even though he has more original information than he could possibly use in a lifetime, he craves more. Brenda hasn't asked him about this, and he hasn't offered any insight. It's a topic they dance around, knowing why they do it, yet neither is willing to bring it up.

Brenda is newly discovering the capabilities of what she's accessed, and is quite satisfied with any and all results. She knows this is about more than enhanced skill. It's about incorporating the gift into her being, taking nothing for granted, appreciating every bit, down to the cellular level. She doesn't have room, at least for now, to want more than she can manage, more than she deserves. Knowing Vincent, she wouldn't be surprised to know he's continually trying to tap into the *Universal Mind* again. She tries not to think about it, doesn't want to know.

So far Vincent hasn't been able to make any progress finding the exact light and time of day to tap in again. He was surprised everything was so perfectly aligned when Brenda tried them on, not having the slightest inkling of what could happen, and BAM, have them connect like the strongest magnets. This is another thing to think about. Maybe he shouldn't be trying all the time; maybe he should just try to forget about it, and only use the glasses as he would any normal pair. Maybe when the time is right, when it's *supposed* to happen, it will. He continues working on a second pair, the ones for Brenda he will give to her as a gift. Even if they never have the same effect, she can still paint them and add both of their initials, a shared reminder of their collaboration.

CHAPTER 13

Brenda doesn't mind so much that Vincent seems to be working more than ever, especially since the time they do spend together is rich, full, and satisfying. This thing, this happening, this situation they share, bonds them deeply. They often don't need to speak to know, perhaps feel, what the other is thinking. It's an easy and special relationship, with both of them engrossed in their own pursuits, and succeeding in ways they also knowingly acknowledge sometimes with a nudge and a wink, knowing more than anyone else could, the deeper recesses.

Brenda now knows Vincent has been repeatedly trying to access the *Universal Mind* again with his sunglasses, and she also knows he's only been able to get what he calls a *blip* now and then. This hasn't deterred any of his other work, and he continues to make remarkable discoveries, in addition to now being in high demand for teaching, sold-out lectures, and symposiums. Truth be told, she's glad he hasn't accomplished tapping in again to the degree he has previously been able to. She feels this has been a gift and not something to be harnessed at will, a balance that should not be tipped.

Vincent enjoys his brief blips with the *Universal Mind,* even though there's been no new information forthcoming, just emotional warmth and a buzzing sense that all is right with the world. When this happens, it reminds him of the times in college when he would smoke a joint and go to class, high on life and knowledge. He toys with the idea of making sunglasses just for this purpose and using them for a brief, drug-free high. This could be used instead of drugs for pain and other ailments. *I'm sure the drug companies would love that,* he laughs to himself.

He feels satisfied with what he hopes is a special pair of sunglasses he created just for Brenda. Even though she says she's very pleased with what she's gained, and not looking for more, he perceives she could benefit with additional insight on an emotional level if another connection is made. Vincent has chosen a retro-type frame for the lenses, and imagines what Brenda will want to paint on her custom pair. Thinking of the place where both their initials will be painted gives him a shared sense of satisfaction, knowing there are only two pairs of these beyond-unique sunglasses in the entire world.

After several attempts with the lenses for Brenda's glasses, he's convinced they'll be able to again bring about some kind of connection with the *Universal Mind* for her. He's fashioned the lenses almost exactly like his pair, with the exception of tweaking what he perceives to be the element that will give her the most emotional benefit. Every time he's made communion using these lenses, the experience has been pleasant, full of mind-expanding feelings about life, but not earth-shattering like the life-altering revelations that were poured into him with his original lenses. This will be good for Brenda, and she can experiment with them, enjoying what he hopes will give her more emotional healing and positive effects.

Glancing at the clock, he sees it's a couple of hours before the lecture he's scheduled to give downtown. If he leaves now, he'll have plenty of time to take the back roads to the conference center, stopping for something to eat at the hotel next door. After cleaning the glasses with a special solvent and polishing them to a shine, he puts them in a case and grabs his jacket. It's beautiful outside, with an hour of sunlight left, one of his favorite times of day.

Once he gets off of the main highway and starts meandering along the back road that runs partially parallel to the highway, Vincent relaxes into his seat and daydreams. His eyes scan the coral and rose-colored sky, beautiful trees, and sunlight filtering through. When the sun reaches the level where it's positioned directly at eye level, blinding him, he reaches into his pocket, takes Brenda's sunglasses out, and puts them on. BAM, everything looks so brilliant, so splendid! The colors, the light; he's never seen anything so clearly, so tangibly, so dimensionally. He can see every ray of light, every color in minute particles.

Vincent is driving on automatic at this point, not cognizant of his actions, just performing them. For several miles he drives like this, admiring his surroundings and noting to himself every color, shape and shadow. When he comes to a sharp bend in the road, not quite slowing down, he realizes the split second of infinite time when the buck jumps into the road, and when he hits it. At point of contact, everything stills and the buck is looking directly into his eyes. Vincent feels himself being pulled into the depths with such intensity, he just lets himself go. The antlers crash into and pierce the windshield; then heat, silence… and fade to black.

CHAPTER 14

Brenda is beyond devastated when she finds out about the accident. Vincent died immediately and was gone, just like that. How can that be? Here one minute, gone the next. She had been finishing up painting a pair of sunglasses for a friend of Caroline's when the accident occurred. Vincent dying was the farthest thing from her mind at that time, and she wonders why she didn't feel it, or at least feel it coming. In some weird way, she feels she should have done something to prevent it happening. At times she's in denial; others, she's overcome with a heavy grief that weighs her down so much she can hardly move. She had been feeling so happy with her life, so fulfilled, and now the rug has been pulled out from under her, and she can't get up.

With the help of the Connellys, and her friend Sarah, they get the Celebration of Life arrangements done, and are by her side at the wake, supporting her and helping her get through it. When George and Caroline bring her to the funeral home, before they go inside, Caroline pulls her in for a long hug. They're both crying and trying to compose themselves. Caroline looks up and motions to Brenda to look at the flock of butterflies hovering and flitting back and forth overhead.

"Yes," Brenda says. "I've been seeing so many butterflies since Vincent died. It's like they're following me. Comforting me."

"Hmmm, yes, like they're comforting you. Interesting, since they're generally long gone by this time of year, you know," Caroline says with a small smile. "Oh, and by the way, did Vincent wear cologne?"

"No," Brenda answers. "But the soap he used has a fragrance of musk and ambergris. Can you smell it too?" Brenda asks as their eyes meet, and more tears come pouring down their faces. Caroline nods and looks up at the sky. They smile a little between the snuffles and nose-blowing and tear-wiping. They have no words; there are none forthcoming for what they both feel.

Brenda's mother and father are standing out front with Sarah, and witnessed the emotional hug between Brenda and Caroline. Her mother is jealous, and can't believe a celebrity like Caroline could care about her daughter so much. She wants Caroline, and George too, to care about her, and fawn over her like they do her daughter. She moves down the sidewalk and puts her hand out to George, and he pulls her in for a hug. She looks around to see who's watching, and forces a few tears for effect. Sarah watches this charade and looks away before her expression conveys her true feelings about Brenda's mother.

Brenda's father, as usual, doesn't know what to do or say, and just stands there until Brenda's mother joins him again. Brenda approaches them and puts out her arms, so needing her mother's caring and love. They hug briefly, and her mother tells her they can't stay long, because they have to get back for something to do with her brothers. Her father hugs her briefly and asks if she's going to be all right. Of course, Brenda nods *yes,* she'll be all right. It's the expected answer.

The Celebration of Vincent's Life is incredible, and several hundred people come from all over. He was well-known and revered by his colleagues for all the work he had done to help humanity, and they feel it's such a great loss—not only as a friend, but for mankind. Vincent's Aunt Carol and Uncle Joe are there, and can't help being astounded by how much more they learn about the greatness of the nephew they'd raised as their son. The energy and love surrounding the throng of people that come to pay their respects is one of grief. However, when any of those who attended are asked about it later, they'll say they have never experienced anything like the other feeling that pervaded throughout. It was somehow joyous, expansive, an all-encompassing love that told them everything would be okay. All was well.

Afterwards, back at Brenda's house, her friend Sarah, the Connellys, and Vincent's aunt and uncle are having a drink, just sitting quietly in their own thoughts. Aunt Carol clears her throat and asks, "Brenda, where are your parents? Aren't they coming?"

Everyone looks at Brenda, then looks down as she says, "They had something more important to do."

Aunt Carol gets up and sits next to Brenda, taking her into her arms. "Oh, honey," is all she can say as she rocks her and smooths her hair.

With the help of her friends, Brenda gets through each day one at a time, often on automatic, often feeling like a heavy veil has been draped over her life, and she can't get out from under it. She tries to continue painting, but everything seems to turn out flat. Her brushes no longer easily transfer the images from her mind to her hand, and every time she tries, it feels like such an effort, with no results. She senses it's unwavering grief holding her back, and wants to rid herself of it. If only she could pour it onto the canvas like she did once before, on the *darkest hurt on canvas* painting she has hidden away in the closet.

Brenda starts thinking about Vincent's sunglasses and how through them, she tapped into the *Universal Mind* by accident. This access caused her to paint the *darkest hurt on canvas* in such a way that she purged the blackest of her inner demons, and became a masterful artist. Could she recreate the flow of the *Universal Mind* again? This is the first time Brenda has really thought about trying to proactively use the glasses like Vincent used to. The more she thinks about it, the more she becomes obsessed with doing it. All kinds of questions about the morality of trying to do this swirl around in her head when she gets up and hunts around in the closet until she finds Vincent's hiding place for the sunglasses. Once they're in her hands she takes a deep breath, puts them on, and walks over to the window. She stands there for a long time… and nothing happens. She starts to cry, though vows not to give up.

Brenda doesn't know about the other pair of sunglasses Vincent had made especially for her. Nor does she know, or suspect, that he was wearing them when he smacked into the buck. There was no way for her to know the glasses came off his face when the airbag deployed, getting wedged down onto his lap. When he was pulled from the wreckage, the sunglasses, along with a lot of glass, fell onto the street. By the time he was loaded into the ambulance, the glasses were kicked to the side of the road, forgotten until the wrecking crew came to tow away the crushed car and sweep up the remains of the wreck. As the tow truck driver was finishing sweeping up the glass on the side of the road, he bent down to pick up what he thought was a decent looking pair of sunglasses. He shook them off, looked around, and put them in his overall's pocket.

CHAPTER 15

The months following Vincent's death are a blur, but Brenda keeps getting up every morning, trying to move on, one step at a time. It mostly feels like baby steps, going around in circles, but at least it's something, better than rolling up in a ball in the corner and giving up. She tries to keep painting but doesn't feel very inspired, and most of what she's done turns out to be toneless and flat. Fortunately, her sunglasses business is at an all-time high, forcing her to keep working on them and giving her a purpose. Getting a pair Vincent had been associated with, posthumously, seems to make them more valuable, and the orders keep piling in. A colleague of Vincent's takes over making the lenses, and Brenda pays him handsomely for his work. The guy does a good job, is thrilled with the extra income, and glad he can do something for Brenda and his old friend.

At first, many of their friends and colleagues check in on Brenda often, always offering to help, inviting her places and asking if there's anything they can do. As much as she appreciates this, she isn't surprised when the attention starts to taper off, and people go back to their busy lives. Her closest friends try their best to be there for her, and this helps her greatly, especially when she doesn't have to explain why she wants to be alone. They sometimes feel she's getting too comfortable with her aloneness and try to help her find the balance, to keep her from withdrawing too much into herself.

Brenda discovers that one soothing way to keep herself occupied, especially when she's lonely and missing Vincent desperately, is to experiment with his sunglasses. Sometimes it gives her great comfort just to have them and wear them, knowing how much they meant to him. Then there are the times she actually gets a *blip,* as Vincent liked to describe it. She feels an infusion of energy in a certain light, but it never peaks or turns into the kind of connection she's hoping for. She tries not to give up, and remembers a saying Caroline has whenever things aren't happening in the timing or way you want them to. Caroline will say, "Don't push the river, Brenda." She thinks of this saying often, and tries hard to feel it whenever her experimenting doesn't bring about the results she wants. At least her painting has improved, and is almost back to where it was before Vincent died. The dimension, light, and emotion now flow more easily, and the inspiration is quite heartening. Brenda knows at least some of this comes from a higher source, a multi-dimensional muse, and wonders if this muse will be everlasting.

Another after-effect of the *blips* comes while she sleeps. When Vincent first died, she would wake up in the middle of the night gasping, thinking she was drowning. She hadn't been just dreaming she was drowning; it was more real than that. She couldn't breathe and felt her lungs filling with water, then woke up gasping and screaming. Her doctor said it was anxiety and prescribed Xanax. She hated taking them, because they gave her headaches and made her tired, so she stopped after taking them only a few doses.

After experiencing a stronger *blip* than usual one day, she feels extremely tired and needs a nap. She falls asleep immediately and sinks deeply into a dream of Vincent. In her dream, they spend several hours talking, and Vincent imparts many secrets to her. He speaks of formulas, light, universal truths, and love. Upon awakening, she immediately starts writing down as much as she can remember, but nearly all of it becomes muddled. She tries hard to remember, and closes her eyes. What she sees is a close-up of Vincent's face, showing every line, every freckle in vivid detail. The more she looks, the more she sees into him, until she feels she's looking at his core, his essence, his very being. She feels herself sinking into him, and then there's a flash, quick and bright. She opens her eyes and feels disoriented, but oddly happy. *I think we've made some progress*, she thinks cheerfully.

As time goes on, it becomes almost routine for Brenda to wear Vincent's glasses whenever she can. The only time she doesn't wear them is when she's driving; she has another pair for that. For some reason, she just knows she shouldn't wear them while driving. She's starting to need glasses for reading and even had a pair made for when she's painting. She doesn't feel she needs them for distance yet.

The way she got the strongest reaction wearing the sunglasses, when she had the blinding light reflected from the mirror into her eyes, never happened that way again. Since then, she's never had so strong a reaction, and wonders if tapping into the U*niversal Mind* like that only happens once. Vincent only had it once from the sunglasses, and then only *blips* after that.

Brenda starts to feel she might be getting addicted to the *blips* that she's now able to access more often than not. Her dreams afterwards almost always involve Vincent. She's sure the *blips* are the cause of the increased communication with Vincent in her dreams, but it's frustrating, because she can never fully grasp what he seems to be wanting to tell her. At times she's satisfied just feeling she's connecting to him, but she wants more. She's thinking about this as she's getting ready to meet Sarah for a drink, wishing she could tell her about it, knowing she can't. This too weighs on her, not being able to share the *Universal Mind* with anyone, ever. That died along with Vincent.

Sarah's sitting at the bar sipping a freshly made drink, talking with the bartender and flirting a little. Brenda smiles, watching her friend and wondering why she's never found the perfect guy to settle down with. She's quite pretty, scarily smart, and funny. *Maybe because she's a psychologist and knows too much about human nature*, she thinks.

Sarah looks over then, spotting her, and her face lights up with a big smile. "Hey Brenda, hope you don't mind that I started without you."

"Hi, beautiful! Don't mind at all. Won't take me long to catch up, that's for sure," Brenda says as she takes off her jacket and puts her purse on the bar.

The crease between Sarah's brows deepens for a second as she thinks about how true that is. She tries not to dwell on the thought of how much Brenda has been drinking lately, as Brenda orders her first drink and settles in. "So, how are you doing?" Sarah asks.

Brenda takes a couple of big sips, then says, "I'm okay. Not bad—some days are better than others, but at least I'm starting to have more good days. Still having strange dreams, still feel this heavy grief feeling, but sometimes, especially when I'm painting, I almost forget about it. It's like it fades into the background, hovering there in case I want to look for it. Does that sound strange?"

"No, not really," Sarah says. "It's all part of the process, the stages you go through when you lose a loved one. It's important to go through them and for you to talk about it when you can, rather than try to squash down the grief and pretend it doesn't exist. I'm sure you feel most people don't want to hear it, because they don't know what to say to you. So you just say 'I'm fine,' when you're not. That can hurt even more, and holds back your healing."

Brenda has signaled the bartender for another drink while Sarah's talking, and Sarah can't help but look disapprovingly at her. "You look like you've lost weight. Are you forgetting to eat?"

"I eat," Brenda says, "when I remember to. I still don't have much of an appetite. Should we order something? Maybe a couple of appetizers?"

"Sure, pick out a few and get whatever you want. You know I'm not picky," Sarah says as she starts to get up. "I have to pee, be back in a minute."

Brenda orders some quesadillas, shrimp cocktail, cheese sticks, and another drink. As soon as the bartender puts the drink down, she sucks up half of it to make it look like her drink looked when Sarah left for the bathroom. She then places it back on the bar and looks around.

As Sarah is making her way back to the bar, Brenda notices a woman sitting alone, and feels like the woman has been watching her. For a split second she makes eye contact, and the woman looks away first, then starts perusing the menu she has in her hands. Sarah sits down and Brenda forgets all about her.

#

The woman *has* been watching them, definitely noticing how much Brenda is drinking, and how she hid the third drink she ordered before her friend got back. Hmmm, they seem like really close friends, and that's not something you do with a close friend, unless you have a problem. *I like people with a problem; it makes them weak, easy targets,* she thinks.

The woman's name is Marlene, and it's the first time she's been here. It's an upscale restaurant in a good neighborhood, and no one knows her here. She's hoping to remain anonymous, at least for tonight, and maybe find an easy mark. *Easy* being the operative word here. She chuckles to herself about the quick getaway she had to make earlier today, and is a little worn out from driving for three straight hours. She figures the ground she covered making herself scarce will be enough for now, and that he'll never think to look for her here. That guy will be really pissed when he finds out how she double-crossed him for the money, and took off with the drugs to boot. Now she has enough to last her a while, ten grand in cash, and a nice place to spend the night down the road where she'll figure out her next moves.

A few more bucks plus some jewelry couldn't hurt, Marlene thinks as she peers over her menu to see if either of them at the bar are wearing jewelry or have expensive purses. Just then, the server appears and asks if she's ready to order. She nods, gives her order, then gets up to take the long way past the bar to the restroom, to get a better look. Neither of them pays any attention to her as she walks by, being engrossed in their conversation. They're definitely getting louder and laughing a lot.

Marlene lingers over her meal, eating slowly as the restaurant fills up. Fortunately, no one bothers her or seems to notice her, and she's really glad she has her paperback to prop up while she eats and observes. A few tables over, there are three men who look like work colleagues, and one of them keeps glancing over. She knows she could easily get him to come to her room tonight, but she really is too tired for that, knowing it could result in a long, drawn-out night for little return. Instead, she waits and watches the two women. Finally, the one she thinks of as the responsible one looks at her watch and motions that it's time for her to go. Then she and her friend seem to have a long exchange that almost looks like an argument. The responsible one gives in, gives her a hug, then says something to the bartender. He nods, then nods again. The woman seems satisfied, hugs her friend one last time, and leaves.

Timing it perfectly, Marlene approaches the bar just as the bartender puts another drink down in front of Brenda. *What a moron,* Marlene thinks with a smile. *Can't he see she's already had too much to drink? Well, it's going to help my cause, so let's see where it goes.*

"Hi, mind if I sit here?" Marlene asks Brenda. "I'm here for work—just finished dinner, and not ready to go back to my room yet."

"Sure, have a seat," Brenda says with a slight slur. "I'll keep you company for a little bit, just until I finish this drink. Then I promised my friend I would take a taxi home instead of driving. Right, Mason?" she asks.

Mason the bartender nods, asks Marlene what she's drinking, then moves on to take care of another customer.

Marlene starts a conversation, and before long Brenda's sharing with her that her partner recently died in a car crash. Marlene comforts her, and orders another drink that she gives to Brenda instead of drinking it herself. When Brenda says she needs the lady's room, Marlene offers to go with her, but Brenda declines, saying she's fine, and staggers a little to the restroom.

While she's gone, Marlene picks up the purse Brenda left on her seat, and starts quickly going through it. She notices that the bartender at the other end of the bar isn't paying any attention to her, so she takes some money out of Brenda's wallet, leaving the credit cards since she feels kind of sorry for her. Digging around, her hand latches onto the sunglasses in their sturdy case. *Hmmm, what's this?* she wonders as she takes them out of the case. She immediately recognizes the painting on the vintage frames as something she's seen in a fashion magazine recently. *Wow, these are worth at least five hundred bucks*, she thinks as she looks around before slipping them into her own purse, and putting the case back into Brenda's bag.

By the time Brenda makes her way back to the bar, Marlene has finished her drink and put Brenda's purse back, exactly as she left it. Brenda climbs back into her seat and looks over at Marlene. "I'm sorry, but it's been a long day and I have an early meeting tomorrow, so time for me to go," Marlene says as gathers up her jacket and purse. "It was nice meeting you, and I'm so sorry about your partner. No one should have to go through that. I can only imagine how you feel. Take care of yourself, and I hope things get better for you." She turns away and signals the bartender. "I think it's time for you to get this nice woman her taxi. It's time for her to go home."

"Will do," Mason says as he goes to call for Brenda, and rings up her bill using the credit card she hands him.

As Marlene bends down to give Brenda a hug, she thinks, *Whew, I'm glad I didn't take any credit cards—she definitely would have noticed, and it could have gotten sticky.* "Bye, dear," she says as she makes her way to the door, patting her bag, feeling the sunglasses inside.

CHAPTER 16

When she gets back to her room, Marlene counts the bills she took from Brenda's purse. *Ninety dollars, hmmm; enough to pay for the room tonight. Not bad*, she thinks. She then puts the sunglasses on and stands in front of the mirror, admiring how they look. She's surprised they look a bit masculine and actually too big for her face, but that doesn't stop her from keeping them on and dancing around the room. She knows they're worth a lot and thinks she can get at least a few hundred for them, plus she loves the hand-painted prism design. Marlene likes nice things, and sometimes has trouble parting with the better items, keeping them for a little while until she gets tired of them or needs the money.

She had forced herself to wait until after dinner before dipping into her stolen bag of coke she'd hidden behind the dresser. She hadn't wanted to ruin her appetite before going to the restaurant, since she hadn't eaten all day. She knows enough about taking care of herself to know she has to eat, and now that she's eaten, she's ready for a line or two to help her plan her next moves. Once she does a couple of lines, she puts the stash back in her hiding place, puts the sunglasses back on to see if they look any better, and dances around a bit more.

She finally settles down and decides to call Charlie. He's a friend of her brother's, and while her brother Noah was in prison a few years back, they got to be friends too. Charlie had promised Noah he would look out for his sister, and they ended up developing a close relationship. Charlie is like a second brother to Marlene. He does find her attractive, but through mutual understanding, they both feel it best to keep romance and sex out of their relationship. Even though her brother is now out of jail, Marlene still always turns to Charlie first. He's a good guy, in the sense that he really cares about Marlene and looks out for her, but he's definitely crooked in his own way. They enjoy "working" together at times, and leave her brother Noah out of the loop of what they're doing more often than not. Since getting out of prison, Noah had been trying hard to stay straight, and they don't want to tempt him, especially since he has a good job he likes as a mechanic.

Charlie answers on the second ring, and she can tell he's glad to hear from her. "Where are you?" he asks. "Everything good?"

"Yep. I'm in a hotel downtown, about two hours from your house. Not sure where to go from here since I can't go back to my apartment right away. I don't think the asshole can find me, but I wanted to make sure he hadn't followed me to see where I live before I took off with the goods. I don't think he thought about not trusting me while I was massaging his balls. He's lazy, and a fool for a pretty face," she laughs.

"Ugh, too much information," Charlie laughs. "So, what are you gonna do? Do you want to meet up? I have a friend who owes me a favor, and can put you up for a week or so if that helps."

As they continue talking, Marlene realizes she still has the sunglasses on and is getting a headache. She takes one more glance in the mirror before taking them off and putting them back in her purse. She's getting tired even though she did the coke, and tells Charlie she'll catch up with him tomorrow to finalize her plans. She turns off the overhead light, just leaving a side lamp on, and lies down on the bed. *Ah, that's better*, she thinks. *I hate that damn fluorescent lighting. This coke must be crap; I bet that jerk must have cut it ten times. It's giving me a headache and only a short buzz. A lot of aggravation for nothing, except the ten grand.*

While Marlene is ruminating about her day, the lousy coke and her ripping off the woman at the bar, she drifts off to sleep. She starts dreaming that she's doing terrible things in her dream, her eyes moving frantically back and forth beneath her closed lids. She's not sure if she's done the killing herself, or if she's the accomplice. There's blood everywhere, and she's not even sure who the victim is, or how they were killed. Then they're on the lam and she's trying to convince her accomplice they need to turn themselves in. She's confused, because she's not even sure what she did, but feels she's done something awful. She tries to see who her accomplice is to ask him, but he keeps drifting in and out of her vision. She tells him she feels sick. Still dreaming, she thrashes about on the bed as though she's running.

#

At almost exactly the same time, Brenda too is deep into a dream. When she first got home, she turned on the TV because she was still too drunk to do anything else. She didn't want to go to bed yet, so she tried to focus on watching a movie. Keeping her eyes open was a challenge, but every time she closed them, her head began to spin, making her feel nauseous. After drinking two glasses of water, she starts feeling better, and reaches into her bag for some aspirin she knows will hopefully ward off some of the hangover she's sure to feel in the morning. She digs out the small bottle, not noticing Vincent's sunglasses are gone, and downs a couple of pills. Sitting in the chair in front of the TV, sleep takes over, and she starts to dream.

Vincent is there, and she's delighted to see him. They go here and there, do this and that as dreams tend to go, until they come to a giant rock he wants to climb. He gets to the top before her, and she marvels at how easily she's able to climb up after him. Once there, he turns to her and says, "You must find a way to do this yourself, from your own source first. You'll find it easier than you think." She's then alone on top of the rock, and scared she won't be able to get down. It seems so very far to get to the ground when she jumps, and she wakes up disoriented, finding herself still in the chair in front of the TV. She stumbles into bed, feeling there's something she's supposed to remember.

CHAPTER 17

The next morning, Marlene decides it's best to move on from the hotel and take Charlie up on staying at his friend's house. She knows the guy and his girlfriend slightly, and that they have an extra room they'll let her use, if she chips in for food and other essentials.

"How are you fixed for money?" Charlie asks.

"I'm good for now. Why, do you need some?"

"I could use a couple of grand. Can you spare it? I can pay you back pretty soon. I have an idea where we can get some more. It'll be a little different than what we normally do, but might be a good change, and it's in an area no one would suspect."

"Okay, I'll meet you before going to Sam's house. Do you want to come with me or should I show up there alone?"

"I think alone is better, since I don't want them to think we're planning anything together. His girlfriend doesn't like most of his friends, and wants him to walk the straight and narrow. Just tell them you're getting your apartment painted, and needed a break anyway. Meet me at the diner before you get into town and we'll talk there."

As Marlene packs up and gets ready to check out, she remembers the weird dream she had, and it makes her shudder. She gets goosebumps, and shakes her head as if erasing the image. *What the hell was that all about?* she wonders. She takes the sunglasses out of her purse, puts them on, and looks at herself in the mirror again. There's just something about them; she can't put her finger on it, but every time she puts them on, she gets an odd feeling. It must be the way they fit on her head or wrap around her temples. As she thinks this, she starts getting a slight headache, and wonders if she's imagining it. She takes the glasses off, puts them back in her purse, and with one last glance in the mirror, takes off to meet Charlie.

#

"I don't know, Charlie," Marlene says with more than a little skepticism. He's telling her about his idea to find some marks at the fairgrounds, not just pickpocketing, but also ripping off some of the vendors too. He tells her he has already wandered the fairgrounds when they were in full swing, and everything was cash exchanges. These vendors don't take credit cards, and if it's a larger, more expensive item, like a rug or antique, they have the customer get cash from an ATM down the street. Some will take a check, but only with several forms of ID and credit card numbers. This is a cash garden ripe for the picking. Plus, there's an area where they serve beer and other alcoholic drinks that's cash only. He saw small cash registers, cashboxes, even cigar boxes stuffed with cash.

"But we'd be so exposed," Marlene says. "What if someone sees us and tries to grab us, or stops us before we get away? There will be too many people around. I'm a pretty good runner, but there's an awful lot of open ground to cover before getting to the street or a getaway car."

"Yeah, I thought of that," Charlie says, scratching his day-old beard and pulling on his chin. "But that place is like a giant maze. You'll see. There are so many vendors close together, with just enough room for a couple people to squeeze through the aisles on the sides and in the back. Then at night, with lots of people, it would be easy to get lost; getting away would be a piece of cake. There's one alley-like area further back that takes you straight to the street, and we could park there."

"I don't know," Marlene says again. "It just sounds so risky. Would we really be able to get enough money to make it worth the risk?"

Charlie sighs deeply and says, "What's happened to you? Getting cold feet? You never used to be like this. You were always up for anything. You're so damn good at this—it's what you do for a living, for Christ's sake. We can go later tonight and check it out. Once you see it, you'll get it."

Marlene doesn't answer for several minutes as they sit at their diner table drinking coffee, each with their own thoughts. She does wonder why she's hesitating. She's always trusted Charlie so far to come up with the right jobs to pull, so why is she hesitating now? She's learned to trust her instincts, and this just feels off. Yet not in the usual way a job would feel off; it's something else, and that's why she's really hesitating.

Finally, she says, "Okay, let's go before dark tonight. I want to see it around dusk. It should be busy for a Friday night, and we can scope it out and mark all the escape routes."

"That's my girl," Charlie says as he leaves some cash on the table.

Once outside, Marlene puts the sunglasses on without thinking, and marvels at how clear everything looks in the bright sunlight. She looks around, trying to remember where she parked her car, when her eyes light on the row of Harleys parked in front of the bar next door. Her eyes follow down the line of motorcycles when the side mirror of the third bike catches the sun at the perfect angle, sending blinding light directly into Marlene's eyes. She staggers back, almost knocking Charlie over, then forgets everything and watches in amazement as the big circle of light becomes smaller and smaller, until it shrinks to a pinprick. She can see inside the pinprick, watching as a gold thread of light whips towards her and then around her like a lasso. The thread of light becomes stronger and thicker, restricting her movements, holding her still. She feels rather than hears information being imparted to her, and at first doesn't understand. Parts are starting to become clear and she feels a certainty, but it's not clear for what.

"Hey, hey, Marlene! What the fuck! What are you doing? Are you sick? Stand up, people are looking," Charlie says as he tries to get Marlene to stand up straight.

Her first thought is to wonder why her body is tingling all over. It's not an unpleasant feeling, yet it's one she's never felt before. She wonders if she's having a heart attack or stroke or something, but then discounts that because she feels really good, just different. Marlene takes a deep breath and says, "Whew, I'm okay. Not sure what that was about. I should have had a bite to eat, not just coffee. I had a few lines earlier and wasn't hungry—probably low blood sugar."

"That was really weird and scary. For a few seconds I thought I might have to take you to the hospital. Are you sure you're okay?"

Marlene assures Charlie she's fine, and they arrange where and when they'll meet up later. While driving to his friend's house, she puts the sunglasses back on and doesn't have the slightest inkling that they had anything to do with what just happened to her. Why would she?

#

As expected, Brenda wakes up with a blinding headache, the bright sun streaming in through the window only making it worse. Groaning, she turns away from the light, putting the pillow over her head, wishing she was dead. *I'm such an idiot,* she thinks. *I am never drinking again.* She knows this is a big fat lie, feeling on the verge of tears when she starts to think about Vincent, and remembers once again that he's dead and gone forever. She forces herself to get out of bed. Once up, she immediately goes to the medicine cabinet and takes out three aspirins, downing them with a full glass of water.

Shuffling into the kitchen, she notices her purse on the floor and picks it up, putting it on the counter while she makes some coffee. Trying to remember as much as she can of the previous night, she hopes Sarah doesn't think too badly of her for drinking so much. Brenda recognizes she has a problem, but only seems to care about it the day after, when she's struggling with a hangover.

She'd purposely picked this house for her home and studio because of all the windows and wonderful light angles, but right now the bright light is annoying. She reaches into her bag for Vincent's sunglasses, wondering if they'll help her with her hangover. At least they'll dim the light without her having to close all of the shades. Her hand finds the sunglasses case and, pulling it out, she can already tell it feels different. She gasps when she finds the case empty, and desperately digs through her bag. Taking everything out, she hopes maybe she put them back without putting them in the case. She already knows this isn't what happened, but can't believe she lost them.

Thinking maybe she didn't have them in her bag at all last night, she starts tearing through the house, looking everywhere for Vincent's glasses. "They can't be gone," she keeps saying over and over to herself. "I know they're here somewhere." Maybe they dropped out of her bag when she got into the taxi last night, or maybe she left them on the bar. She calls the restaurant, she calls the taxi company, and no one has found any sunglasses.

Brenda is trying not to get hysterical, but she's on the verge, and feels herself starting to hyperventilate. With shaking hands, she gets another glass of water and forces herself to sit down and breathe. "Think," she says to herself, "think." She closes her eyes and suddenly remembers part of the dream she had when she first fell asleep. She remembers Vincent saying, "You must do this yourself," but she can't remember what else he said. She tries, but can't remember, then starts to cry.

CHAPTER 18

Charlie and Marlene stroll around the fairgrounds like a couple on a date. She has a scarf tied around her head, hiding most of her long brown hair, and Charlie has on a baseball cap. She admits to Charlie she's impressed with his idea, and notes all the areas where she thinks they'll find the most cash. She's doing this on automatic, and for some reason feels like she's on the outside looking in—like it's not really her here at the fairground, but someone else. This makes her think she should stop doing the coke she stole, that maybe it's cut with something that's giving her weird reactions. Her plan had been to just keep the coke for herself, doing a little bit at a time instead of selling it. She's fooled herself into thinking she can quit any time she wants, yet for the first time in a very long time she's realizing she may be addicted, or at least on the verge of being addicted. Not good.

While looking around with these thoughts swirling in her mind, she notices a small, exotic-looking tent with a sign outside advertising a fortune teller. It's a little off to the side, and there are no people close by it. She moves closer to read the small sign. *Get a Reading for $10* is all the sign states, and it looks handwritten. Something makes her want to go in, and she pulls on Charlie's arm to slow him down. "I want to go in here and get a reading," she tells him.

He looks at her as if she's lost her mind and says, "I don't believe in that shit. They're bigger scammers than we are!"

She laughs and says, "I want to try it anyway—I think it'll be fun. Go wander around some, have a beer, and meet me back here in about twenty minutes. Can't imagine it'll take even that long."

Charlie wanders off, and Marlene sticks her head into the tent, calling, "Hello, anyone here?"

A voice that seems to come from far away, even though the tent isn't that big, replies, "Come in, dear, I'm back here. I've been waiting for you."

"Oh," is all Marlene says as she walks to the back of the tent, and sees a tiny old lady who looks like she's at least ninety years old, maybe older. She's so wrinkled Marlene has to bend down and squint closely to see her features.

The old woman raises her bright eyes from the table where she has cards laid out and says, "Please sit and give me your hands."

Marlene gets settled across the small table from the fortune teller, and reaches her hands out across the table. When the old woman takes her hands, she feels a soft jolt of the most pleasant kind go into her hands and up her arms. So far Marlene hasn't said anything, asked any questions, or offered any information as to why she's sitting there. The old woman asks no questions either, and they sit like this for several minutes with their eyes connected.

"You will need to stop doing it," the old woman finally says, still holding Marlene's hands. "I don't know what it is you are doing, but it is only hurting you. You must understand, I cannot see your future; I can only see your past and your now."

"What do you mean?" Marlene asks, puzzled. "I thought you were a fortune teller."

The old woman barks a short laugh and says, "We will begin now," as she lays out the cards. For the next fifteen minutes, the old woman tells Marlene what she can see of her past, bringing her to tears, dredging up so much hurt. She talks about how she can see her mother, so important to

Marlene, leaving when she needed her the most, without a backward glance, never to be heard from again. She sees two important male figures, her father and her brother, both broken souls. Her father, an alcoholic, did his best to raise them, but booze was the only thing he wanted to nurture. Her brother tried to protect her, but didn't know how. Neither of the kids had anywhere to turn or other role models, except for an old man down the road they used to run to when their father got violent. This old man hid them, fed them when he could, and tried to help them. But he was old and unwell himself, and died when Marlene and her brother were in their early teens.

The old woman stops and lays out more cards, closes her eyes, and continues. She speaks of a third man, who's also broken, leading Marlene down a path she doesn't really want to go. He means well, and has a good heart like Marlene, but he's given up. He's been beaten down as well, from the time he was a young child, and now he sees nothing beyond his feet. She goes on to talk about all the hurt Marlene endured throughout her life so far. She speaks with a matter-of-fact cadence, but not without emotion, though certainly without judgement. She tells Marlene there's hope for her, just like her brother, who's trying to change his life, and that they both have been given a gift. Her brother's gift is a strong spirit that he's found how to get a hold of again. Her gift is of a different nature. Even though she has a strong constitution and is a survivor, there's something more, something so few have been fortunate enough to acquire.

Here the old woman stops, not sure how to continue. She turns over another card. "Your gift," she says slowly, "comes from the same place that allows me to see into you, to receive the messages I impart to you. I am just interpreting the messages."

Marlene is nodding her head, feeling what she's being told is of supreme importance. She's trying to take it in, and finally asks, "What *is* my gift?"

"You have allowed the *Universal Mind* into your soul, but you are not yet aware of it. In time, you will see how much more you know, and what to do. I cannot tell you what to do or what your future holds; I'm just the messenger. But I do know that what you thought to do in your now will change, must change, as every now becomes."

They're holding hands again when Charlie sticks his head into the tent and says, "Hello? Marlene, are you in here?"

"I'm back here, Charlie, give me just two more minutes."

The old woman pulls back from Marlene, and starts to gather up the cards. "Wow," Marlene says, "I'm blown away. You gave me a lot to think about. Thank you so much."

"Thank *you,* my dear. Your energy is beautiful, and it has been my pleasure." She looks up as Marlene rises, and smiles when she's handed a twenty-dollar bill. She reaches into her pocket to give Marlene her change, but Marlene just shakes her head, says, "Keep it," and walks out.

"What took you so long?" Charlie asks.

Marlene doesn't answer, and instead asks him, "You see any good prospects?"

"Yeah, follow me and I'll show you. It's starting to get dark, so if it feels right to you, I got a plan."

They walk down to the area where the food and drink vendors are, and it's getting crowded. One of the beer vendors has two guys working the taps and taking the money. The money is being stuffed into a box with a lid, like a cigar box, and it's on the opposite end of the booth from where the taps are. When one of the kegs goes empty, one of the guys has to prime a new one while the other has to wait on customers by himself. This leaves the money box unattended for a short time, easily within reach without being noticed. The booth is really just a makeshift tarp on poles, with open sides and a table. With quick hands, one could easily reach in without being noticed. Marlene and Charlie are watching all of this when they see one of the guys take the almost-full box and dump the contents into a canvas bag. He then stuffs the bag behind a chair before going back to work and putting the box back.

"What do you think?" Charlie asks. "I could snatch that bag so fast, turn and take off before anyone notices."

"I don't know. Doesn't seem worth it. How much can they accumulate at two dollars a pop? And it looks like most people are paying in small bills. That box was full of mostly singles."

"Yeah, but he must have dumped the cash into that bag at least four times since I've been watching. I almost feel like telling him to get a bigger box," Charlie laughs.

"I don't know, Charlie. Doesn't feel right to me. Seems like you'd have to wait around a while until that box fills up a lot more times to even make it worth any kind of risk."

"Well, maybe I'll do just that. I told you, I need some cash, and this feels ripe for the picking. Why don't you go get something to eat, and I'll meet you back at the car in about an hour. Do you remember the back way I showed you to get to the car?"

"Okay," Marlene says. "Give me the keys. Check your watch, and make sure you meet me in an hour. If you're more than ten minutes late, I'll come looking for you."

They separate, and Marlene checks out the different food vendors, trying to decide what she feels like eating. She feels weird. She feels like she doesn't belong here and wants to leave, but doesn't feel like waiting an hour in the car, so she wanders a little while, then decides what she wants to eat. While finishing her chili, she hears some kind of preacher start speaking over a loudspeaker in the sing-song chanting way that preachers preach, and she rolls her eyes. *That's it,* she thinks, *I'm out of here.*

Walking back to the car, she realizes it's almost totally dark by the alley she needs to walk through to get to the street. She wishes she'd brought her pocket flashlight, and makes a note to herself to put it in her purse for the next time. She thinks Charlie made a good plan as far as this being a getaway path, because it really is dark, and she instinctively puts herself on high alert. Adjusting her shoulder bag, she heads into the dark alley, and hears footsteps up ahead. She stops and listens, then gasps as she's grabbed from behind and pulled further into the blackness. She starts to thrash around, but the guy is strong, and before she gets her bearings, he has her arm held painfully high behind her back, his other arm around her neck. His breath stinks, and she tries to kick him and come down hard on his instep, but his grip is too strong and she can't move.

"Got us a live one, Donnie," he says as a figure comes out of the shadows. "She's a fighter. It'll be fun taming her," he laughs, spraying his saliva and smelly breath over the side of her face.

CHAPTER 19

Once Brenda finally gives up trying to find Vincent's sunglasses, and knows they're truly gone, she withdraws into herself and endures a sense of paralysis. She cannot paint, has no energy, and can't even pick up a pair of sunglasses to work on for her business. Oddly, it's not a state of depression; it's more like a paralyzing shock, a tangible thing holding her down.

Her friend Sarah has tried repeatedly to find out what drove her to this state, but is seriously baffled. She feels there's something Brenda isn't telling her that's behind it, somehow knowing it's more than her grief from Vincent's death. She thinks back to the last time Brenda seemed more like herself, and that was the night they met for drinks in town. She saw that Brenda was drinking too much that night, and wonders if somehow the alcohol messed her up more than seemed possible. She knew she was drinking alone every night, maybe even during the day too, but still, this is more than that. She flat-out asks Brenda if she's drinking every day, and Brenda says no, insisting she's not drinking at all. Although she did say she was taking an antidepressant the doctor gave her after Vincent died. *Could that be causing her strange state of mind?* Sarah wonders.

Caroline Connelly is also very concerned about Brenda, and puzzled as well. She too knew Brenda was drinking, but now she's acting like she's no longer there—like her body is there, but the rest left. She's almost robotic, and Caroline feels like shaking her, even slapping her to bring her out of it. She tries to get Brenda interested in painting the sunglasses again, and feels a little guilty stressing about the backorders that are piling up. Strangely, every time she even tries to hand Brenda a pair of sunglasses, she recoils as if they're poison or will burn her.

The two friends get together to try and figure out what to do to help Brenda. There must be *something* they can do. Caroline comes up with the idea for both of them to take Brenda to a yoga class, and then a meditation session afterwards. Sarah mulls this over, thinks it can't hurt, and agrees its worth a shot, assuming Brenda agrees to go.

Surprisingly Brenda does agree to Caroline's plan, without any fuss or excuses. The yoga class actually feels good to her, and she feels the stretching loosening up some of the paralyzed feeling. After class, they go to another room to sit through a guided meditation. The meditation instructor is doing an emotional release meditation this evening, designed to help one let go of negative emotions by locating them within, then releasing the associated tension.

As Brenda focuses on her breath and the teacher's voice fades, she feels a comfortable buzz, and lets it embrace her until she's fully immersed. Vincent parts the mist like a curtain and walks towards her. His arms are outstretched, and she feels his essence surround her with warmth. She feels so relaxed and secure; then he starts to speak.

"Your talents and gifts are yours, and cannot be taken away. Use them to help yourself and to help others. No effects are lost; they are everlasting. You do not need props anymore." Vincent fades into the haze, turning into a smoky swirl of color that dissipates into nothingness. Just a touch of his voice reverberates, then is gone as well.

#

While Brenda's in her meditative state, Marlene realizes she must slow her breath, become calm, and come out of this situation alive. She knows screaming won't help because there are two of them, and they can easily silence her. Instead, she focuses and breathes, focuses and breathes, until she's in a higher state of calmness. Her eyes are now accustomed to the dark, and she can see her assailants. She can more than *see* them; she can feel inside them, feel their weaknesses as she winds up her body to a tautness she's never experienced before. Marlene sees what she must do, and what the outcome will be, before she even acts.

Donnie comes closer and grabs her breasts, while the guy holding her laughs. Her knee comes up into Donnie's groin with a strength she didn't know she possessed. She then brings her leg down in one fluid move, stomping on the instep of the guy who's holding her. Almost simultaneously, they both groan with pain and surprise; this gives her an edge for the next move. She spins out of the one guy's grip and kicks Donnie again, finishing the spin by kicking the other guy under the chin, making his head snap back. They're both disoriented and confused by her strength and skill.

She fights like a ninja, or a warrior, Donnie thinks, and this makes him mad. *Who the fuck does she think she is? I'll show that bitch.* He comes back to grab her, trying to throw her to the ground. Except she's too fast for him, and punches him right in the middle of his face, breaking his nose, the bone shattering. As he stumbles, the other guy jumps on her back, and starts punching her on the side of her face, pulling out handfuls of hair. Marlene yelps, and bends down, flipping him over her back, right into Donnie, and they both fall.

She thinks of running now and figures she'll easily get away, but she's really pissed. Really, *really* pissed. Marlene feels like a superhero fighting the bad guys, and wants to make sure they don't hurt anyone else. She bends over, grabs Donnie's head by his hair, and slams it into the pavement, hearing a thud that tells her that's enough. The other guy gets up and tries to run, but Marlene is too quick for him. Grabbing his leg, she pulls him to the ground and gives him a hard kick to his gut, doubling him over into a fetal position.

Okay, that's enough, I don't want to kill them, she thinks, *although maybe I should.*

Staggering towards the end of the alley, Marlene then starts to run, reaching the street where the car's parked. Jumping inside, she locks the door, starts the engine, and moves the car away from the mouth of the alley, further down the street. Once she's sure she hasn't been followed, she pushes the seat back and turns on the overhead light to access the damage. Amazingly, what hurts the most is where that creep pulled her hair out. Her blouse is torn, her face is scratched, her eye is starting to swell, and she aches all over. She feels lucky, though, knowing it could have been a lot worse. She lays her head back, closing her eyes while she waits for Charlie.

She realizes she must have fallen asleep when she hears Charlie pounding on the window, telling her to unlock the door and let him in. "Jesus, why did you move the car? I thought you left me, or it got stolen or something. What the fuck!" he says breathlessly. "Let's get out of here quick, someone saw me. You're not going to believe this," he continues, "but I think I saw a dead guy in the alley. I tripped over him, and almost did a faceplant. And there was another guy there trying to sit up, moaning and groaning. Jesus, did you see them when you went through there?"

"See them?" She asks. "Did I *see* them?" she laughs lightly to herself.

Marlene is only half listening as Charlie tells her about nabbing the bag with the money in it, only to look up and see some middle-aged woman watching him. He smiled at the woman and put his finger to his lips, while saying *shhh*. At first, she smiled back, but when he turned to run, she started yelling, and he says he never ran so fast in his entire life. He's still nervously laughing, now that he thinks he got away with it, and he finally looks over at Marlene and says, "Hey, what happened to you? What happened to your shirt? Your face is scratched, your eye looks swollen. Were you in a fight?"

"You could say that," she says again laughing. "But you should see the other guys."

"Was it those guys in the alley?" Charlie asks doubtfully.

Marlene thinks for a few seconds before answering. “Nah, I tripped and fell in the alley because it was so dark. I didn’t see any guys there.”

“Oh, geez, must have happened after you came through. Sorry I picked such a dark place, but maybe that’ll make them think it was one of those guys that stole the money. Ha,” he says, already forgetting about Marlene’s injuries.

“Yeah, maybe,” she answers quietly.

CHAPTER 20

When Marlene gets back to where she's staying, only the girlfriend is home, and she's glad. Even though she doesn't know her very well, after staying there a few days, she's starting to like her more and her boyfriend less. There's something untrustworthy, almost creepy about him, so she's kept her distance. But the girlfriend, Donna, seems okay.

Seeing that Donna is watching TV in semi-darkness, Marlene's hoping she can get by without having to explain her torn shirt and swollen face. She just wants to clean up, and go to bed. But Donna's in the mood to talk, and it looks like she's had a few beers. She says hello and asks Marlene to join her for a little while. "Hey, have a good night?" she asks.

Marlene can't decide yet what to tell her, so she says she has to pee and will be back in a couple of minutes. In the bathroom, under the bright light, she throws water on her face, and examines her swollen eye and scratches. She wonders if maybe the sunglasses will cover her eye and hide some of the swollen part, so she puts them on and looks in the mirror. She realizes she's starting to get a headache, so she downs a couple of aspirins, then looks again to decide if she should keep the sunglasses on. While looking in the mirror, she has an odd feeling come over her. It's like the quick static-electric shock you get when touching something after you walk across a carpet in the winter when there's no humidity. This makes her step back and take the sunglasses off. She then goes to her room, changes her shirt, and joins Donna in front of the TV. She has an overwhelming feeling she must tell Donna the truth, at least part of it. She starts with, "No, I've had an awful night. How about you?"

"Oh, what happened?" Donna asks, ignoring the second part of the question.

"I was at the fairgrounds just enjoying myself, and when I was on my way back to the car, two guys jumped me."

"Oh my God," Donna says sitting up, and taking a better look at Marlene. "Is your face swollen? Are you hurt? Did you call the cops?"

"Yes, a little, and no," Marlene answers with a slight smile. "I'm okay, but something really strange happened. If I tell you, you have to promise not to tell a soul. No one, not even your boyfriend." Now she's looking squarely at Donna, to gauge if she can really trust her, and her gut tells her she can. Oddly, she feels not only that she can trust her, but certain that she *must* tell her. Donna meets her look and nods solemnly.

Taking a deep breath, Marlene begins her story of what happened that evening. She was walking around the fairgrounds enjoying looking at all the stuff the vendors had to offer, even though she wasn't buying anything. She said for a laugh she went to a little old lady fortune teller, and was surprised at how much she seemed to know about her past, but didn't really tell her anything about her future. Then she had something to eat, and when she heard some preacher guy start preaching, like he was giving a sermon, she decided to leave. Marlene conveniently left out that she went with Charlie, that they were planning to rip off some money, and that the fortune teller lady freaked her out with all that she told her.

"So, I had parked my car by the back of the fairgrounds, and didn't realize how dark it would be going through the alley on my way back. It was light out when I parked, and I didn't have a pocket flashlight or anything with me. As I started to go through the alley, I couldn't see a thing, but I thought I heard someone up ahead. Before I knew what was happening, one of them grabbed me." She stops to gather her thoughts.

"Oh my God, how did you get away?" Donna asks.

"That's the thing," Marlene says slowly, once again looking Donna in the eye. "That's the weird thing. I knew they were going to rape me, beat me up, maybe kill me. I knew they were really bad, and meant to fuck me up. Then this feeling of calm came over me, as if I was expecting this, and knew exactly what to do. That it was somehow my purpose to take care of it. So I did."

"What do you mean?" Donna asks, not understanding. "How?"

"Well, I kicked the shit out of both of them. It was like I was watching myself in a movie. I had these amazing moves, knew what would hurt them and bring them down. It seemed to happen in slow motion with a lot of forethought, if that makes any sense. I had the strength of a superhero, maybe adrenaline-driven. I don't know, but I think I almost killed one of them, or maybe I did."

Donna's looking at her with a shocked face, trying to take it all in. Finally, she says, "And you're not really hurt, and you left them in the alley, and you drove yourself back here?"

Marlene takes a deep breath and says, "Yeah, incredible as it sounds, that's what happened."

"What are you going to do?" Donna asks.

"Right now, nothing. What am I supposed to do? No one would believe me, for one thing. I need to think about it. I still can't believe it happened. Like I said before, it's like it was meant to happen. Like all of a sudden, I discovered I have this hidden talent. I took a self-defense class when I was in high school years ago, because my father was abusive when he was drunk. But that was sort of good for if you just wanted to get away. What I did tonight, Christ, that was different. I really hurt those guys. I wanted to fuck them up so they would never try to do it again, and I knew exactly how."

"Wow, unbelievable," Donna says as she shakes her head. "Are you sure you're all right?"

"Well, I'm shook up more than anything. My scalp really hurts where one of them pulled my hair out, but the other stuff only hurts a little. I'm just so baffled at how strong I was, or how strong I *am*, and how skilled I was. I can remember every move, and I think I could do it again. It's really spooky."

Donna doesn't say anything for a while, and looks as though she's mulling over all this. Finally, she looks at Marlene and says, "Don't worry, I promise not to tell anyone, even though I'm really impressed. Can I tell you something, and ask that you in turn not tell anyone?"

"Of course. What is it?"

"Sam hurts me, but he does it in a way that doesn't leave marks. Not much, anyway," she says as she lifts up her shirt. "You can still see some bruises here. He doesn't do it all the time, mostly when he's drunk. Then he's really sorry, and says he won't do it again, but he does."

"Oh, Donna, you can't keep letting this happen! Why don't you leave him? Do you really love him that much, and love yourself so little to let this keep happening?"

Donna starts to cry, and Marlene moves over to hold her and let her cry it out. After a few minutes Donna pulls herself together, and Marlene gets her some tissues to blow her nose. Neither of them has said anything for several minutes, and finally Donna looks at Marlene and says, "Can you teach me to defend myself?"

"You bet I can, girlfriend. You bet I can. We start tomorrow."

#

While Marlene promises to teach Donna self-defense, Brenda's in her studio, painting. Ever since Caroline and Sarah took her to the yoga and meditation class, she's slowly come around and begun to heal. Her friends have no idea that it was losing Vincent's sunglasses that put her over the edge, and Brenda knows she'll never be able to tell them. *Well, maybe when I'm old and gray, and they think I'm senile,* she laughs to herself.

Yes, she's even starting to get her sense of humor back, and feeling like painting, although her work isn't quite up to what it was before Vincent died. She still has a large backlog of sunglasses to work on, but is slowly coming around with that as well. Brenda attributes her healing to the guided meditation classes, and finds that often—not every time, but often—she can bring herself into that place between here and there where she can see Vincent. The times she doesn't see him, she tries to not get depressed, and is slowly becoming more able to stay positive. Sometimes she still dreams of Vincent, but those dreams are more and more infrequent.

She often wonders what happened to the sunglasses, and who has them. When Brenda thinks back to the evening she lost them, she can remember that there was a woman who sat with her. She remembers talking with her for a little while, but not much else. She doubts she would recognize her if she saw her again, but is pretty sure she's the one who took them. Next time she sees Vincent she'll ask him; she's sure he knows who has them.

CHAPTER 21

Marlene makes her way into the kitchen, badly needing a cup of coffee. It's still early, but she can't sleep anymore; her mind is going a mile a minute. As she shuffles into the kitchen, she's surprised to see Sam sitting at the kitchen table, arms crossed, deep in thought. When he sees her, he just nods, then notices her scratches and bruises, and asks, "What happened to you?"

"I fell," Marlene says looking away.

"Oh yeah, looks like more than that," he chuckles. "Someone show you who's the boss?" he asks, still chuckling.

"No, nothing like that," Marlene says, facing away from him to get her coffee.

"Well, it wouldn't surprise me. You women sometimes have to be shown who's the boss."

Still facing away from him, Marlene clenches her fists, and wonders how Donna can stand him. What a lowlife creep he is. She wonders if Charlie knows that he beats Donna. *You're in for a surprise, asshole,* she thinks with a smile. *It'll be the surprise of your life.* She doesn't say a word, just gets her coffee and goes back to her room.

I have to get out of here, she thinks, *but maybe it's better I stay until Donna can better defend herself*. Marlene's surprised at the level of rage she felt towards Sam when he made that comment, and knows she needs to rein herself in. She doesn't know where this newfound fighting instinct comes from, but she does know it's a game-changer, maybe even a life-changer.

Going back out to the kitchen, she's relieved to find Sam's gone to work, and she has the place to herself. Donna's working early shift at the café, and will be back this afternoon, so Marlene starts thinking about how and where she can teach Donna some self-defense skills. She's never really looked at the backyard here, and is disappointed to see that it looks like a small fenced-in patch of dirt and weeds. It's a bright, sunny day, and she puts the sunglasses on before stepping out to get a good look. Looking around, she's trying to see if they can somehow make it work when she notices the next yard over. There's a low see-through fence, and she sees two large, very pale people in lounge chairs, sunbathing. *If they had any less on, it would be indecent,* she laughs to herself. *Christ,* she thinks, *doesn't anyone work around here?* She should talk. She hasn't had a job in several years, and doesn't even know what she could get a job doing. Marlene realizes she's looking up at the bright sun, so as not to stare at the almost-naked people next door. Even though it's warm, she suddenly gets goosebumps and feels lightheaded.

Going back inside, she thinks for a second she might be getting sick, but the feeling passes as fast as it came. She takes the sunglasses off, and finds herself suddenly obsessed with the idea of getting a job. She starts humming that song *Get A Job*, and can't get it out of her head. She starts dancing around and singing, not knowing why she feels so good.

Back in the house, she has an idea and calls the local Y. She finds out they do have a gym, and for a small fee she can join. That would be the perfect place to get started with Donna. Now that she has a plan, she showers and gets dressed. Leaving a note for Donna, she tells her to meet her at the Y at 3:00, so they can *exercise.* She leaves the note vague in case Sam comes home early, but she knows Donna will get it.

Her next idea brings her to the bookstore in town. *What's up with me today?* she wonders. First, I can't stop thinking about getting a job, and now I'm in a freaking bookstore. She asks the clerk where she can find books on martial arts, and he points to a section in the back. Marlene had no idea that there are more than 170 forms of martial arts, and ends up spending over an hour there, perusing all of the different books. The guy working there is pretty helpful, and knows enough to steer her in the right direction. She finally decides on a Mixed Martial Arts book, and asks if there are any classes offered locally. He says not that he knows of, but to check at the Y.

Marlene gets to the Y about 20 minutes before it's time to meet Donna, and goes inside to see what the gym looks like. It's larger than she expected, and she sees an area where there are mats that they can work on. She puts her stuff down to claim their spot, then walks around to see if she can find the office, or someplace to sign up. She wanders down a hallway and doesn't see anyone in the office, so she continues to the end of the hall, where there's a door that leads to the outside. She hears people talking loudly outside, and pushes the door open.

Two men are shoving a third around, and he has blood coming out of his nose. All three look at her, then the biggest one comes towards her and says, "Get the fuck outta here, bitch!"

The second man is still holding the one they were beating, who is struggling, trying to get away. "What's going on here?" Marlene asks, hoping to diffuse the situation.

"None of your business, bitch, I said get outta here!" the big man says again, coming towards her.

Without thinking, Marlene takes a step forward, and waits until the big man is within range. As soon as he takes the next step to try and intimidate her, her arm shoots out and she chops him right in the throat. He immediately recoils and starts choking, grabbing his throat and falling to his knees. The other man lets go of their victim, and looks around, trying to decide what to do. He looks at Marlene, and she can tell he's going to run. She moves towards him with a forward kick right to the gut, and he too is down. The man who was getting the beating looks at her in awe, then runs away. She decides to run after him, because she doesn't want to be around when these guys are able to get up.

He runs around the side of the building, and she easily catches up to him. "What was that all about?" she asks, grabbing the back of his jacket.

"You tell me, lady! Where did you learn to fight like that?"

"Don't change the subject. What's going on? Wait a minute, don't I know you?"

The guy looks at her without recognition, and says, "No, I don't think so."

"You're the guy who preaches at the fairgrounds. I've heard you. I recognize your voice."

They start talking, and Marlene takes him to her car so she can wait for Donna and keep them out of sight at the same time. Preacher Bob tells her she can just call him Preacher or Bob, whichever she likes better. He tells her he owes money for a gambling debt, and doesn't know what to do. He says he volunteers at the Y a couple of days a week, counseling people in need, and Marlene just shakes her head listening to him.

"I'm actually a good counselor," he says defensively, "I just need counseling myself. I have an addiction. I know I do, and I'm really trying to stop. If I can just pay off this last one, I know I can stop."

"You're pathetic, you know that, right?" Marlene says.

"You're right, I am. I stole money from a guy in my congregation to pay off my last debt, and he thinks I invested the money for him. And now, if I don't pay those other guys, I'm a dead man. Especially since you kicked their butts. Geez, thanks for saving me, but they'll be back and twice as mad. I won't be able to go back to the Y, and I'll have to stay low for a while."

Marlene's listening to him, and glances over to see Donna getting out of her car. She hurries over and tells her everything that's transpired. Donna's amazed and worried that Marlene's beat up two more guys, and they decide to all take off together, to figure out what to do next. They end up at the fairgrounds and walk over to the park across the street. Interestingly, Donna and Preacher Bob hit it off, and seem to enjoy talking with each other. Donna tells him they were going to meet at the Y so that Marlene could teach her self-defense, then that leads to why she needs to be able to defend herself. Preacher talks about his addiction, and Marlene talks about how she wants to change her life around. Before long, they know more about each other than the best of friends would. The conversation goes on for almost two hours, and the cathartic baring of their souls is the beginning of a strong relationship between the three of them.

CHAPTER 22

Back at the apartment, Marlene apologizes to Donna for not being able to start teaching her self-defense. Donna laughs it off, saying she's not to blame, since neither of them had any idea how crazy the rest of the day would turn out. "I really like that Preacher guy," Donna says.

"I know," Marlene laughs. "I can tell. Actually, I like him too, although he really has to beat his gambling demons. They'll ruin him if he doesn't. Funny, but it does seem like he would be a good counselor, yet it's weird that he needs help as well."

"Not really. Don't you know most shrinks have more problems than their patients?"

"True, ha. Hey, do you want to do a few lines before Sam gets home? I have some coke, although I think it's pretty shitty, and it does kind of give me a headache."

"Well, if you put it that way, then no," Donna laughs. "I don't do drugs—well, not much anyway. Maybe smoke a joint once in a while, but never wanted to do anything else. But I will have a beer. Want one?"

Marlene decides she doesn't want to do any coke either, and resolves to give the rest to Charlie. He'll easily be able to sell it if it doesn't all end up up his nose. She starts thinking about Charlie, and realizes she hasn't missed him these last few days, and is glad he hasn't been around. After he gives her some money for the coke, she'll start keeping her distance from him.

The rest of the evening Marlene and Donna just hang out talking, and Donna doesn't even notice that Sam hasn't come home from work yet. She hopes he doesn't come home if he's been at a bar all night, then remembers she has Marlene to protect her, and vows to scream if he tries to put a hand on her.

The next day, they decide to go to the Y two towns over, and are pleased that it's nicer than the one they were going to use. Preacher comes with them, and talks with the manager to see about offering his counseling services, and anything else he might do. Marlene gets Donna on the mat, and they begin her training. It turns out that Marlene *is* a good teacher, and what she wants to teach Donna just flows. She feels more in her element on the mat with Donna than she ever has, and marvels at the feeling. She's light on her feet and her moves are impeccable, as though she's been training for years.

Donna's trying her best to keep up, and after lots of repetition, has a few moves down. Marlene calls for a break so as not to overwhelm her, and both are surprised when they see several people around who've been watching them. Preacher's also impressed, having come over with the manager to watch. The manager approaches and says, "You've really got some moves, young lady. Who did you train with?"

"Uh, no one—not yet anyway."

"I find that hard to believe. If I didn't know otherwise, I'd think you were a high-level, seasoned instructor. You're a natural."

"Thank you," Marlene says. "I'm hoping to find an instructor to fine-tune my skills, and then become an instructor myself. I'm pretty much self-taught." She doesn't add that it's only been a matter of days since she acquired her skills, that has no idea where they came from, and feels like she's been in a science fiction movie ever since. The words just come out of her mouth, so she goes with it.

"Well I can help you out with that," the manager says. "I have a friend who can instruct you. Come to the office when you're done here, and I'll give you his contact info. He has a small studio on the other side of town. I'm thinking too, if you can work it out, maybe teach a couple of self-defense classes a week here in the meantime. You would do just fine with that—it would be a beginner's class. The pay isn't much, but it would get you started."

Marlene doesn't know what to say, so she just nods, trying to stifle a huge smile. Preacher and Donna have heard the whole thing, and the three of them move aside to talk it over. Preacher tells them the manager gave him access to do counseling sessions a few evenings a week, and to also do a group session, as long as it's not a sermon. They tease him that he won't be able to make it less preachy, and he blushes. They're all excited about how well the pieces are falling into place, only Donna is a little quiet. She tells them she feels she has nothing to contribute, but is glad she at least has the job at the café, and looks forward to Marlene's classes. Marlene tells her since she's her first student, she'll get extra special one-on-one training, no charge.

As they continue laughing and joking and marveling at their good fortune, Donna looks at Preacher and says, "Preacher, do you think you can give *me* some counseling? I need help."

"Of course, my dear. We can do it anytime you like. Meeting you both has been a turning point for me. We're good for each other. I feel like I have a real purpose again, and maybe now I'll finally be able to help myself, too. We can all lean on each other. Deal?"

After working out the details with the manager, they leave the Y in high spirits. To add to their good mood, it's a gorgeous sunny day, and Marlene digs into her bag for the sunglasses. Once she finds them, she pulls them out, but takes a long look at them before putting them on. Donna notices, and asks her about them since they're so unusual. "Where did you get those?" she asks. "I've never seen anything like them."

"They were a gift," Marlene answers. For a moment, she flashes back to the evening she stole them, and feels a pang of guilt. She wonders if the woman she stole them from really misses them, and feels even worse about it.

"Can I try them on?"

"Sure. You'll be surprised how clearly you'll be able to see. Usually sunglasses are harder to see out of, unless they're prescription. But these have some kind of super-lenses."

"Oh, cool," Donna says as she puts them on and looks around. "Wow, these are amazing. Must have cost a lot."

Marlene doesn't offer any answer, so Donna gives them back, when Preacher asks if he can try them on too. Marlene hands him the sunglasses, and watches his reaction as he puts them on. "Holy smokes," he exclaims. "These are marvelous. I usually can't see well out of sunglasses, but these really are amazing."

He continues to look around, pointing at different things, and talking about how well he can see. He then decides to look up, directly into the sun. Marlene's still watching him, and sees his neck slightly snap back; his body then stiffens, and his head is cocked as though he's listening for something. She gets a shiver through her body, and continues watching him. It's only a matter of seconds before he turns to her, takes the sunglasses off, and returns them to her outstretched hand. Their eyes meet as he hands them back, and she thinks for a split second that something about him has changed.

Preacher shakes his head slightly, then quietly says, "Those sunglasses are so good, I think I saw God." He then laughs so hard it comes out as a cackle, and both Marlene and Donna start laughing too.

"I don't think they're quite *that* good," Donna laughs. She hadn't been paying attention, and didn't notice anything unusual.

Marlene doesn't say anything, but she can't help feeling spooked, and she has a really odd feeling she can't put her finger on. *Something about the sunglasses,* she thinks. What is it? *Nah,* she says to herself, *it couldn't be.* There's just no way her brain can wrap around some of the thoughts that flash through her head. Once she's alone, she feels she needs to think about the fortune teller, timelines, and changes, and whys, and when. This is a genuine puzzle.

CHAPTER 23

Brenda's started going to the meditation classes every day on her own, and hasn't been able to see Vincent for several days. He also hasn't come to her in any dreams, and she feels like she's starting to go through major withdrawal. She feels on the verge of tears, and can't understand what's changed. For weeks she was able to communicate with him almost at will, and now it's as though he's disappeared. *What am I doing wrong, or differently?* she wonders as she settles on her mat, getting ready for the day's meditation. *Maybe I'm trying too hard.*

The guided meditation begins, and Brenda's breathing slows. She feels her mind settle, and focuses on nothing but her breath. From far away Vincent materializes, and as he comes towards her, she sees he has what looks like a black scarf, or maybe a sash, tied around his waist. His clothes are white and loose-fitting. Brenda's so happy to see him, and calls out to him. She tells him she's missed him, and he tells her he's always with her. She feels such relief, and so full of love. As he starts to vanish, he says, "Yes, the woman has the glasses. It's as it should be. Be joyous. It's on the path for good."

As she brings herself out of the meditation she's smiling, and feels especially relaxed. She looks around, and the woman who's seated on the mat next to hers is looking at her strangely. Brenda gives her a shrug and asks her what's the matter.

"You were mumbling, very softly. At first, I thought you were chanting, but you were saying words. You said *Vincent,* and some other words. Please, if you're going to talk, don't sit near me next time. It's distracting."

#

Marlene, Donna, and Preacher become fast friends, always helping each other out, and it's the best kind of friendship any of them has ever had. Through all of their weaknesses they gain strength, drawing from each other, and giving back in kind. Only Marlene knows her new talents come from somewhere else. She often ponders how much her life has changed these last several weeks, and she always feels there's something else she needs to pin down about it. Yet whenever she tries really hard to think about it, she gets a slight headache, and only finds her thoughts going around and around, with no conclusions—at least, none she can accept. As time goes on, she thinks of *how can this be* less and less, and just goes with the gift she's been given.

Preacher still struggles somewhat with his gambling addiction; however, Donna reins him in often enough to keep him from being foolish and getting further into debt. It helps that he has a renewed purpose keeping him busy, with less time to indulge, plus he just doesn't feel right trying to sneak in a bet behind Donna's back. The two of them have become really close, and a romance is teetering on the edge, waiting for the tipping point to take it to the next level.

Donna's still in the apartment with Sam, and it's obvious to both of them that their relationship is on the rocks. She's felt this way for a while, but hasn't had the courage to leave. She was afraid he would come after her and really hurt her. She felt there was nowhere to run, no one to help her. She would tell herself she loved him, and that he would change, but she's tired of lying to herself. Starting over on her own has always been a terrifying thought—until now.

Now she's much stronger, she has friends, she feels loved, and she can fight, literally. Sam hasn't tried to beat on her for several weeks now, and she thinks she knows partly why. He notices that something about her has changed, and he's been keeping his distance. She doubts he's afraid of her, but maybe senses a new strength in her he'll have to deal with, like maybe she's learned to fight back. It's more than that, though, as she now knows he's seeing someone else, and that's keeping him from paying much attention to her. She's ready to use this as leverage, and knows Marlene or Preacher will take her in when she needs a place to stay. She could even stay at the Y if she has to.

It's late, after 1:00 AM, and Donna's been waiting for Sam to come home. Tonight, she'll confront him about the affair, and tell him she's leaving him. When he stumbles in, it's obvious he's been drinking, and she tells him calmly they need to talk. As expected, he goes into a rage and she stands facing him, prepared to defend herself.

"Can't you see I'm tired, bitch? I'm not talking to you now. I'm going to bed."

"No, Sam, we need to talk. I'm leaving. I know you're seeing someone. You don't love me, and you don't need me. I have to go. I can't live like this anymore."

"Fuck you! You don't know what you're talking about, stupid whore. You're not going anywhere." With that he lunges towards her, but she's too fast, and sidesteps, so he ends up crashing into the door. He rights himself, turns around, and tries to throw a punch to her face. Donna ducks, and when he comes towards her, she knees him in the groin, really hard. Sam falls to the ground, yelling obscenities, and promises to kill her. She grabs her purse and runs out the door, leaving Sam still cursing on the floor.

Donna knocks lightly on Preacher's door, assuming he's already gone to bed. She's surprised when, a few seconds later, he opens the door as though he's been expecting her. Pulling her inside, he asks what's wrong, and she fills him in, proud of herself for not crying through the whole story. She doesn't break down until he pulls her in for a hug. This is the tipping point moment they both've been anticipating, and they hold each other tightly, the energy around them an aura of love.

When they finally separate, Preacher says, "Tomorrow we go get your stuff, and you're coming here. It's so strange, but I went to bed a couple of hours ago, and I had this dream that you were in trouble. I felt I had to save you, but I couldn't move, I was paralyzed, and couldn't get my legs to work. So I had to just watch someone grab you, and he was shaking you. Then you got this glow, and you fought back, and you literally picked him up and threw him up and over a fence, where he landed with a thud. You then turned around, looked at me with a smile, and said, 'So there!' When I woke up, I couldn't get back to sleep. I thought about calling you, then thought maybe I'd go to your apartment. I was deciding what to do when I heard your knock on my door. Incredible."

Donna laughs with tears in her eyes, and says, "I was ready for him! I used what Marlene taught me, and left him on the kitchen floor. He'll be hurting for days. I knew it was time. You helped me love myself again, and Marlene helped me defend the decent person I am. Thank you, Preacher."

Preacher pulls her into his arms again and whispers to her, "We make a beautiful pair, Donna. I love you. But promise me you won't kick me in the groin if I fall off the wagon. I don't think Sam's going to get laid for quite some time." They both burst out laughing, and the rest of the early morning hours are finally spent together as they were meant to be.

Marlene's been teaching her beginner's self-defense class at the Y, and the attendance is at an all-time high. The students love her, bring their friends, and there's often a small crowd of spectators, marveling at the strength and fluidity of her movements. Observing her is like watching a beautifully choreographed dance, with mostly the students down on the mat, unless she chooses otherwise. Marlene's whole demeanor has changed. She carries herself differently, she's more poised, and has even become more beautiful.

She'd given the coke to Charlie, and he sold about half of it; at least, that's what he told her. He gave her some money, but then disappeared with the rest, and she's glad. She was looking for a way to disengage from him, and this worked out for the best. She found the martial arts master recommended to her to be exactly what she needed. He's a grueling teacher and helps her fill in the missing pieces of her skills. Although he hasn't told her, the master is in awe of Marlene's level of talent, and feels someday, possibly soon, she'll surpass him. They say a good teacher often is the one who learns the most, and this is what's happening more frequently between them.

Before long, Marlene's sending her more skilled students to train under her teacher, and that's expanding his business quite nicely. Following the natural course of events, he asks Marlene to come work for him, and they eventually become business partners, although she still keeps teaching her self-defense classes at the Y.

Donna catches Preacher buying a large number of lottery tickets one day, and they have a big argument about it. They talk well into the night, until they both understand each other's stance on it. Preacher's argument is, at least he isn't gambling with the big boys, as he puts it. What he's doing isn't dangerous, it's only lottery tickets, and he's just trying to win some money so they can have a better life. Donna feels he's better off going cold turkey. She says you're either a gambler or not a gambler. Otherwise it's like saying you're not a smoker, but you sneak in a couple every day. They both agree he still has work to do, and Donna says of course she'll help him—they're in it together.

CHAPTER 24

One thing Preacher does confide to Donna is that he feels like he's been blessed, literally blessed. He feels it's partly because Marlene and Donna came into his life, but it's more than that. He asks her if she remembers the day he and Marlene got new jobs at the Y, when things started to really come together. He tells her that that day, he honestly felt like he got a glimpse of God, or some other kind of universal thing. He sometimes hears a voice in his head that isn't him. It's subtle, not glaring or moralizing, yet he feels it helps guide him. That day is when he remembers it started.

Donna isn't sure what to think of what he's confessed to her, and doesn't remember any earth-shattering revelations that day—although she does think his counseling has become better, maybe even more inspired and caring. He's beginning to build a practice of regular clientele beyond what he's doing at the Y. He also continues his sermons at various small venues, and she has to admit they're rather motivating and thought-provoking.

Another incident happens to convince Preacher he truly has been blessed. It begins when a woman comes to him for counseling on a personal matter that she can't divulge to anyone else. She's 52 years old and in love with another woman. They started out as friends, but after her husband divorced her, their friendship blossomed. She needed a friend and never consciously felt attracted to women. This is what she tells Preacher, but he intuitively knows this isn't true. When the woman became lovers with her friend, she suffered a tremendous amount of guilt, and made her friend promise to never tell a soul. She tells Preacher she's ashamed of her unnatural feelings, and yet ashamed for being ashamed. Through several sessions, he brings her to a place of acceptance, even celebration, of who she really is, and she's tremendously grateful.

This woman owns a beauty salon, and she tells Preacher she wants to give him a new hair style, and *the works,* as she puts it, on the house, as a token of her appreciation. At first, he protests and won't accept, but Donna talks him into it, telling him if he turns it down, he's depriving the woman of showing her gratitude, and that's not helping. Donna has an ulterior motive, though; she thinks Preacher *could* use a haircut and some sprucing up. So he gives in and accepts her offer.

From the minute Preacher walks into the shop, he feels at home. There are women all over the place, in various states of being groomed and pampered. Some are getting cuts, some are getting dye jobs, some are getting pedicures, and the noise level between the blow dryers and women's voices permeates the place like a house full of people during a party. There's laughter, and the vibe is so positive, Preacher smiles as he looks around for Jesse, the owner of the salon. He sees her, and she motions him over. Before he knows it, she has him seated, cape fastened, and her best stylist asking him what style he wants. Jesse is smart enough not to do the job herself in case he doesn't like it, but stays close by to supervise.

By the time Donna comes in they're almost done, and she can't believe the transformation. She always thought Preacher was handsome, but now she thinks he looks like a movie star. As they take the cape off of him, brush him off, and admire how he looks in the mirror, he tells Donna she should get her hair cut, too. She doesn't want to take advantage, so just dismisses the idea until Preacher gets up from the chair and spins her around, so she's now sitting in it. He whips the cape around her, and fastens it at the neck. He starts to run his hands through her hair, and everyone in the salon is now watching.

"So, what do you think we should do, my dear? Maybe bring up the length, and add a few layers?" he asks, while twirling a pair of scissors around.

Donna looks at him as if he's lost his mind, and says, "Preacher, quit fooling around, they probably need this chair for another customer."

"Trust me, I know how to do this," he says with a twinkle in his eye.

"You're acting crazy, I don't think this is a good idea. You never told me you know how to cut hair," she says, as she tries to unsnap the cape and get out of the chair.

"Oh, but I do, I do. Don't ask me how, but I do know how to cut hair. Please trust me."

Jesse's been watching this closely, and cuts in. "Donna, let him try. As soon as I see him messing up, I promise I'll take over."

"Really? Are you sure?" Donna asks. "Okay what could possibly go wrong?" she asks with a smirk, and everyone around laughs. "You promise you'll take over as soon as he messes up, and fix his mistakes?"

Jesse nods, Donna relaxes, and Preacher picks up the scissors again. The salon becomes very quiet; all talking has ceased. A few clients are still being worked on as Preacher brushes out her hair and makes the first cut. You can hear an intake of breath and the sound of scissors as he goes to work. Jesse is hovering, waiting to take over, but she doesn't need to. Everyone's jaw drops when he's finished, and Donna is speechless. It's the best haircut she's ever had, and she looks beautiful.

From then on, Preacher's days are overflowing. He still counsels at the Y, does his motivating sermons, and works three days a week at Jesse's salon. He's too busy to think about gambling, too happy to wonder much how all this came about. But if you asked him, he would tell you he was blessed by God one sunny day, and his life has never been the same.

One of Preacher's clients is the events manager at the biggest hotel in town, where all the main events and conferences are held. He arranges for Preacher to do one of his motivational talks there, and even though it's a notably large venue, it sells out quickly. Donna and Marlene go together, and are so proud and excited to see Preacher up there, looking like he belongs, speaking astounding words of wisdom to a rapt audience. At one point, he talks about receiving a gift from the universe, and how this gift opened all the doors to where he is today. He doesn't know why he was chosen for this gift, but a voice tells him the gift comes once, opens the door, and the rest is up to him.

As he's talking, Marlene is listening carefully, and realizes he's also talking about the gift *she* was given. She starts to think about where and how this gift comes from, and thinks back to when it all started. There's that woman's face again, the one in the bar she stole the sunglasses from. She thinks of her more and more lately, and every time, she gets this overwhelming feeling of guilt. She realizes somehow that it's all connected, but she can't imagine how.

Once Preacher's talk is over, Marlene and Donna make their way to the stage to congratulate and hug him for doing such a fine job. They have to wait a few minutes while others do the same, and finally he's free to get his hugs from them, before they leave by a side door. Marlene realizes she's left her purse under her chair, and runs back in to get it. She sees it right where she left it, and when she picks it up, it's upside down, and everything falls out. She quickly throws everything back in, and runs to meet up with her friends.

It isn't until days later that she realizes the sunglasses are missing. She flashes back to the event, and figures that's most likely where she lost them. She immediately goes to pick up the phone to call them and ask if they found them, when she suddenly sees that woman's face again, so sad from having recently lost her partner. She puts the phone back down, deciding not to call. She never tries to find them after that, and somehow knows she did the right thing.

CHAPTER 25

The janitor whistles while he works, not in a hurry, since this events room won't be used until tomorrow morning for an antiques show. He's got plenty of time, and doesn't feel like rushing anyway. He likes when the Preacher guy uses the room for his talks, because he seems like a regular guy who gives good advice, not one of those doom-and-gloom, you're-going-to-hell-unless-you-give-me-money scammers. He comes early just to hear Preacher Bob talk, and finds there's not much of a mess to clean up afterwards. Seems he draws a crowd of decent people, and there sure was a full house tonight.

The hardest part is stacking up all the chairs and getting them into the storage area before tomorrow's event. There sure are a lot of chairs, and when he's halfway through, he sits down for a breather, and decides to eat his sandwich. It would definitely be quicker with two guys stacking the chairs, but he's happy the young guy they just hired is doing something out front, where they had some kind of light-fixture problem. He likes working alone, and the young guy talks too much anyway. He's thinking about some of the things Preacher said during his talk while he eats, when he notices there's something under one of the chairs on the other side of the room. He walks over to look, and sees it's a pair of sunglasses in a cheap plastic case. He picks them up and decides to take them to the front desk, so he can leave them in their lost-and-found box.

No one's at the front desk when he gets there, and this is surprising because there always seems to be someone there. He looks around and notices the front desk clerk is by the entrance, talking with the young guy working on the light problem. He waits a couple of minutes, then starts looking around behind the desk, to see where the lost-and-found box is. He finally finds it on a bottom shelf in the back, and throws the sunglasses in. *Okay, I've done my good deed for the day,* he thinks as he walks back to the events room to finish his work.

The main doors to the antique show open at 10:00 am sharp, and Arnie's among the first to be let in. He's probably been to hundreds of these shows as a customer, and been on the other side of the table as a vendor about the same number of times. He prefers being the customer and looking for bargains rather than standing on his feet all day being nice to clueless people, who more often than not want something for nothing. *Well, today, I'll be one of those people, but I'm not clueless*, he laughs to himself.

Arnie's really good at this. He's been dealing in antiques and what he refers to as *old junk* for many years. He has a sort of love/hate relationship with *old junk,* and sometimes feels like he's selling a gently used piece of crap, just like the guy at the used car lot on the corner. He doesn't really get why people want antiques, or how some old collectible dishes can all of a sudden be worth twenty times what he paid for them. What he does get is that there's money to be made without too much effort, and he feels no guilt when some poor sap hands over three times what he paid for something. Hey, that's the name of the game: eat or be eaten, like in the jungle.

His strategy is to circle the room, checking out the vendors on the periphery first, then slowly making his way to the center. The first several vendors don't have anything that interests him, and he lets out a deep sigh, thinking it's going to be a long morning. Looking around, he sees something that catches his eye a few tables over, and heads towards it. He stops in his tracks and just stares at the Chinoiserie hand-painted table lantern. It stands about two feet high, looks to be in perfect condition, and is worth a pretty penny. He knows this just from looking at it, because his mother had one almost exactly like it on a table in the living room for years. It had been his grandmother's. When he was around nine years old, he almost broke it, and he thought his mother was going to have a heart attack. From then on, he was never allowed in the living room unsupervised.

Everyone in the family coveted that lantern, and when his mother died suddenly, he was the first one to go back to the house. He was alone and he helped himself to many of his mother's items, knowing the rest of the family would be there soon, like vultures doing exactly what he was doing, before the will was read. His aunts and cousins were the worst. His mother lived alone when she died, his father long gone, and his siblings spread around the country. But her sisters and their offspring had this sense of entitlement, and he never liked them. He remembers carefully wrapping the lamp and putting it in the back seat of his car before going back to take several other things. His mother really took care of her things, and fortunately didn't throw much away. When he went up to the attic, he was delighted to find it full of well-preserved vases, paintings, furniture, china, silver, and collectibles. That was when he decided to go into the antiques business.

He stands looking at the lantern, reminiscing, until the guy manning the table comes over and starts telling him about it. Arnie tells him he knows all about it, his mother had one, he's just looking. It brings back memories. He wanders off and continues to circle the room, but he's distracted. In his mind he sees all his mother's things that he ended up selling for a high profit, and he's feeling nostalgic. The nostalgia is not about his mother, though; it's about the treasure trove of pieces he got for nothing that brought in so much money. He finally realizes he's been daydreaming when it comes to his attention he has to pee. This shakes him out of his reverie and he goes in search of a restroom, cursing his weak bladder.

He looks around for a sign, and not seeing one, asks the closest person if they know where the restroom is. They tell him he has to go through to the lobby, and down the side hall. Once he gets to the lobby, he sees a guy at the front desk asking the desk clerk if anyone turned in a set of keys. He's very distressed, sure he lost them somewhere in the hotel, as he hasn't driven since he checked in. The desk clerk tells him no one's turned in any keys during his shift, but he can take a look in their lost-and-found box. He takes the guy behind the desk, and they dig through the box together, looking for a set of keys.

This interests Arnie, and he stands by the front desk to see if the guy's keys turn up. While watching them look through the box, Arnie gets a glimpse of what looks like mostly items people left behind in their rooms. The clerk holds up a decent-looking watch and says, "I'll bet someone will be back for this." A light goes on in Arnie's head, and he thinks he should find a way to look in that box—there might be something good in there, and it doesn't hurt to get something for nothing. He still has to pee, so he thinks about how to do it while walking towards the restroom.

On his way back, he's surprised to see the desk clerk walking towards him. For some reason, Arnie thinks he knows what he's up to and looks down, not making eye contact. The clerk walks past and into the restroom. Arnie starts walking faster, and finds the front desk unmanned. He quickly slips behind the desk, finds the lost-and-found box, and starts rifling through it. He grabs the watch, then thinks he hears footsteps from the hall. He takes one last look, grabs a pair of sunglasses in a cheap plastic case, and runs out from behind the desk with both items in his pocket.

CHAPTER 26

Arnie walks quickly out to his car and puts the stolen items under the front seat. He thinks it's funny he got away with it, feeling a rush from the thrill, like he's one of those jewel thieves in the movies. He doesn't know if the watch and glasses are even worth anything; it's the getting something for nothing that he enjoys. Locking the car doors, Arnie decides to go back into the show, to see if there's anything worth picking up. From what he's seen so far, he feels most of the antique dealers seem to know the value of their items, but you never know.

He does flea markets and shows all over the state, and sometimes further, depending on the season. He classifies his goods by category, value, and size, and that determines which shows he sells at. Sometimes he puts some pieces on consignment if he doesn't have room to store it all, or tote it around in his van.

He laughs when he notices his hands are still shaking from the adrenaline, and starts looking seriously for some bargains. Arnie buys a few coins and old foreign currency he feels sure he can make a profit on from a young couple, and then wanders over to look at some antique bottles. He picks through a few more things, until he realizes he has to pee again. He's afraid to risk walking past the desk clerk another time, no reason to push his luck, so he decides to leave.

By the time he gets back to his car he has to pee pretty badly, and looks around for the closest place. He spots a small cafe down the block, but doesn't think he'll make it if he walks. He drives there in less than a minute, swings into a spot right up front, and rushes into the café, asking for the bathroom. The server points to the back, and he runs to the men's room, barely making it. While he's peeing, he thinks about the stuff he stole from the hotel, and is looking forward to getting a better look at it, but he's dying for some coffee. So, when he's done, he asks the waitress for a large coffee to go. Once back in the car with his coffee, he reaches under the seat, then lays the watch and sunglasses out on the dash.

First, he examines the watch and sees it's a fairly decent Timex, nothing great, but worth keeping. He puts it on his wrist and pockets the cheap old watch he's been wearing. Now for the glasses. He doesn't have high hopes for the sunglasses, especially if they're prescription, making them too personalized. The plastic case is cheap, and he figures the sunglasses will be too. He's pleasantly surprised when he gets a good look at them, and realizes they have some kind of custom painting on them. He knows nothing about their value as mostly a high-end fashion accessory, since that isn't what he deals in, but he knows instinctively that they have some value. He's intrigued by them, and tries them on.

They're still warm from sitting on the dash, and he likes the way they gently hug his temples. He moves the rearview mirror to get a better look, but isn't especially pleased with what he sees. The lenses are dark enough to hide the bags under his eyes, but they do nothing to make his fleshy nose look smaller. He looks around and is impressed by how much better he can see, and wonders if maybe they *are* prescription. He's always been too cheap to get a prescription pair, always depending on the inexpensive drugstore kind. The crisp clarity is new to him, so he decides to keep them on. Finishing his coffee, he starts the car and decides to drive home, with a stop at the deli for a sandwich.

Arnie has forgotten about the construction being done on the highway, and wishes he'd taken the back roads. With another eight miles to go, he struggles to be patient, and turns the radio on trying to find something worth listening to. After crawling along for another few miles, he realizes he has to pee again. "Shit, shit, shit," he yells, slamming his hand onto the steering wheel. "I don't think I'm going to make it." He decides to get off at the next exit, but it's at least a half-mile away. He's starting to get desperate, so he inches out to the side of the road and slowly makes his way along the shoulder, passing the cars in front of him along the right. He's getting closer to the exit lane, when he hears the siren behind him. Looking into the rearview mirror, he sees the flashing lights and just stops. There's no room to pull over. The cop comes to his door and Arnie rolls down the window.

"You do know it's illegal to drive on the shoulder like this, correct?" the cop asks sarcastically.

Arnie nods and says, "Officer, this is embarrassing, but I really have to pee. I have a small bladder, and I didn't know it would be all backed up like this."

"Yeah, right, license and registration, and take off those sunglasses. Have you been drinking?"

"No sir, I'm just on my way home."

"Stay in the car. Don't move," the cop says, as he walks back and gets into the cruiser to check on Arnie's license and registration. He's in there a long time, and Arnie starts to feel a bit of leakage. He looks around the car for a bottle or can, and finally finds an old empty soda can. He unzips and lets loose, splashing some on his pants, and hopes the cop takes a little longer. Arnie sees him starting to get out of the car and zips up, knowing the front of his pants are wet.

"I'm giving you a ticket for driving illegally on the shoulder, in a construction zone. The instructions to pay are on the ticket, and by the way, the fine is $200. Can't believe you didn't know better than to do that." Arnie just takes it and nods. The cop walks away shaking his head, the upside being that this will help with his quota for the month.

Arnie finally makes it to the exit and takes the back roads. *Ah, almost home*, he thinks, as he slows for the stop sign. Looking left, then right, he starts to accelerate when BAM, a car pulling out suddenly side swipes him, bouncing off his passenger side door. Oh shit! Arnie takes the sunglasses off, throws them on the seat, and lays his head down on the steering wheel, feeling like he's going to cry. Someone's knocking on his window, but he stays like that for a minute more, trying to get a grip.

#

The first time Arnie puts Vincent's sunglasses on, Brenda's in her studio painting what she saw in a vision the last time she meditated. Vincent's in the painting, although only visible by a seasoned eye knowing where to look. Brenda's paintings are becoming more in demand, and she's becoming renowned in elite art circles, with continually positive reviews in all the major publications. She's still in business with Caroline producing and painting the vintage sunglasses, although her interest in them is waning, and she thinks of telling Caroline she needs a break. She steps back to view her work in a different light at the precise moment Arnie is stopped by the cop. She gets a peculiar feeling, and sort of chuckles, but feels it's not really funny. It's sort of like slapstick, where a person slips on a banana peel and falls down hard, maybe hurting themselves, but you can't help laughing.

That's weird, I wonder what made me think that, she wonders as she continues to paint. This one is coming out beautifully, and she's especially pleased with how she's hidden Vincent's formulas in the clouds, knowing that even if someone does see them, they won't know what they're looking at. The light and shadow are perfect. At the moment she turns to put down her brushes, Arnie has his head on the steering wheel, wondering why his day is turning out so badly. Brenda gets a flash of Vincent's sunglasses. For the first time in a long time, she can see them clearly, and knows something's different.

CHAPTER 27

At least I still have my van while the car's in the shop, Arnie thinks as he starts it up. *Otherwise, I wouldn't be able to get to the flea market.* This is his least favorite venue because the buyers tend to be cheap bargain hunters, and he feels like telling them to go take a hike when they whine about wanting a better price. This flea market is mostly where he tries to get rid of his old junk that he purposely leaves a bit dusty, to look more like valuable antiques. Any savvy buyer will know the difference, but you don't see that many of them in a place like this… although sometimes the educated ones play dumb, and end up walking off with something the seller doesn't know the value of. That's why he always has an eye out for what everyone else has on display, and throws in a few more valuable pieces, in case there actually *is* a buyer with some money.

It's a beautiful sunny day, and Arnie decides to wear the sunglasses he nabbed from the hotel. He gets his space set up and looks around at the other tables. *Same old crap*, he thinks, as he looks up at the flock of birds flying overhead. His eye catches the bright sun, and he feels a quick flash before looking away. He asks the guy who always sets up next to him to watch his stuff while he goes to take a leak, and quickly heads to the port-a-john. Once done, he takes his time getting back, scoping out what the other vendors have to offer. He spots a young guy about thirty, polishing some coins and putting them back in their display cases. Arnie leans over to get a better look, and does a double take. Is that what I think it is? He takes the sunglasses off and puts his magnifiers on. That looks like a 1943 Lincoln Head copper penny; it's worth thousands, and the guy has it just laying around with other considerably less valuable coins.

"Hey there," Arnie says to the young man. "I don't remember seeing you here before. You have some nice coins. Did you buy them from several different dealers?"

"No, my grandpa was a collector, and he left me all of these when he died last year. I've been learning a lot about their value, and it's interesting, but I decided collecting wasn't for me. Figured I'd sell some of them, since I could really use the money."

"Can't we all?" Arnie says amicably.

"I don't have the real valuable coins with me, but if you're genuinely interested, I can meet with you to show what I have."

Arnie pretends to peruse the various cases, and finally allows his eyes to settle on the 1943 Lincoln Head copper penny. He tells the young man he generally doesn't deal in coins, but might want to try at some point, when he has more capital to lay out. By the way, how much is he asking for the penny? The young man looks at which one Arnie's asking about, and says he left his guide at home by mistake, but thinks it's worth about $300. Arnie pretends to gasp and says it sounds rather high, and the young man sort of laughs and says he's pretty sure it's worth that much.

"Hmmm, let me think about it," Arnie says. "I'll come back after lunch."

"How about $275 cash, would that work?"

Arnie can barely contain his excitement, and nonchalantly says, "Not sure I have that much cash on me. I'll have to take a look, see what I got. Maybe this will get me started on a good collection. This is bad for me, since I'm supposed to be selling today, not buying."

They both laugh as Arnie goes to get the money from his van. He tells the guy watching his stuff he'll be right back, and goes to buy the penny. He keeps thinking the young guy will change his mind, or suddenly realize the value of the coin, but he doesn't. They make the exchange, and the young guy seems happy taking the cash and putting it in his pocket. Arnie goes to stash the penny in a safe place, and can't believe his luck.

Back at his table, Arnie puts the sunglasses on and talks to a few people perusing his goods, but no one is buying yet. He's bored, and looks around, rearranges stuff on his table, then looks up towards the sun that comes out from behind a cloud, and gets that flash again. Looking away, he thinks it's not good to look at the sun directly, and wonders why he keeps doing it. *These sunglasses don't work for shit, I shouldn't keep getting blinded.* He turns quickly when he hears two guys arguing behind him, and bumps his leg really hard on the edge of his table when his ankle twists, and he almost falls.

"Shit, ouch, that hurts," he says out loud. The guy at the next table looks over, but Arnie just waves him off, signaling he's okay. But damn. that really hurts. *I'm going to have a nice big bruise*, he thinks. rubbing his leg.

Arnie's good at sizing up his potential customers, and has a natural feel for when he can overcharge someone. He gets that eager feeling when a middle-aged woman and her teenage daughter approach, knowing there's good potential for exactly that. They're touching and handling everything, and he finds it annoying, but doesn't say anything. They ask for the cost of a few items, and Arnie inflates the price every time. He purposely doesn't have any pricing on his goods, and makes it up based on what he knows it's worth, and what he thinks they're willing to dish out. The daughter's spoiled and whines a lot, saying she wants everything he quotes a price on. The mother wants to oblige, but hesitates, telling her she can get one item, to pick out just one thing she really wants. The teenager picks up an antique hand mirror, admires herself in it, and says she wants it. *This* is what she wants. The mother asks Arnie how much, and he gives her a price three times what he would normally charge. He can barely keep from rubbing his hands together greedily.

The woman holds up the mirror, looking at it closely, examining every inch of it, when she suddenly says, "Hey, are you sure this is worth that much, that it's really an antique?"

"Oh yes, I got it from a man older than me. He said it was his mother's."

"Really?" she says indignantly. "Then why does it say *Made in China* on the handle here?"

"What? Let me see that." Arnie grabs the mirror from her, and as he turns it around, the bright sun bounces off, and pours a powerful stream of light directly into his eyes, blinding him for a few seconds.

"That's it, we're done here," the woman says as she reaches for her daughter's arm. "You're a lousy cheat," she yells as they walk away, with one quick backward glance of disgust.

Guess I shouldn't have done that, Arnie thinks, as he puts the mirror back. He looks around at a few people still looking at him, shrugs and turns away. *Nothing to see here, folks. Oh well, you win some you lose some.* He takes the sunglasses off, polishes them on the hem of his shirt, and looks at them thoughtfully, shrugs again, and puts them back on. He feels no remorse for getting caught out.

By mid-afternoon, Arnie's thinking about packing it in. He's tired, his leg hurts, and he's not even sold enough to make up the $275 he laid out for the penny. He makes one more trip to the port-a-john, and when he comes out, a huge Rottweiler on a leash looks over at him attentively. The dog starts to approach, pulling hard on his leash, and before Arnie realizes what's happening, the dog lunges at him. Arnie falls back against the port-a-john, and the dog claws at his face, growling. The sunglasses are pulled off his face, and as soon as they fall, the dog stops growling, and his owner pulls him back with all of his might.

"Oh my God, are you all right? I'm so sorry, he never does that! He's usually very friendly, and we spent so much time and money training him! I'm so sorry, are you okay?"

Arnie is shaking as he dusts himself off, backing away from the man and the dog. "What the fuck, man! That dog was trying to kill me!"

"I'm so sorry. Are you hurt? I don't see any damage, just a small scratch on your face. I'll pay for any doctor bills," the man says worriedly.

"I should fucking sue you, and that dog should be put down, for Christ's sake!" Arnie says, already thinking about how he can make a profit out of it.

The guy reaches into his pocket and takes out a hundred-dollar bill, and says, "Here, this should cover a doctor visit if you need it. Once again, I'm really sorry."

Arnie pockets the hundred and decides to just walk away; he's too shook up to fight it. Before he leaves, he says, "You ought to do something about that damn dog."

As he turns to go, one of the vendors who saw the whole thing stops him, and hands him the sunglasses he's picked up from the ground. "Here, these are yours, came off when the dog jumped on you."

"Oh, yeah, thanks," Arnie says as he goes to put them on. As soon as they're on his face, the dog starts growling again, and Arnie high-tails it away from them.

Back at his space, he definitely feels like leaving, but needs to calm down and take a breather. He gets a bottle of water from the van and sits for a minute, trying to bring his heart rate back to normal, while examining the scratch on his face. He takes the sunglasses off and looks at them, realizing he's had nothing but bad luck ever since he swiped them. *These fuckers are bad luck, I think someone put a spell on them or something, they're cursed. Damn, I have to get rid of them.* He polishes them on his shirt one last time, and puts them on the table next to the fake antique hand mirror. *Good riddance,* he thinks as he starts to pack the bigger items into the van.

A young man in his late twenties walks by and stops at Arnie's table. Something has caught his eye, and he comes closer. He picks up the sunglasses, and immediately tries them on. He then picks up the hand mirror to see how they look. *Hmmm, not bad. Not bad at all,* he thinks, putting the mirror back and looking around. He takes the glasses off and admires them closely, then notices the tiny initials inside, and the intricate prism design. He recognizes them as similar to a designer pair his mother bought a few years ago. He remembers they were all the rage among the movie stars, and those who could afford them at $500 a pop. He remembers his father didn't even blink when his mother told him how much they cost. As long as she was happy, his father was happy.

Arnie comes over, and the young man asks how much the sunglasses are. Arnie is delighted at the prospect of getting rid of them, though he thinks it's really weird that someone comes along wanting them within minutes of his deciding to sell them. *Everything about these glasses is just so fucking strange,* he thinks, *cursed or something for sure.* He tells the young man the price is $250, and when he doesn't even blink, Arnie realizes the guy really wants them. He then wishes he'd quoted a higher price, forgetting for the moment about them being cursed.

The old guy isn't going to budge on the price, the young man thinks, *and it's annoying the way he keeps insisting they're meant for me. Funny, though, I don't think he knows their real origin, or he would've said something about it. Plus, he handles them like they're on fire or something, like he can't wait to get rid of them.* The guy's really strange, and definitely acting like he's a bit unhinged.

Once the sale is made, the young guy puts them on again before he walks off. Arnie watches him go, and breaks out in a sweat, thinking, *Good riddance*!

The young man hurries off, glad to get away from Arnie, satisfied with his purchase. He can't wait to show off his cool new sunglasses.

Arnie finishes packing up, chuckling to himself about the young guy paying so much for those stupid sunglasses. *Good riddance,* he thinks again. *I had nothing but bad luck once I swiped those things. One bad thing after another. Oh, except I forgot about the penny. Yeah, the penny. It's worth thousands,* he thinks. *The one good thing, yes, the penny. Now where did I put that damn thing*? he wonders, now that he's remembered about it. *Where did I put that penny?* Arnie starts searching frantically, but for the life of him, he can't remember what he did with it.

CHAPTER 28

Carter swings the car adeptly into the parking space in front of the restaurant. He firmly puts it into park, turns it off, takes his sunglasses off, practically slams them onto the dash, and turns to look at Kristin. She's holding onto the door handle, not sure what to do. Carter's still looking at her, so she finally says, "What's wrong?" She's a little afraid of his temper, and is hoping it's not something she's done to annoy him. From the moment he picked her up he's barely said a word, and keeps looking at her with some kind of expectation.

"You didn't even notice," he says, putting the sunglasses back on. "I got these today at the flea market—they're real designer hand-painted sunglasses, even signed, and worth twice what I paid for them. My mother got a pair specially made a few years ago. Don't you recognize them?"

"Sorry, I'm not familiar with them. But they really do look special on you, and they make you look so handsome. You always look so handsome, though, so I didn't realize. I don't know as much about cool fashion as you do. Sorry."

Carter is somewhat appeased by this, and doesn't even realize how solicitous Kristin has learned to be, telling him exactly what he wants to hear and getting awfully good at it. She knows he constantly expects to be fawned over, like he has been his entire life. He's still slightly annoyed and is starting to think it's time to dump Kristin. She's nice and all, passably smart, really cute, but she's definitely not hot like he likes his women. He's mentioned to her several times how he likes red lipstick and the smoky-eye look on women, but she doesn't change her makeup for him, although he *has* noticed she's been wearing a push up bra lately.

While waiting to be seated, Kristin has her own thoughts about dumping Carter. He's a spoiled mama's boy, an egotistical, arrogant, know-it-all, sometimes-mean-to-her, high-maintenance pain-in-the-ass, unless everything's going his way. She goes on and on in her mind about everything wrong with him, and the list is quite long. She almost laughs out loud when she asks herself why she even puts up with him. While they peruse their menus and he orders a bottle of wine, Carter finally seems to relax. Sitting in an upscale, expensive restaurant always makes him feel like he's in his element. This is how he grew up, surrounded by the finer things in life.

He finally breaks the silence and starts telling her about his day. He works as a property manager for a friend of his father's, who got him the job, and naturally he feels the job is beneath him. He tells Kristin how he had to spend the day coordinating all kinds of maintenance work, and that half the guys are idiots, don't show up on time, do shit work, and can't be trusted. Kristin half-listens and nods sympathetically at the intervals she's supposed to, once in a while touching his arm in understanding. What she's really thinking about is how delicious the wine is, and how fortunate she is to be eating in a restaurant like this. She grew up middle class, and being in a place like this was reserved only for very special occasions; if wine was ordered, it would be the least expensive one in the ten-page leather bound wine list.

Once their dinner arrives and Carter has the sommelier bring another bottle of wine, they're both relaxed, starting to enjoy each other's company. He openly takes a good look at her, then smiles, and tells her how beautiful her eyes look in the candlelight. She thanks him and looks up at him under lowered lashes, and tells him how special and wonderful he is. By dessert and coffee, they're holding hands across the table, looking like any beautiful couple succumbing to the make-believe world that a delightful ambiance of candlelight, excellent wine, food, and wealth can provide. The funny thing is that Kristin doesn't know his father is the one paying for tonight's dinner. Carter has one credit card with a very high limit that his parents give him as an *allowance,* with the bill going directly to his parent's house every month. It gets paid without him ever seeing it, and only occasionally is he reprimanded for going over what they think is a reasonable limit. In many ways, he's even less of a manly man than what Kristin sometimes allows herself to think. However, she's still smitten with his good looks and what she believes is a chance of a life filled with the finer things. She also loves his physique, and that he's a highly skilled skydiver. No doubt, there's nothing sexier than Carter in his jumpsuit organizing a group of formation jumpers. Then he looks so strong, self-assured, and where he belongs.

Once the waiter brings their check, Carter makes a big show of signing for it with his expensive gold pen, then waits for the sommelier and maître d' to acknowledge and thank him profusely. *At least he's a good tipper,* she thinks, *I'll give him a few points for that. Except for practically expecting them to kiss his feet.*

They're both more than tipsy, but not quite drunk, when he pulls out of the parking lot and onto the main road. It's civil twilight now, and most people have their headlights on. Since it's Friday night the traffic is still heavy, yet not congested, and flowing smoothly. Carter decides it's best he take Kristin home instead of having her stay over at his apartment, seeing as he has a full day of skydiving scheduled, and needs to get an early start. He would definitely like to have sex, although that usually leads to staying up later than usual, and his being a little off his game the next day. The weather is supposed to be perfect tomorrow, and his passion has to come first. He tells Kristin he thinks it's best to take her home, that he has to get up early, and is really tired from a long day at work and the wine. She's a little put off, but also relieved in a way. She's tired too, she works hard too, so she agrees without whining, knowing that would just annoy him. Her agreeing rubs him the wrong way, even though that's what he wanted. He also expected her to say how much she wants him, and how hard it will be to wait until they can be together again. But she doesn't, and ironically, this annoys him.

On the freeway, everyone drives over the speed limit. Carter glides into his lane and keeps up with the traffic. They're mostly silent, absorbed in their own thoughts, when two cars that seem to be racing pass them on the left, going well over the speed limit. The cars start zigzagging through traffic, and drive like this, with no consideration for others, for several miles. When both cars are finally out of sight, Carter breathes a sigh of relief. The last thing he needs is to be in an accident.

Kristin has been holding on to the seat, white-knuckled, and she relaxes as well. This gets them chatting again, and the next few miles are just small talk. When their exit comes up, Carter puts on the directional signal and slows to take the exit. About a quarter-mile past the ramp they see smoke and two cars in a tangled mess of metal, no movement coming from either one. *Oh God, it's those two cars that were driving like maniacs on the freeway,* she thinks. *It looks bad, really bad.* "Oh my God!" she yells. "Pull over, they need help, we have to help them. It looks like it just happened. Call 911, pull over! They can't get out, they're hurt. Oh God."

Carter slows the car and looks over at the wreckage. The smoke concerns him, and he thinks maybe something will explode or burst into flames. He really doesn't want to get involved, and to be honest, thinks it serves them right for being jerks, so he starts to pick up speed and drives past. "What are you *doing*? Turn around, for Christ's sake," Kristin says as she dials 911. She starts talking with the dispatcher and Carter pulls over. He's already decided to drive away as soon as she's off the phone. They've been drinking, and he's more concerned about himself and not getting a DUI.

So far there are no other cars coming down the ramp, but Carter thinks someone will be along soon and they can help the jerks in the car. He's tired and wants to make sure he gets an early start tomorrow, and he's not going to allow this to mess up his day. Kristin gives the operator as much information as she has, and is told there's already an ambulance and fire truck being dispatched. She looks over at Carter when she hangs up, then looks down at her lap and starts to cry. When they hear sirens in the distance, Carter starts the car and heads towards home. Kristin turns in her seat, still staring at the ghastly mess of metal, when three emergency vehicles come speeding in from the opposite direction.

"See, that's good. You did the right thing calling 911. Now they can do their job and we don't have to get involved."

Kristin looks at him, deeply dismayed at how heartlessly he's behaving. "Have you no compassion?"

"Of course I do," he says defensively. "We did everything we could, and I didn't want to get involved, blown up, or end up with a DUI."

She shakes her head, thinking how screwed-up he must be, thinking only of himself when his actions could have possibly saved someone's life, and then being so coldly logical about it. This disheartens her greatly as she tries to absorb everything that's happened. When they get to her apartment, he turns off the car and pulls her in for a hug.

"I'm so sorry you had to witness such a horrible thing, especially after such a nice evening together. It was quite a disaster, but they're being helped now."

Kristin just hugs him back, still in shock from seeing what happened and how Carter handled it. Like so many inexperienced young women, she's already forgiving him, thinking for sure she can change him.

Carter makes certain to have his new sunglasses when he gets out of the car. He wants to see what he looks like wearing them with his jumpsuit on. He's going to wear them tomorrow, and he can't wait. Later, standing in front of the full-size mirror on the back of his closet door, he parades around modeling the look, and is very satisfied with the result. He's already forgotten about the accident when he turns all the lights on in his bedroom, as high as they'll go. As he looks again at his reflection, the light catches his eyes at such an angle that he has to look away. The flash is blinding, and he pulls the sunglasses off, wondering why they didn't filter the light better.

Lying in bed moments later, he finds he's having a little trouble falling asleep. He thinks of Kristin for a few minutes, wishing he was having sex with her now. Then his thoughts touch briefly on the accident, and he fleetingly feels a pang of guilt, thinking maybe he should have tried to do more. On that note, he succumbs to sleep.

#

At the exact moment that Carter feels the flash and absorption of light through the sunglasses, Brenda's sitting at home quietly reading a book, with a glass of wine on the side table. She feels content and relaxed after a rewarding day of painting. Suddenly, she feels a strong shift in the air. Brenda puts the book down and concentrates. *Something's changed*, she thinks. *I'll ask Vincent, he'll tell me.*

CHAPTER 29

Carter's father is a renowned heart surgeon, in high demand. He's a master at what he does and truly loves his profession. He often feels *godlike* when performing surgery, and to him it does feel like he *is* performing, every single time. He prepares, he practices, he studies, and then he gives the performance of a lifetime, every single time. If you have to have heart surgery, it would be a good thing to know him.

Many surgeons who feel this *godlike* feeling often act like they believe they *are* God, and expect to be treated as such. But not Carter's father; he's a really nice, caring guy who tends to be naive in just about everything but his profession. He feels blessed to have a beautiful, loving wife and is content to give her just about anything she has a need for. He rarely questions what she wants or what she's doing, and genuinely loves her. Many of her friends are envious of their relationship, and their husbands sometimes call him a sap, a milquetoast genius. Could be they're jealous. He works exceptionally hard without complaint, and when not working, can be found grilling some chicken, swimming in his huge pool, or catering to his family. To him life is good, and he's happy to help keep it that way for those around him.

Carter's mother is still lovely to look at, and seems to grow even more beautiful as she ages. Her beauty has always been the main thing people remark about and remember her for. She learned from an early age that her beauty was significant, powerful, and what she would be judged on. Taking care of and preserving her beauty meant everything. Participating in countless beauty pageants from an early age resulted in many first and second place wins for her. She disliked coming in second, mainly because her mother would take it personally, as an affront to her, and that made Carter's mother feel badly. She almost made it to the coveted Miss America win, but was topped by Miss Arkansas. Looking back, she'll tell you she's glad she lost, because that evening was when she met Carter's father. She was finding it extremely difficult to be an accepting loser, and made a great show of not falling apart. After a brave front of congratulating the winner, she finally got a chance to escape to the restroom, to pull herself together. She shed countless tears, then wiped her face and peeked out the door to see if anyone was around. When she opened the door, Carter's father was standing there looking as though he'd thought about coming in. He asked if she was all right, as he'd heard someone crying. He held out his arms, and she fell into them and started crying again.

As it turned out, his family had attended the pageant because his sister was participating (Miss Idaho) and they all came to support her. They were getting ready to leave when Carter's father said he needed the restroom, and it took him a while to find it. When he heard the sobbing, he wanted to help; and when Carter's mother peeked out the door and he saw her tear-stained face, he knew it was love at that very second. If you asked her, she wouldn't say it was love at first sight, because she'd been crying so hard and so much her sight was all blurry, and she couldn't really see. She gave him her number and ran off to find her mother, which she was dreading. He caught up with his family, told them he met the woman he was going to marry, and off they went. To this day, Carter's father always says it was such a fortunate coincidence he was there at the same time she was. If you believe in fate, it might be that… but coincidence? There's no such thing as coincidence.

When Carter was born, his mother vowed to be as good to him as she possibly could. She wouldn't push him and shame him into being what she thought he should be, or chide him when he didn't come out on top every single time. She'd give him positive reinforcement at every turn, and ensure him he was a worthy, wonderful individual they loved with all their heart. Carter's father, being a kind soul, knowing Carter's mother wanted the best for him and didn't want him to suffer through his childhood like she did, went along with it.

They did a good job of adhering to those vows, not realizing the fine line between growing up confident and loved, and growing up feeling entitled. There are so many other variables that determine the type of person one will be, and this proved true with Carter. He was a beautiful baby and grew into an extremely good-looking child, the kind who makes you do a double-take when you see him. By the time he was seven, he knew the power of his looks, and used them whenever he could. At school, he learned that a smile with his dimples showing and a polite manner went a long way, especially with the women teachers. The men teachers, he felt at times, could see through him, but mostly seemed charmed as well, especially if he called them *Sir*. He was quite good at figuring out how to manipulate people and getting out of things he didn't want to do. He spent a great deal of energy on this, and got away with more than he should have. He believed he was really something special, and didn't understand that his looks would only take him so far.

As a young adult, he's started to realize he has to rely on more qualities and strengths to get by, and he does the best he can, but hasn't been able to realize the balance between entitlement and humility. He knows he's special and should be more grateful, because people tell him so, but he mainly feels deep down that he comes first, and that's not going to change. He's also been blessed with a nicely proportioned physique and athletic ability. In high school, he did better than average in practically every sport, but not quite good enough to get a scholarship or be able to make it a career. His grades were above average, just barely, and his SAT scores nothing to brag about. When it came time to talk about college, he told his parents he wasn't sure where he wanted to go, or what he wanted to study. Fortunately, his father had contacts, and he ended up pulling some strings to get him into USC. Carter did passably well academically at college, and had a good mind for business.

Of course, he was quite popular with the ladies, but was surprised that some of the more *earthy girls*, as he likes to call them, weren't especially attracted to him. Carter learned a great deal while away at college, and enjoyed the freedom of being away from home. He was surprised to learn how many people out there didn't have supportive, wealthy parents like he does, and wondered how they got along without an allowance like he got. He kind of felt sorry for those guys who had to work while in school, and didn't know how they did it. It's not that he's lazy by nature; he's spoiled, and that makes him lazy.

Carter never expressed a strong passion for any one thing, and generally moved through life doing more or less what he was supposed to, what was expected of him. Right before he graduated, a friend of his suggested they go skydiving. This sounded like an adventure Carter had never thought to try, and he was up for the challenge. They got a group of guys together and drove an hour to the nearest drop zone to do tandem skydives. They went up two guys at a time, attached to their tandem instructor, and Carter could barely wait for his turn. While he was waiting, his tandem instructor went through the drill with him, and Carter took in every word. He loved the feel of the drop zone, and watched all the real skydivers coming into the hangar from their jumps, their parachutes over their shoulders, their helmets high on their heads, and an exhilarated look of accomplishment on their faces. He wanted to be one of those guys. They were the coolest group of people he'd ever been around, and there were women skydivers too. The whole experience was almost giving him a boner, and he hadn't even had his turn yet. One of the guys he was with was having second thoughts about doing it, and kept saying he was afraid of heights. But not Carter; he could barely contain himself.

Finally, they were all packed into the Twin Otter and Carter started to get a queasy feeling in his gut; *Here we go.* His tandem master chatted with him the remaining fifteen minutes it took the plane to get to altitude, and before he knew it, they were crab-walking their way to the door. With one last deep breath, head held back, they launched—and Carter was flying! They weren't falling; they were hurtling through space, and it felt so good. *Don't forget to breathe*, he told himself as he tried to look around and keep his back arched. He felt his instructor pull his arms back, and he remembered he wasn't free falling on his own. Just as he thought this would go on forever the instructor pulled the ripcord, and the parachute opened, bringing them up like a bungee cord with a sliding jolt.

The instructor asked Carter how he felt; he smiled and said *Fantastic*. Now he could see all the postage-sized patches, roads, and mountainous terrain below him, and realized it looked just like the aerial photos he'd seen in the movies. It was beautiful, stunning, and he was speechless. When he became aware of others around him and heard his friend whooping a few hundred feet away, he started laughing, and couldn't stop until they slid on their butts over the ground to a stop. They detached him and he jumped up, knowing he was going to do this again and again. Carter was going to become a skydiver, and he ran to the hanger to find his friends to let them know.

That was how Carter found his first real passion, and he never tires of telling the story. It's hard for him to believe that was more than five years and a thousand jumps ago. Now he's an experienced skydiver, organizing formations, highly skilled and respected in the sport. He likes telling the story, but doesn't mention how he struggled in the beginning, and almost gave up after his first few solo jumps.

Driving to the drop zone with his new sunglasses on, he reminiscences a bit about the early days, and is glad they're behind him. He thinks about the accident they saw last night, and feels mostly confident that Kristin doesn't still think they should have stopped to help. Surprisingly, he feels something gnawing at him, and faintly realizes it's guilt. When he gets to the drop zone, he checks how he looks in the mirror, then grabs his gear from the trunk. He looks up, watching the guys from the four-way team come in for final landing. At a perfect angle, the early sun suddenly glints off of his sunglasses, and a static-like flash passes directly into his eyes. He looks away and steps back, almost losing his balance. *That was weird*, he thinks as he makes his way to the packing area in the hangar.

CHAPTER 30

Carter drops his gear by the packing mat, and walks around to see who's here, and who's ready to do some jumps. He sees his buddies RJ and Tony, and asks if they're ready to jump and where the other guys are. They're ready, and Tony wanders off to see who else he can round up. A few minutes later there're five of them, and Carter's thinking about the formation that will work best based on their skill levels. There's one new guy, Pete, who only has thirty jumps, but he seems to be doing well for a newbie. RJ and Tony are both more experienced, and he can put them anywhere, but Billy is the wild card. He has a lot of jumps, but still always manages to either screw up the exit, miss his slot, or drop like a brick. When doing formations, it's key to put the right person in the right slot based on skill and strengths, so Carter figures out who to put where, and they start to practice the dirt dive on the ground. To an outsider watching, the dirt dive looks almost like they're doing a touch-and-grab square dance. Envisioning these practice moves being done in free fall, trying to stay stable at 120 mph, gives you an idea of the expertise required to pull it off.

After repeating the dirt dive until everyone is certain of what they'll be doing, they hang around talking and waiting for their load to be called. Normally by now, they would be securing their parachutes, checking their chest straps, and making sure they have their altimeters, goggles, and helmets ready. But after the first load came in, with guys being thrown around from wind gusts, the drop zone manager put out a wind hold until things calmed down and it was safe to jump again. This could mean waiting anywhere from twenty minutes to a couple of hours before they can jump. There tend to be many reasons not to jump based on safety, and this is one of them.

With a few groans, the guys separate, with just Tony and RJ hanging around with Carter. Tony's the first one to notice Carter's sunglasses. "Hey, what's up with the sunglasses? They look like something my grandmother would wear," he teases.

RJ chimes in and says, "Dude, really? They're kind of big and have paint on them or something. Where'd you get them?"

"They happen to be one of a kind," Carter says. "If you had any kind of fashion sense, or good taste, you would know what they were."

He takes them off and looks at them admiringly before handing them to RJ, the more responsible one, and tells him to try them on. "Whoa, these are awesome," RJ says as he looks around. "I can see so clearly, and they fit my face just right." He walks to the end of the hangar and looks up, then around. "I want a pair. Here, Tony, check them out," he says as he hands them over to Tony.

"Okay, give them back," Carter says nervously. He doesn't trust Tony, and worries he might break them. It's too late; Tony already has them on as he runs off, whooping and acting crazy. "Shit, what an asshole. Get back here!" Carter yells as he runs after him. Finally, he catches up with him. Tony takes them off and throws them to RJ, who's behind Carter. They start throwing them around, and Carter's getting really mad. "Give them back!" he says angrily.

Then an odd thing happens: he starts to calm down. He realizes getting mad is doing no good, and what's the worst that can happen anyway? He turns his back on them and walks away. He sees a woman he knows whom he helped train, and goes over to talk with her. He's really proud of himself for not throwing a tantrum. *Oh man, I think that's a sign of maturity,* he tells himself, *or could it be something else?* For some reason, this thought gives him an odd feeling. He shakes it off when Tony comes back and hands him the sunglasses, perfectly intact. Without a word, he puts them on, and goes to manifest to see if they have a band he can attach to the glasses, to hold them on tight around his head so they don't fall off.

When the wind hold finally lifts, the guys get into their gear, and carefully check that everything is in place. They do another quick dirt dive to make certain everyone has remembered what they're supposed to do, then head off to the boarding area. Carter has his sunglasses securely fastened and looks around. Without really thinking, he starts checking everyone's gear, confirming to himself everything is as it should be. His eyes go from one person to the next, until they settle on Steve, a guy with about a hundred jumps, who happens to be a pretty good skydiver for the amount of experience he's had. Carter realizes Steve's chest strap has been misrouted, and if he doesn't fix it, he could literally fall out of his harness on deployment. Carter immediately goes over to him, and grabs him, telling him to look down at his chest strap. When Steve realizes it's misrouted, he gasps and immediately fixes it.

"Man, thank you! I've never done that before, thanks for catching it," Steve says, taking a deep breath. Carter pulls the strap to make sure it's tightened properly, and steps back to look at him. Steve thanks him again; Carter nods and takes another look around to make sure everyone else's gear is as it should be. While they're boarding the plane, Carter's lost in thought for a few minutes, thinking about what he just did. He feels really good that he helped someone and possibly saved their life. He can't wait to tell Kristin, and hopes it makes up for being a jerk the other night.

The exit goes well, and the formation is starting to build, except they're missing one guy. Where's Billy? Oh, here he comes, but he's coming in too fast, and BAM, he takes out the formation. As it breaks apart, Pete, the newbie, gets hit and ends up spinning on his back. Carter sees this, and soars over to him as Pete rolls over onto his stomach. He can see that Pete is aware, but looks dazed, and is trying to gather himself. He finally looks over, and Carter signals him to pull, which he does. Knowing Pete seems okay, Carter pulls too, and tries to calm down and focus on his landing.

Once he's on the ground, he waits in the landing area to make sure Pete makes it down safely. Pete comes in a little wobbly but stands up his landing, and Carter cheers, genuinely impressed. He goes over to him to see if he's all right, and makes a point of telling him he did an excellent landing, especially after what happened in the air. Pete's shook up, but tries not to show it as he walks back to the hangar with Carter. He thanks him for saving him, and pulls his arm to stop him. Carter turns around and Pete gives him a quick man-hug, and thanks him again. Carter just shrugs and nods, then continues walking with a barely discernible smile on his face.

His first instinct is to find Billy and punch him in the face, but amazingly he keeps himself from doing this, and decides to wait and see if Billy will come over and apologize, realizing how badly he messed up. Carter has almost completed his packing before RJ and Tony come over. They're surprised he's being so quiet and not giving Billy a load of shit for screwing up the jump, and almost causing a major accident for the newbie.

"Hey, you okay?" RJ asks Carter.

"Yeah—pissed, though. Where's Billy?"

"Last we saw he was out back, having a cigarette. He hasn't started packing yet."

"Man, he fucked up," Tony says. Carter just nods and finishes packing. RJ and Tony walk away, knowing Carter needs time to process, but stay close by to see what he does.

Sheepishly, Billy finally comes over to Carter and says, "I fucked up. I don't know what happened. I'm so sorry. I saw Pete and apologized."

Instead of dressing him down in front of everyone, Carter pulls him aside and they have a long talk. Carter tells Billy he needs to get more training; even though he has a lot of jumps he screws up too much, and if he doesn't do something about it, Carter says he'll recommend Billy not be allowed to jump at that drop zone any more. For most skydivers, being banned from a drop zone is like a jail sentence, and this hits Billy hard. He wants to argue about it, but Carter's quiet, calm manner unsettles him, and he just nods.

Tony and RJ come back to see what was said, and Carter just shakes his head and tells them Billy's going to get more training. They realize they're not going to get anything else out of him, so they let it be and start looking to put another jump together, minus Billy. The rest of the day turns out better, and after three more jumps that mostly go well, the winds kick up again and everyone decides it's time to pack it in. Just as Carter decides to call Kristin, he sees she's already there, and talking with some guys he doesn't recognize. He feels a pang of jealousy at how attentively they're looking at her—and suddenly realizes he's the fortunate one, not the other way around. It's an epiphany, and he doesn't realize that what he's feeling is appreciation. It's a relatively new feeling for him, and it makes him feel satisfyingly good… and amazingly, it's about the other person. *Am I gaining maturity?* he wonders. *Okay, let's not get too carried away here*, he laughs to himself.

CHAPTER 31

Brenda has become a master at meditation, and believes it's become her saving grace. She doesn't need the class anymore, but she still goes once in a while to be around other people. They've even asked if she would like to lead some of the guided meditation classes, but she's declined the offer. Although she's flattered, this is something she wants to keep to herself. Meditation is how she communicates with Vincent; this is where she comes to feel him inside of her being, hear him impart marvelous wisdom she feels humbled to be privy to. Through these sessions she learns about the journey of the sunglasses, the ripple effects, the purpose that has become so much more than initially intended, all on their own. She can feel when they leave one person to go on to another, to influence and impart what comes from who they really are. She now knows the residual effects continue as meant to, taking the best of what's already inside a person and bringing it to the surface.

As she paints, she draws on this knowledge, feeling a multifaceted force at work within her. She doesn't want to be ungrateful, and tries to make all of this enough. She has so much more than others, in so many mystifying ways they would not be able to fathom, even if she were able to describe it. Except she doesn't have Vincent, not really, and that's what she wants more than anything, to be close to him in this realm.

#

While Brenda paints, Carter's having an early breakfast with his parents. His mother makes a big deal of them sharing breakfast on Sunday mornings, and sometimes this is the only time they get to spend together. They're willing to have an early breakfast so Carter can get to the drop zone, and hopefully his father doesn't have any emergency surgeries to perform. His mother gets up at the crack of dawn to have all the preparations ready, so his favorite omelet and side dishes can be put together quickly. There have been times Carter complains about this routine, but his mother is insistent, so he complies to keep the peace.

This morning he finds he's actually looking forward to it, and wants to tell them all about what happened yesterday. He tells his mother about the sunglasses he got at the flea market and shows her how cool they look on him. Normally he's not that talkative, and they have to play twenty questions to find out what's going on with him, but not this morning. He's like a chatterbox, and his parents exchange several looks of wonder and pleasure at how he's behaving. His father attributes it to Carter's passion for skydiving, but his mother senses it's something else, although she doesn't know what. Even though breakfast is usually only an hour at most, Carter's enjoying himself and stays longer than usual. When he realizes the time, he jumps up and his mother walks him to the door. After saying goodbye to his father, he gives his mother a hug and thanks her for the breakfast. She looks into his eyes and thinks, *Yep, definitely something different about him.* Mothers know these things.

It's another sunny day, and the winds aren't kicking, so when Carter gets to the drop zone, it's already humming with activity. He finds a few of his buddies and goes to manifest to sign up for a load. There are six guys total for their first jump, and he's thinking about the best formation based on what he knows about them. RJ and Tony he can put anywhere, but the other three he hasn't jumped with yet, and he can only go by what they tell him. Raj and Mike both have over a thousand jumps, but Marcus has less than a hundred. Normally, Carter would tell Marcus he only jumps with more experienced guys, but today he decides to let him jump with them.

He's usually the organizer who always asks, *How many jumps you got?* before he'll even consider letting you in on the formation. Today he's feeling more tolerant than usual.

For this first jump he doesn't plan anything too difficult, and the dirt dive goes well, with everyone understanding what they need to do. He still has a few minutes before their load goes up, so he walks to the landing area to check the windsock, and take a look at the sky. As he starts to turn away, a bright beam comes from behind a wispy cloud, and he can't look away. The light is beautiful, with a pinkish hue, and he feels no blinding sensation, only a surprising coolness wash over his eyes. He blinks, and it passes. He takes his sunglasses off and looks at them carefully. There's a barely visible nick towards one of the edges which he rubs with his thumb, then polishes with his shirt. He puts them back on, marveling at how clear everything looks.

On the way up, there's the usual laughing and joking until they get close to altitude. Then things quiet down considerably and everyone checks their gear, focuses, and gets ready to jump. Carter looks at all his guys and they nod in confirmation; they're ready. It's their turn, and out they go. Right out of the door on the exit, Carter sees a guy tumbling, and when the guy continues to tumble, Carter breaks away from the others and chases the guy until he catches up with him. Carter grabs onto him and finds he's unconscious, flips him over, points him towards the drop zone, and pulls his parachute. He then immediately pulls his own parachute and tries to stay with him and follow him down. He can see the guy is slumped in his harness, out cold, and hopes he comes to before landing.

Carter sees the patch of trees, knowing they're off course, but there's nothing for him to do but follow. He watches the guy land in one of the trees, and sees some branches that might cushion his fall, then loses sight of him. Carter steers away from the trees and lands safely, dumps his gear, and runs over to where the guy's lying on the ground. The good news is that the branches did help to break his fall. The bad news is, one of the broken branches punctured his arm, and blood's gushing from the wound like water from a fountain. Carter immediately tears off his jumpsuit, and rips his belt from the pants he has on underneath. He wraps his shirt around the wound and tightens his belt around it, making a pressure bandage. He then wraps part of his jumpsuit around that, and continues to apply as much pressure as possible.

The guy's now conscious, but very disoriented, and asks what happened. Carter tells him he fell through a tree upon landing, but doesn't go into a lot of detail. He asks the guy if he remembers hitting his head, but he can't remember anything but being on the plane. Carter carefully feels around his head but doesn't find anything, and is glad the guy was wearing a helmet. He continues to do a body check and runs his hand over first the guy's other arm, and then down his legs. Carter can see on the left leg, before he even puts his hand on it, that something's wrong. He carefully puts his hand on the guy's leg, and can feel even through his jumpsuit that his shin is broken. The guy starts to moan and says he hurts so bad, and he's sure he's dying. Carter thinks he may also have some broken ribs, but doesn't want to jostle him around too much to find out.

Fortunately, Kevin was at the drop zone that morning watching, and saw the two parachutes open one after the other, much higher than usual. He tracks them, sensing there's something wrong, and watches as they go way off course, at least a mile from where they should be. When most of the guys who were on that load are on the ground, Kevin goes around asking them who's missing. He has a reputation for being extremely observant, always knowing where people end up when they land off the designated area, and whether something's wrong. He's that guy who's really good at watching, and has been instrumental in finding just about anyone who's ever had an off landing. Before long, they know it was Carter and a guy named Roger. Kevin runs to the office, tells them what he knows, and where he thinks they are. It's obvious that if Carter did an off landing something was definitely wrong, so they grab the first aid kit and radio, and jump in the truck to go find them.

By now Roger has lost a lot of blood, and is passing in and out of consciousness. Carter continues to apply the pressure, and tries to stanch the flow as much as possible. He's laid Roger down with his head resting on his bunched-up parachute and speaks calmly, continuing to tell him he's doing good, and it will all work out. In the meantime, Carter's praying someone will find them soon. He's afraid to move Roger, and knows he wouldn't be able to keep the pressure on at the same time. Without the pressure, Roger would surely bleed out. So, Carter continues the pressure, talking softly and even telling a few jokes, trying to keep Roger conscious.

Finally, he hears people calling and yells back, letting them know where they are. The truck zooms up, and before they even get out Carter tells them to radio 911, they need an ambulance. He never lets up applying the pressure, and tells Kevin there's a lot of blood-loss and he needs help keeping the pressure on. Kevin takes off his shirt, wraps it on Roger's wound, and holds the pressure so Carter can get a break. When he's finally able to move away from Roger for a minute, he's surprised to see how badly his hands are shaking. He remained calm throughout the ordeal, but now that help has arrived, he feels the reality of the situation go through him.

The ambulance comes in record time, and Carter quickly fills them in on what he knows of Roger's injuries. The main concern is stopping the blood flow from the puncture, and the EMT guys have that under control before they attempt to get him in the ambulance. Time is of the essence, and they're ready to take off within minutes. As one of the EMTs is pulling the door shut he says, "Good job, man, you saved his life. He would have been a goner if you hadn't done what you did."

Before getting in the truck to go back to the drop zone, Carter reaches up, feeling around, and realizes he doesn't have his sunglasses. He goes back to where he'd been with Roger and looks around, trying to find them. The only time he can think of when they might have come off was when he flipped Roger over; he remembers Roger's arm hitting him in the face. He asks Kevin if his face is bruised, and his friend nods and says it looks like he's going to have a black eye. With Roger bleeding out the way he was, no one thought to ask Carter if he was okay.

"Yeah, I'm good," Carter says quietly. "It was like time stood still and everything around us stopped, but I knew what I was supposed to do. When I was following him down, I knew he was unconscious, and it was like I was outside of myself watching. I saw him land and then fall through the tree, and knew before I saw him on the ground that I would know what to do. The only time I started to get a little nervous was when it really struck me that it was up to me to keep him alive. Then it became the most important thing I ever had to do in my life, and I did the best I could."

"You did great, man," Kevin says. "In fact, more than great. How did you know what to do?"

"It all just came to me, like I was guided or something. Wait until I tell my Dad. Now he's going to want me to go to medical school!" They all laugh, and Carter sits back in the seat, suddenly very tired.

Word gets around at the drop zone about what happened, and everyone's saying that Carter's a hero. He has to admit he likes the attention, but doesn't feel like a hero. He feels there's another element involved that should be given some credit, but he keeps this to himself. Only to Kristin does he partly reveal what he's really been feeling about it. He tells her he's learned a lot these past few days, and how good it feels to be the giver instead of always expecting others to cater to him. Giving didn't come naturally to him, and he honestly didn't know how good it would make him feel. But now that he knows this, he's still a little confused about something. "If I feel so good helping others, am I really doing something good if I'm getting so much out of it? Isn't it still selfish?" he asks Kristin.

She thinks about this before answering, then replies, "I think every single thing we do, we do because we think it will make us feel better."

"But I didn't know what I was going to do. I just did it."

"I guess a part of you knew it would feel good if you tried to help someone, if you did the right thing. So you figured out what to do, and did it. You could have just gone on with your jump and not helped Roger."

"How come I didn't know this before, though? I should've known it would make me feel good to help others."

"Well, you know it now," Kristin says, laughing.

"So, even Mother Theresa? She does what she does ultimately because it makes her feel better?" he asks skeptically.

"Yes, even Mother Theresa. But it's anything *but* selfish on her part. It makes her feel better to do something about others' suffering; she couldn't live with herself otherwise, if she weren't helping others. But yes, ultimately I would say it does make her feel better."

"Man, did I underestimate you," he says, pulling her in for a hug. "Oh, did I tell you I lost my sunglasses? They came off when Roger's arm whacked me, I think. They're probably lying in a field somewhere. They're probably broken. It's too bad—I really liked them."

CHAPTER 32

Ollie grips the edge of the blanket in his teeth and pulls, stepping backwards until Helen groans and pulls back, letting him know she's awake. He jumps on the bed, tail wagging and happy, as he always is when it's just the two of them. Giving him hugs and kisses, she then pushes him away to enable her to get up and get her day started. Padding into the kitchen, she gives Ollie his breakfast, then makes some coffee for herself. Watching him eat, she smiles a little, thinking how lost she would be without him. She feels there's no other soul on Earth right now who loves her, except for Ollie.

The farm is a little over three acres of useful land, providing a variety of vegetables throughout most of the year, making just enough to keep them going and Jake's mother in a decent nursing home. Jake's parents ran the farm for years, and when his father died last year, his mother signed over the land, including the house, free and clear. In return, all she wanted was to be taken care of in a nice place. They have a few full-timers working the fields, with Jake handling the business end and Helen keeping the books, plus everything else to do with the home. Every morning, without exception, she walks the perimeter of the fields with Ollie, making sure the work is being taken care of while her husband is out and about *taking care of business*, as he calls it. She knows he's away from the farm to be away from her, and closer to whatever women he can find who are willing to succumb to his attention. He *does* take care of business in between, and the farm is genuinely well-run between the two of them, even though their relationship is like the broken-down, rusty old tractor they have out front for decoration.

"Wait up, Ollie," Helen calls as he takes off in a flash after something that catches his attention. The morning inspection is one of his favorite jobs, and he takes it seriously. He must smell and inspect everything as if it's the first time, and run ahead to protect Helen every step of the way. It's a glorious bright day with a few puffy clouds and a slight breeze—the kind of day when you want to be outside, and the perfect temperature for a long, take-your-time reconnaissance. Ollie agrees, running and wagging, then checking behind him to make sure Helen's keeping up. He spots something in the grass along the border of the corn section, and starts pawing, trying to dig it up. Helen comes to see what he's dug up, and it looks like a pair of sunglasses. She reaches down and is surprised to see they're intact, wondering how they got there. It almost looks like they were partially buried. Maybe by an animal? Hard to tell. She wipes the dirt off and sees that these are no ordinary sunglasses. They're intricately painted and even have something, looks like initials, painted on the inside. Damn, she should have brought her glasses. She doesn't normally need distance glasses, just uses them for reading and close work.

After wiping them some more, Helen puts them on and is quite startled at the clarity of vision they provide. Looking around, she thinks maybe she *does* need glasses for more than just reading, because she can't believe how well she can see. Everything looks crisp and bright, yet with enough shadow to provide the kind of lighting photographers strive for. It's interesting how it changes depending on where she looks, and she suddenly feels like she's been missing seeing the real world until she looked through these glasses. She doesn't think she's ever seen the world around her look so exquisite, so captivating, so full of something she can't put her finger on. The feeling this gives her, the feeling that she can't identify, is hope—something she gave up on a long time ago, so long ago she forgot what it feels like.

Ollie is jumping around her legs, wanting attention and some pets for making such a good find. She absently bends down and pets him, telling him what a good boy he is, feeding him a treat from her pocket.

After taking twice as long as usual on their reconnoiter, Helen and Ollie head back to the house. She's mentally going through the list of tasks she needs to accomplish before starting dinner, and realizes she's way behind. Taking the sunglasses off, she looks around for a good hiding place for them, and finally decides to hide them under the cushion of Ollie's doggie bed. She's not sure why, but she knows she needs to hide her find from Jake. As she buries them under the cushion, Ollie watches as if he knows he must protect them, and gives Helen a look telling her the glasses are safe with him.

First order of business is catching up on the books, so she heads into the back room they've set up as an office. After several hours of going over invoices, payroll, and taxes, Helen decides to take a stretch and make a cup of coffee. While drinking the coffee and massaging her sore neck, she gazes out the kitchen window, wondering how she let herself get stuck in such an unhappy place. It all started when she'd just turned sixteen, and her friend Lisa talked her into running away from home. Lisa was her best friend, her only friend, and at the time, Helen felt she had nothing to lose.

She'd been born prematurely, and everyone thought she wasn't going to make it. After almost three months in the hospital, she was finally able to come home. Her parents did the best they could as far as taking care of her and keeping her alive, but made sure to mention, often, how hard it had been on them financially, and that she was the reason they never had any money. Without actually placing the blame on her, it was often alluded to, and when she became old enough to start deciphering things and make conclusions, she developed a feeling of guilt that she was too young to fully understand.

Her parents spent a lot of money on cigarettes and cheap wine, often lamenting they couldn't afford better wine, and the other things they felt they deserved. Helen even felt guilty about this, and vowed to save her babysitting money to give to her parents so they could buy better wine. She never went to anyone else's house, or even had any friends other than Lisa, so she thought this was normal behavior, that all parents were like hers. She was glad they weren't like Lisa's parents, especially her stepfather. He was pure evil, pushing her mother around and touching Lisa inappropriately every chance he got. When things began to get out of hand, Lisa started talking about running away, but she was only fifteen and had no place to go. They would talk about it after school, and it became a goal that Helen thought would never really happen.

She felt sorry for Lisa but was afraid to run away, and felt she was okay where she was—until the night she heard her parents talking in a drunken stupor. She usually stayed in her room at night doing homework or watched TV in the living room, not paying attention to her parents, who spent the night drinking. She was good at being alone, used to it, and mostly didn't mind. But that night she had gotten her period, and her cramps were really bad. She just laid on the beat-up couch, TV turned low, hoping the cramps would subside. Her parents started arguing, and before long she could tell it was about her. She forced herself to get off the couch and stood outside the kitchen, listening.

"You know we were *both* hoping she'd die," her mother slurred. "Admit it. It's her fault we had to get married, and it's her fault things turned out so bad. The hospital bill wiped us out, we were too young, and now look at us. It would have been better if she'd died."

Helen didn't wait to hear what her father said. She slowly backed up and crept to her room, tears rolling down her face. If she had some place to go, she would have started packing right then, but she didn't. When she saw Lisa the next day, she told her what she'd heard, and they started to plan their getaway in earnest.

Deep in thought, the loud ringing of the phone startles her, and she jumps up, almost spilling her coffee. *Shit, it's Jake*, she thinks when she hears his voice.

"Why are you still home?" he asks angrily. "Why the *fuck* are you still home? You're supposed to be at the home visiting Mother!"

"I was just getting ready to leave," she lies. "It took longer than usual to get the books done."

She hears Jake sigh deeply and waits for his tirade, but it's not forthcoming today for some reason. "I'll leave right now," she says, and just before she hangs up, she swears she hears a woman's voice in the background. "Asshole," she says out loud as she gathers her keys and purse and heads out the door. She's halfway to her car when she turns around and runs back inside to get the sunglasses. Ollie looks at her questioningly as she comes over to where he's lying in his bed, and starts wagging as she reaches under the cushion for the sunglasses. Giving him a few pats on the head, she runs out the door.

The home where Jake's mother resides is a 20-minute drive from the farm, and fortunately traffic is light this time of day. She rushes inside, and the receptionist seems to eye her accusingly, saying Marian's been waiting for her. *I can't win,* Helen thinks. *No matter what, someone's annoyed with me.* Sighing deeply, she takes a breath and taps lightly on Marian's door.

"Hello, dear," Marian says from her bed. "You're late. I thought you forgot about me."

"I'm so sorry, Marian, I had extra work at home. I got here as soon as I could."

Marian looks away with that look she gets, twisting her lips tightly like she's trying to keep from spewing awful thoughts. Which she probably is. She clears her throat and starts telling Helen about a dream she had, where she was playing her beloved piano, and how wonderful it felt to be able to play again, even if it was just a dream.

This gives them something to talk about, and gives Helen a chance to tell her how she wishes she had heard more of Marian's playing, how wonderful her playing was, and how good she takes care of the piano that sits in the corner of their living room. They talk about how one day, when Marian is feeling up to it, Helen can bring her home so she can play. Neither of them ever expects this to happen, but they go on and on about it, ending with Helen promising to get the piano tuned, so it will be in perfect condition when Marian comes to play.

Outside, Helen takes a deep breath, glad the visit is over, although she really doesn't mind visiting Marian. What she minds is that she goes to visit Jake's mother a lot more often than Jake does, and his mother makes excuses for him, saying how busy he is running the farm. If she only knew what her Jake was really up to, giving that priority over visiting his mother... She shakes her head to clear her thoughts, thinking *erase, erase, erase*, a trick she learned when she lived on the commune to block out negative thoughts. *Let's not go down that rabbit hole*, she thinks as she digs around in her purse looking for the sunglasses. She can't find them, and starts to feel anxious. Unlocking the car door, she spots them on the passenger seat, realizing they must have fallen out when she threw her purse there in her haste to get going. *Whew, so glad I found you*, she laughs, thinking she's really lost it if she's now talking to a pair of sunglasses. She puts them on and starts driving back to the farm to continue her chores and get dinner started. She figures Jake will be hungry after this afternoon's *activities*.

Helen's about halfway home when she notices that everything looks much larger than usual. Glancing around, the trees appear to be almost twice their normal size, and the car in front of her looks as big as a garbage truck. She slows to a crawl and takes the sunglasses off. Within a few minutes, things start to go back to their normal shape and size, and she wonders if she's having a stroke or something. Feeling somewhat rattled, she looks around carefully when back at the farm, and everything looks like it normally does. Once inside, she carefully puts the sunglasses back in their hiding spot, now with yet another thing to wonder about.

CHAPTER 33

While making dinner, Helen thinks about how the trees and cars took on warped shapes when she was driving home, and is somewhat concerned, considering she's never experienced anything like it before. She feels fine—better than fine, actually—and is puzzled by that as well. Usually she finds herself dragging through her days because she's sad and lonely, finding it exhausting to put on a good front when she's so miserable. Yet now, she's feeling a form of enthusiasm she doesn't know how to describe; almost an anticipation of something, and *not* like waiting for the other shoe to drop. It's more like that hopeful feeling she's afraid to feel.

Jake still isn't home, and dinner is keeping warm in the oven. She'll wait another half hour before she starts without him. He'll either be pissed about it or won't notice; she's never sure how he'll treat her. While waiting, she's drawn into the living room, and over to the far corner where the dusty piano that belongs to Jake's mother sits, almost hidden. Interesting that Marian dreamt about playing; must be hard being stuck in the home knowing she'll never feel the keys beneath her fingers again.

Helen had been given a few piano lessons in grade school, when they allowed the children to try different instruments, in hopes they would get serious about one of them. She remembers a few notes, but never learned how to play. No way her parents would pay for lessons, and her mother said it would be a snowy day in hell before they ever got a piano. They would ask if she'd lost her mind, thinking they could get a piano. *Don't you know how much they cost?* So that was the end of that. She goes back to the kitchen and gets a dust cloth and some polish, and starts really cleaning up the piano. It's not a Steinway, but she knows this is a good piano, and Jake's mother kept it in excellent condition. She never played professionally but was classically trained, playing since childhood, and even gave recitals when she was a young woman. That was mostly before she married Jake's father and became a farmer's wife.

This thought gives Helen a melancholy sinking feeling; she finds it chilling how this mirrors her own life. Jake's mother seems to have accepted being a farmer's wife willingly, but who knows really what's behind the fronts people want you to believe? Helen remembers promising Marian she would get the piano tuned, and she makes a mental note to do so. *It's the least I can do for her*, she thinks, feeling a little ashamed she hasn't taken better care of the piano, having pretty much forgotten about it.

It's been an hour now since dinner's been warming in the oven, and Helen decides to eat. She's perfectly happy eating by herself, and prefers it that way. She hopes Jake doesn't come home until late, so she can enjoy the evening on her own. There's so much wrong with their relationship, but Helen feels she owes a lot to Jake for marrying her when she found out she was pregnant, and not kicking her out when she miscarried. It doesn't really occur to her that he's partly to blame, partly responsible, and that she's more than carried her weight in their marriage. The deeply embedded sense of guilt planted early in her life flows over into every relationship she's ever had. Even Ollie knows how to play on her guilt at times, although he's kinder than most in that regard. Emotionally, she's very confused, and could really use a friend. She still misses Lisa, and wishes things had turned out differently. She feels guilty about Lisa as well, even though she couldn't have prevented what happened to her.

They were both barely sixteen when they ran away from home. After the night Helen heard her mother say she wished Helen had died, instead of beating the odds of her premature birth, she was determined to leave. She was hurt, angry, and—of course—filled with guilt, even though a part of her knew it wasn't her fault. She was coming to the age when she started questioning things more, even though she was sheltered and socially inept. She was starting to believe that not *everything* could be her fault. The anger fueled a newfound courage, and they plotted their escape.

Lisa was unable to keep her stepfather at bay any longer, and had barely escaped him forcing himself on her a few weeks prior. It would have been full penetration, but Lisa's mother came home and interrupted his intentions. He pushed her aside and whispered that he would kill her if she told her mother. There was no chance of that happening, since Lisa knew her mother wouldn't believe her anyway, and make it out as all her fault. It was time for them both to leave; at least they had each other.

They started saving every penny they could, and stole a few dollars here and there they hoped wouldn't be missed. Lisa even sold her bike and some old dolls. They pooled their money, and in their young minds thought it might be enough until they could find people that would help them. Lisa talked about going to a church for help or maybe a teacher, but they couldn't think of who would help them without telling their parents. Then one day after school, they decided to go to the bus station to see how much tickets cost, not even knowing where they wanted to go. There was a teenager there a few years older than them, with long hair and a scraggly beard, sitting outside waiting for a bus. Lisa, being the braver one, asked him where he was going, and he mentioned a town she'd never heard of, over in state she'd never been. He told them he lived on a commune, and they took people in who needed a place to go. They grew their own food and shared everything. Everyone chipped in and worked, and there were even young kids running around.

He had a guitar and a nice smile. All of a sudden, there was hope. They couldn't leave right then, but the guy told them to gather whatever they had to bring, which bus to take and which day, and someone would be there to pick them up. The girls were delighted, and could hardly contain their excitement. They grilled the teenager with everything they could think of, and told him they would see him next week. He said they only had one phone but not to worry, to just take the right bus, at the right time, on the right day, and someone would be there to pick them up. Helen started feeling a little hesitant once it looked like they could actually do it, but Lisa was determined to go whether Helen came or not. It was her only option, no turning back; she couldn't take the abuse any longer.

After much deliberation and planning, they decided what they would bring, and where to hide it until it was time to go. Both of Lisa's parents worked, and they had an old shed in their yard that was mainly for storage. They stashed their bags and a few other items in the rundown shed, behind stacks of old newspaper. They knew what bus they were supposed to be on, so they bought their tickets in advance, and waited. When the time finally arrived, Helen snuck over to the shed behind Lisa's house, where Lisa was waiting. They got their stuff and hurried quickly to the bus stop, where they could catch the bus that would take them to the main terminal. It was a short walk from Lisa's house, but they were worried someone would spot them and ask where they were going. One old woman kept looking at them while they waited for the bus, but finally lost interest when a one-legged man on crutches gave her something else to gawk at.

Once the bus took off from the main terminal and they were on their way, they relaxed and talked non-stop about what they thought it would be like. Even with only one stop, it took over four hours to get to their destination. They were hungry, tired, and no longer enthusiastic by then. Looking around the desolate bus station, the reality of what they'd done began painfully sinking in. They were scared being this far out from their comfort zone, far away from home and anything they were familiar with for the first time in their lives. Not knowing what else to do, they gathered their stuff and walked out onto the main street, looking up and down the road, hoping their savior would be there.

All the other passengers were long gone when, finally, a pickup truck that had seen better days pulled up to the curb. There was the guy they knew with the long hair and nice smile in the passenger seat! He hopped out and they scrambled in, while he loaded their stuff in the back, and off they went. It crossed Helen's mind that not a single soul knew where they were; even she didn't know where she was. But not Lisa; that thought never occurred to her. She was too busy looking at the handsome older guy who was driving, happy to be away from her smelly step-dad.

At the commune, there were two quite large, shabby warehouses that had been partitioned off inside to accommodate everything from sleeping quarters to common rooms, kitchen, and bathhouse. Lisa and Helen were given beds in the women's dormitory, where there were already six others occupying the same space. Helen already hated the lack of privacy, and had to keep reminding herself why she ran away. Everyone was kind to them and very accommodating, but it was made clear that they had to earn their keep, and they were given jobs right off. Helen was given various tasks in the fields and was outside every day, where she learned a great deal about farming. Several others worked alongside her, and the women were expected to work as hard as the men. She liked being outdoors, and enjoyed the feeling she got using her muscles and becoming stronger. Her hands became calloused, her skin darker and freckled. At meal times, she felt proud that she'd done her part to help grow the vegetables that were laid out on the long wooden tables.

Lisa was put to work in the kitchen, and spent her days preparing and cooking meals for the entire commune. She too worked alongside others, but didn't enjoy her work nearly as much as Helen enjoyed hers. She tended to talk too much and goof off a bit, often getting reprimanded by the others, who told her she needed to pull her weight or she'd get into trouble. Lisa wasn't all that concerned about it, because she couldn't imagine who she would get into trouble *with*, as everyone was generally nice.

The head of the commune was called Mister Masters, and they usually only saw him when they all gathered in the largest common room to hear him speak. He was an enthusiastic, influential speaker, using the power of persuasion to control his little empire. Mister Masters spoke of unity, oneness, enlightenment, spiritual peace, and how they would be taken care of and respected at the commune, more than at any other place on Earth. They took care of their own and shared everything, he said, willing to take in anyone who truly wanted to belong and share. This was their family now, the only family they needed, the only one that truly loved them. The members were mesmerized whenever Mister Masters spoke, and revered him to an unhealthy degree. He was extremely charismatic and handsome, with an uncanny ability to know each individual's weak spots, exploiting them accordingly. He already had his eye on Lisa.

Helen and Lisa were rarely alone together, and it was extremely difficult to have any private conversations. One evening, they both headed to the bathhouse, to find the women's side empty. They immediately found a corner in the shower and started whispering, keeping an eye out for any intruders on their conversation. Helen told Lisa she needed to stop being lazy, that word was getting around that she would be punished if she didn't pull her weight. She advised Lisa to ask to work outside with her if she disliked her kitchen duties so much. Lisa just shrugged and said the farm work seemed too hard, and she would try to do better. She was surprised Helen had heard about her, and this seemed like the motivation to get her going. Problem was, she felt really bored and confined being there, and was fantasizing about leaving, but didn't know where to go. Going back home wasn't an option. She was jealous that Helen seemed to be adjusting better than her, and didn't voice her true feelings when they spoke.

A week after Helen told Lisa she'd better shape-up, Lisa was called to have a private meeting with Mister Masters. It was done very surreptitiously, as one of his aides took her out of the kitchen on a pretext of preparing a special meal for their leader. Lisa was scared to be alone with him and thought he was going to kick her out, so she stood shaking in front of him, not saying a word, until he finally spoke. His voice alone was hypnotic enough to sway practically anyone, and Lisa was no exception. She listened carefully as he locked eyes with her, although later she wouldn't remember most of what he'd said. He came forward and embraced her in a warm hug, then, releasing her, he gave her a pill to take and some tea to drink. He said this was a special formula for a special young woman, that he cared for her deeply, and hoped she became more productive and compliant. Of course, she agreed she would.

Back in the kitchen, Lisa felt different, but not necessarily in a bad way. The others watched her jealously, knowing she'd been alone with Mister Masters. During the next week, Lisa behaved and worked harder, not shirking any duties, trying her best. Before long, she was brought to Mister Masters several times a week, spoken to, hugged, and—she realized much later—drugged.

Helen continued working in the fields and gardens, developing relationships with her fellow workers. One man in particular paid a lot of attention to her, and before long, had her sneaking out at night to meet him in the large shed where they kept their farming tools. He was ten years older than Helen, and the first man to ever show any real interest in her. They kissed and touched a lot but it never went further… at least, not right away. Oftentimes she'd wish they had, being naive about the possibility of getting pregnant. Then, one evening, Jake just couldn't control himself and they ended up going all the way. Helen didn't like it as much as she thought she would, but continued with their trysts to please him.

Mister Masters didn't make his move until he knew Lisa was sufficiently dependent on the tenderness of his embraces, and the high of the drugs. The night he decided to have his way with her, he was rougher than he intended, and so turned on it set the precedent for future sessions. Lisa was shocked that this was happening, and felt helpless to do anything about it. She couldn't believe she'd run from the horror of her stepfather into the trap of something even worse. He had her brought to him almost nightly, and Lisa became withdrawn, depressed, and even more addicted to the additional pills he fed to her afterwards.

One evening, about a month after the horrid abuse began, Mister Masters insisted Lisa drink a large glass of wine after he was sure she had taken the pills he gave her. He liked seeing her really out of it and so easily controlled. When he was done with her, he led her out of his home and told her to go to bed. She hated him so much in that instant that she wanted to spit in his face, to kill him for making her feel like such a whore, like a useless no-good whore. Instead of going to bed she went outside and started to run towards a nearby stream. She was sobbing uncontrollably, running in bare feet along the chilly, rough ground. In the pitch black she couldn't see where she was going, and slipped on the rocks.

She was found the next morning, face-down, with her head split open from forehead to chin.

Helen now has tears spilling down her face, thinking of the morning they found poor Lisa dead in the streambed. They said she had gone out walking alone, and must have just fallen. Helen knew Lisa was seeing Mister Masters, but she was too busy with Jake to really concern herself with it. She hardly saw Lisa, and wasn't aware there was any need to be concerned; but when she found out she died, she felt she was partly to blame for not watching over her friend better.

Wiping her eyes, she hears Jake's car coming up the driveway and quickly throws some water on her face. Helen grabs one of her magazines and pretends she's reading when Jake comes through the door. She looks up, asking him if he's hungry. He grunts a yes, and she busies herself getting his dinner out of the oven, and getting his place setting just right for his dinner. She doesn't ask where he's been, and he offers no conversation. She takes her magazine into the living room, wishing she was anywhere else but here.

CHAPTER 34

Helen and Ollie stand by the back door, gazing out at the fields and gardens. Sipping her coffee, she watches Jake talking with their head field-hand, observing how relaxed he looks, smiling and gesturing, while Pete nods and they both look out over the farm. Helen thinks about Jake and how she once thought she really loved him, and tries to imagine again what it felt like, and what it would feel like now. She starts to feel guilty for not loving him the way she's supposed to love her husband—but a funny thing happens. She squelches the guilt, and instead turns to Ollie and says, "Let's have some music!" Ollie doesn't really understand what she's saying but he likes the enthusiasm, and wags furiously, waiting for what happens next.

Helen figures Jake will be talking with Pete for a while longer, and doesn't want to make her rounds while he's still out there. Instead, she decides to listen to her favorite radio station while getting a few chores done inside. She has to keep the volume low, because Jake doesn't like her listening to the radio and has no appreciation for music. This was always a disappointment for his mother, who couldn't understand Jake's lack of feeling for most music. He did like a good, catchy country song now and then, but classical music gave him a headache and made him feel melancholy.

Helen's favorite station plays only classical music, and today's selections are mostly piano concertos. Surreptitiously listening to the station for the last few years, Helen's discovered how much she favors piano and cello, although she hasn't yet mastered knowing all the famous composers, or can identify them when she hears their music. She's familiar with Mozart, Chopin, Beethoven, and has recently discovered Rachmaninoff. As she starts dusting and polishing the piano, she thinks of talking with Jake's mother about the different composers. This is something she's never done, because she's afraid Marian will mention it to Jake, and she couldn't bear it if he took her music away. Although now that they've spoke of Marian's dream where she was once again playing her beloved piano, she *could* broach the subject that way. Marian has years of musical knowledge, and would be glad to speak of what she thinks she would have devoted her life to if she hadn't given it up to be a farmer's wife. These thoughts remind Helen that she promised to get the piano tuned, and she goes back to the kitchen where they keep the phone book. Once she finds a listing that's not too far from where they are, she sets up an appointment for tomorrow afternoon, when she's almost positive Jake will be out. Helen finds herself excited and restless for the first time in a long time, feeling she has something to look forward to.

Finally, Jake gets in his truck and drives away, leaving Helen relieved that she can now go out and make her rounds with Ollie. Before she has a chance to call him, he's at the door, wagging away with his nose pressed to the glass. She grabs the sunglasses out of her purse, and puts them on as they walk out the door. Another glorious sunny day, and Helen feels happy to be alive. She's been feeling less depressed and lonely lately, attributing it to the nice weather mostly, as she can't think of what else it could be.

As usual, Ollie forges ahead, nose to the ground, tail wagging, tongue lolling, loving life in that way dogs have of doing. Helen follows, looking around, still marveling at the clarity of sight the sunglasses provide. Everything looks so beautiful, with that perfect contrast of light and shadow, and she swears she can see particles of light dancing. An impulse to look directly at the sun cannot be resisted, and BAM, there it is. The flash, and then the stream of light goes directly into her eyes, a rainbow of undulating light fluidly streaming, separating into memory that starts to unfold like a film, with her as the observer.

She intently watches a baby too tiny, a miniature doll. This baby lies in an incubator, hooked up to wires, all red and squirmy, barely keeping up with being alive. On the other side of the glass her parents, so young, are looking in anxiously, not knowing what to think, not wanting to recognize how they got there and just wanting it all to be over, to get on with their lives. The scene changes and the baby has grown into a girl, somehow beating the odds. She sits on the floor playing while her mother looks on with a regretful look on her face, holding a glass of wine with tears in her eyes. The girl looks up, knowing she's the cause of the tears, yet not knowing why. Fast forward: the girl is now a teenager listening at the kitchen door to a drunken conversation her parents are having, her mother slurring the words that caused her to run away, the words that spoken out loud could never be unheard, ever.

Riding on the bus with Lisa comes into view next—both of them so naive and full of hope. The commune looks alluring to their inexperienced eyes as they swallow their fears and jump in feet first, not yet knowing how to dive. Lisa starts to fade from the scene and Jake takes over. He's a decent man, kind to Helen in the only way he knows how, following his instincts with a simple-minded ignorance. The sheltered, guilty teenager falls for this decent man, ravenously sucking in the attention and caring, after starving for most of her young life. Lisa appears again, smiling, hugging her friend, telling her it all worked out as it should; she's safe now, the abuse forever over.

The scenes continue and the teenager has a huge belly, although it's not stopping her from working in the field. She bends over with an aching back, and has trouble standing up straight again. The decent young man comes to her, saying he's spoken to Mister Masters, and they're free to leave. Masters is seen being heavily interrogated, with a lot of answering to do regarding Lisa's death. The commune is hanging on a thread, gradually crumbling while he's seen behind closed doors planning his cowardly getaway. The young man tells the pregnant teenager his mother has agreed to help them, and is pleased he'll be coming home after all these years. The teenager's parents are seen looking horrified at the *history repeating itself* situation she has gotten herself into, and refuse to have anything to do with her. She's *dead* to them, and when her mother says these words, she sounds disgustingly pleased. The teenager is relieved there's someplace to go, someone who will take care of her, and she's grateful. Hugging the young man, she vows to always love him with all her heart.

She watches the teenager having a difficult time with the birth, and then sees her tears of despair when the baby is stillborn. The loss of hope is so palatable, she can almost see it tangibly draining what's left of aliveness within the teenager. An ugly shadow of guilt joins the mass of what's already there, settling like a rock when the doctor tells the teenager she'll never bear another child.

Seeing the teenager walking, she watches as she grows with each step, aging until it becomes now, the shadowy burden she carries on her back through all the transitions becoming heavier and heavier. Stopping, she looks up as she is now, wipes her brow, and casts the burden she's been carrying on her back aside. Satisfied, she wipes her hands on her pants and thinks she hears a dog whimpering.

She *is* hearing a dog whimpering, and it's Ollie. Both of his paws are on her legs and he's gently clawing, trying to get her attention. Helen looks down at him, takes the sunglasses off, and sinks to the ground. She lies back, looking up at the sky, trying to remember everything she saw. She's shaking inside, and the vibration of it hums throughout her body. Ollie lays down next to her, and puts his head on her legs. Helen feels so calm, and yes, as if a weight has been lifted. Interestingly, she doesn't feel afraid, think she's losing her mind or anything like that. She's curious and relieved, and has never felt better in her entire life.

Brushing herself off, she gets up and they continue their mission, with Ollie leading the inspection. Helen feels like she was in her altered state for a long time and that it must be late, so she signals Ollie to get a move on, and they head back to the house. Looking at the kitchen clock. she has a hard time believing only a half hour has passed, and goes into the bedroom to look at the alarm clock on the dresser. Sure enough, the time is correct, and she tries to make sense of what happened. Without any proof whatsoever, she intuitively knows it had something to do with the sunglasses. But her logical mind is disallowing this suspension of disbelief, searching for other avenues of thought.

The afternoon goes quickly, filled with chores and cooking. Helen doesn't dwell on the episode she experienced earlier, and like the mind often does, she stashes it in a compartment to be examined later. Her little radio softly plays piano concertos in the background, synchronizing comically with Ollie's snores. The cooking smells fill the kitchen, and Helen has a sense of peace come over her. With dinner warming in the oven. she decides to rest a little and put her feet up. She digs through her magazine basket and pulls out last month's fashion and entertainment edition. She's been getting this particular magazine for years, and enjoys fantasizing like a teenage girl when reading it. She wishes she had someplace to wear the latest fashions, and likes knowing about the various trends. This edition has a photograph of an attractive woman wearing an unusual pair of sunglasses on the cover. She looks at the photograph, and then looks for her reading glasses to get a better look.

She puts the glasses on, then Ollie perks up and she hears Jake's truck coming up the driveway. She quickly throws the magazine back in the basket, turns the radio off, and goes into the kitchen to check on dinner and set the table. She's surprised Jake's home early, and tries to imagine why, when he comes through the door. He has a smile on his face, comes over, and gives her a kiss on the cheek. "I just came from the accountant," he says happily. "We're getting a decent tax refund this year, and he was impressed with how well you've been keeping the books."

"Oh, good. Nice to hear," she says, smiling.

Jake looks at her sheepishly and says, “Thank you. We make a good team. I couldn’t run the farm without you.” He then quickly looks away, going into the next room to take off his boots. For a few seconds, he looked like the decent young man she once loved.

Huh, Helen thinks. *The world is sure showing a different face today.*

CHAPTER 35

During this morning's inspection rounds nothing unusual happens, even though Helen has her sunglasses on the entire time. She finds herself swiveling her head around, looking up then down, but nothing changes except that she gets the beginnings of a sore neck, and Ollie starts looking at her curiously. She laughs to herself when she thinks it's a good thing no one's watching other than Ollie, yet she can't shake the feeling that the sunglasses are somehow connected to the vision she saw. And how can she explain the feeling of wellness surrounding her? After Jake went to bed last night, she took the glasses out and thoroughly examined them, thinking she could find some kind of clue. All she saw was a beautifully constructed pair of sunglasses with an intricate miniature painting, and a pair of what looked like initials. She then remembered the magazine with the woman in sunglasses on the cover, and wanted to take another look. Reaching for the basket, she hears Jake stirring, and quickly puts the sunglasses back in their hiding place, saving the magazine for the next time she's alone.

When they return from their rounds, Helen gives Ollie some treats, and mentally goes over everything she has to do today. There are several errands in town, plus phone calls to make, and she decides to get the errands done first. Before leaving, she consults her *to do* list and sees the appointment for the piano tuner this afternoon that she'd forgotten about. If she leaves now, she should have plenty of time to get everything done before the appointment. Hustling Ollie to the car, she then runs back to get her sunglasses. Jumping in, she puts the glasses on, and they head out. It's not as sunny today and she really doesn't need sunglasses, but she likes wearing them, and leaves them on. Before going into the store, she takes them off, carefully putting them in her purse, forgetting about them until she's heading back home.

Suddenly remembering the first time she had the sunglasses on while driving, and the size distortion she experienced, Helen thinks maybe it's best not to wear them while driving. Her curiosity takes over, though, and she leaves them on for the next twenty minutes with no changes, no oddities occurring. "Maybe I *am* losing my mind," she says to Ollie. He looks at her and bobs his head as if in agreement, and she laughs while he wags his tail happily.

Helen still has a half-hour before the piano tuner is due to arrive, so she turns the radio on to her favorite station, delighted to hear today's selections will be compositions for cello and piano, her two favorites. As she listens, she finds the strings and keys pulling on her emotions with a force she's never felt before. The tears spring from her eyes, cascading down her face, dripping off her chin and onto her shirt. She's wrapped in the feeling with all of her senses, seeing the notes as tangible things she can touch.

The doorbell startles her, and she jumps up. Grabbing a dish towel, she runs to the door and greets the piano tuner. Wiping her face, she tells him she was just chopping onions. He laughs and tells her the same thing happens to his wife, as she leads him to the piano in the corner. He looks approvingly at the piano so polished and shiny, waiting to be tuned to perfection, and says, "That's a fine piano you have there. Who plays—is it you?"

"I had a few lessons as a child, but have been thinking of taking it up again. My mother-in-law was on her way to becoming a concert pianist before she had to give it up. She's now in a home and gave us the piano to take care of for her. I promised her I would keep it tuned."

“When was the last time it was tuned?” he asks, tapping on a few of the keys.

“I honestly don’t know—a long time ago, I think. My mother-in-law has been in the home for over two years now.”

“Oh, a pity her not being able to play. Well, I need to get to work. If you don’t mind, would you please turn the radio off? I need to focus my hearing.”

Helen turns off the radio and leaves the piano tuner to his job. She mulls over what she said about considering taking lessons. It just came out of her mouth, but now when she thinks of it, she feels it really is something she wants to do. Her enthusiasm is dampened when she considers the pushback Jake will give her, but then an idea begins to form. She’s due to visit Marian again tomorrow, and she’ll tell her all about getting the piano tuned. Maybe if she asks her to put in a good word about it, she’ll be able to sway Jake into going along with her having lessons. *Maybe it’ll touch on her sensibilities of not being able to pursue her own career and passion, and she’ll want to help me aspire to do something for myself. If I appeal to her kindness and promise it won’t take away from my duties, she may want to soften up Jake to the idea. Plus, Marian has never understood Jake’s lack of appreciation for any kind of music, and she should be happy someone is playing her beloved piano. Or maybe she’ll be bitter, and not want to help me; because if she can’t play, why should she help me?*

Helen considers all angles and finally comes to the conclusion that she has nothing to lose by asking for Marian’s endorsement. She knows it would be too taxing to try and do it behind Jake’s back, and she really doesn’t want to do it that way. With newfound courage, she resolves she’s going to do it either way, then peeks in to see how the tuning is going.

The piano tuner tells her he’s almost done, and she asks him if he’d like something to drink. He shakes his head no and she leaves him alone, but not before grabbing the magazine she’s been wanting to catch up on. There’s that woman with the sunglasses, and Helen scrutinizes the glasses the woman has on in the photo closely, and can’t help but see a resemblance to her pair.

Just when she's turning to the page where the article starts, the piano tuner interrupts her, telling her the tuning is done. He leads her to the piano, and guides her to sit on the bench. He tells her to play some scales, and when she's not sure what to do, he leans over and plays back and forth to show her. Helen then tries, and the sound coming out of the piano is exquisitely rich, resonating with a vibration that goes straight through her. She runs the scales back and forth several times, looking up at the tuner with a smile, not even needing to look at the keys. He smiles back and starts packing his things, and she asks what she owes him.

After handing him a check, she can't wait until he leaves so she can touch the keys again.

Helen turns the radio on, again listening to piano and cello selections, separating the piano part from the cello, trying to hear where they fit and where they separate, then where they combine seamlessly. She closes her eyes and listens for several minutes. Sitting at the piano, she puts her hands lightly on the keys, and closes her eyes again. When the next selection comes on, she opens her eyes and starts playing the piano part perfectly. She watches as her hands fly over the keys, astonished and thrilled with the way it makes her feel. It's like in a dream, where one can leap over buildings, fly, climb mountains, do amazing things. Only this is not a dream, and she can feel every touch of the keys, knowing every place to put her fingers, every note she's trying to pull from the piano. She knows all this as though she's been doing it her entire life, and the tears start to flow again.

She's doing this, but she doesn't know how it's possible. For the moment, she doesn't care as she sways before the keys, playing with the precision and feeling of a virtuoso. The piece ends, and there's a station break on the radio. Helen jumps up, runs outside, and looks up at the sky, "Is that You, God? Are You doing this? Oh God, is that You?"

She runs back inside, finds the sunglasses, puts them on, and runs back out. Looking up again, she asks, "Is it these? Is it You, God? Is it You in these glasses?"

Ollie comes running over, practically knocking her down, and Helen starts laughing. She can't stop laughing, with the tears still rolling down her face. Finally, she pulls herself together and goes back to the piano. She tries to think of something to play, and realizes the only songs she can think of are basic songs. She finally settles on *You Are My Sunshine,* and begins to play hesitantly. She quickly realizes she can't play it as well as she played the piano piece she was playing along with from the radio. She closes the piano, gets up, and walks back outside, calling Ollie to walk with her. "I need to think," she says to herself.

#

Brenda's sitting in a cafe having afternoon coffee with Caroline and Sarah. She's just dropped off some new paintings at the gallery, where her friends met up with her. She'll be doing a new show at the gallery this weekend, and they came to see the paintings and provide their support. Brenda's doing well, very slowly having adjusted to Vincent being on the other side. She still sees him in her dreams and communicates with him sometimes when meditating, but has learned to journey on without his physical presence. She's now a renowned artist known for her paintings as well as her sunglasses, and the recent article in the magazine spread has increased the demand for her artwork even further.

The three friends are huddled together at a small table talking when Brenda suddenly sits up straight, gazing blankly out the window. She looks without seeing, a small smile playing on her lips. For a few seconds her friends don't notice, but after a minute Caroline nudges Brenda and says, "Earth to Brenda, come in please."

Both Sarah and Caroline laugh, but it takes a few more seconds before Brenda shakes her head slightly, turns her gaze from the window, and says, "Huh?"

"What do you mean, huh? You were in another world. What were you thinking?"

"Oh, I guess I was thinking about the show, and the placement the gallery has decided to do," Brenda replies.

Her friends look at her curiously, kind of shrug, and they all go back to chatting away, drinking coffee and enjoying each other's company. On the drive home, Brenda's smiling to herself, and can't wait to get settled enough to deeply meditate the way she needs to, enabling her access to Vincent. Something's happened; the sunglasses have changed hands again, and a phenomenon of the most wonderful kind is occurring.

#

Helen tosses so many thoughts around in her head during her walk, still reeling from everything that's transpired. There's just no obvious explanation, or even an obscure one, of how she has the ability to play classical piano when she's never even had a real lesson. She's come to the conclusion she may never know the how, or the why, or the what. Instead of driving herself crazy, she decides to formulate a plan and see what happens. First, she'll go see Marian tomorrow at the home, and tell her about the piano being tuned, and how that gave her the desire to learn how to play. She'll convince her to get Jake onboard for her to take lessons. The rest will come to her, and she'll take it one step at a time. With at least a little plan of action decided on, Helen feels better, and realizes it's time to start dinner. She can't help one more peek at the piano, now so much more than just a piece of furniture needing to be dusted. It now has a life of its own, just like her.

CHAPTER 36

Helen usually avoids Jake in the mornings, as they both need their space, but this morning she's in the kitchen making coffee when he comes in. He nods as she hands him a cup of coffee and mumbles a good morning. She never mentioned getting the piano tuned, and figures now will be a good time, so clearing her throat, she says, "The piano tuner came yesterday. The last time I visited Marian she talked a lot about the piano, and about dreaming she could play again. I promised her I would get it tuned. She kept asking me, and I couldn't say no."

Jake looks at her, surprised, and says, "What did you do that for? How much did it cost?"

Ignoring the second question, Helen replies, "I promised her I would—it's the least we can do for her. She's been really good to us, and it was important to her."

"Well, it's a waste of money. You could've just told her you did it. She'd never have known."

"You'd want me to lie to her?" Helen asks incredulously. "I can't do that. I won't do that."

Looking down, Jake just shakes his head, not sure what to say. Now that he's somewhat chastened, Helen continues, "I could learn to play the piano. I could take lessons. Then the money wouldn't be wasted, and the piano wouldn't just sit there taking up space."

Jake looks up quickly, with an annoyed look on his face. "Forget it, there's no time for that, and it's a waste of money." He gets up from the table and stalks out of the room.

Helen figured this would be his reaction, and isn't surprised or deterred. She's already decided she's going to get lessons, one way or another, whether he wants her to or not. She follows him out of the room and says to his back, "I'm going to see your mother today, letting her know the piano's tuned. I think it will make her happy."

Jake turns around and says, "You don't have to go today. I was going to go tomorrow."

Helen doesn't answer him; she just leaves the room. *I'm going today anyway*, she tells herself. *Actually, this will work out even better, because it will give me a chance to plant the seeds with Marian before Jake visits her.*

As soon as he leaves, she calls the home to let them know she'll be there today, instead of later in the week, asking them to let Marian know. Satisfied, she then calls Ollie and out they go to begin their rounds. Helen puts her sunglasses on and does her swiveling, looking-up-and-down act, while Ollie rushes ahead like the dog on the job that he is. It's a sunny morning with a few scattered puffy clouds, and Helen breathes deeply, enjoying the feel of the sun on her face. Ollie takes off into the corn and she lets him, figuring he's after a rabbit or some other critter, and she continues looking up at the sky while she waits for him to come back. She identifies different shapes in the clouds, and laughs to herself when she sees one that looks like a dragon breathing fire, thinking that must be Jake.

The dragon shifts and is no longer a dragon, just a passing cloud, and the sun becomes more visible. Helen can't help herself as she looks directly at the sun, and nothing happens. She continues to look, wondering how bad it is for your eyes to look directly at the sun. Just as she's ready to look away, she feels a slight *blip*, a tiny flash, and she closes her eyes. Waiting for more, nothing else happens. She doesn't feel different or see visions, she just sees spots from staring directly at the sun. Shaking her head, she calls Ollie, and he comes quickly, looking proud about something, she knows not what.

Once inside Helen goes directly to the piano and tries to play *You Are My Sunshine.* First, she hums the tune, and then plays haltingly, like she did the previous day. Nothing's changed, and she's disappointed. Turning on the radio, she waits for an appropriate selection. With hands hovering over the keys, Beethoven's *Moonlight Sonata* comes on, and she listens carefully as she's done before, separating the piano in her mind, until she begins to play along seamlessly. Beyond thrilled to know she can still do it, she plays the entire piece with no hesitation, flawlessly, with profound feeling. Once again, the emotional tears flow, only this time she's smiling and truly joyful, not concerned at all about how she can do this, just grateful that she can.

Later that day, Marian tells Helen she's pleased to see her, and notices something different, and wonders if maybe she's pregnant. She knows Helen can't have children, but she has a kind of look, that glow pregnant women have, and she senses something's happened. She tells Helen she was somewhat concerned when they told her she was coming today, and asks her if everything's all right. Helen nods, and they make small talk for a few minutes, with Marian telling Helen she looks well, and asking if she's been taking vitamins or spending more time outdoors.

Finally, Helen tells her she's had the piano tuned as promised, and it sounds wonderful. "How do you know it sounds wonderful?" Marian asks.

"The piano tuner had me play scales, and it now has a rich lovely tone that I don't remember it having before."

"Can you really tell?" Marian asks excitedly. "How can you tell since you never played, and don't really know what a finely-tuned piano sounds like?"

Helen thinks carefully before replying, feeling this will be a pivotal point. "I don't think I ever told you, but I love music, and always wished I could play an instrument. I especially love piano and cello, and listen to the classical music station every chance I get. Except when Jake is home," she says, looking down, not wanting to meet Marian's eyes for fear she'll take offense.

Marian sighs deeply and says, "I didn't know. I'm sorry I didn't play more for you, but by the time Jake brought you home, I had pretty much stopped playing. I too only played when my husband was out. And Jake would kick up a fuss as a child whenever I played. He disliked the classical pieces, only liked silly songs like *Old McDonald*, and even then, would tire after hearing it once. Most times he didn't even care about that; he would leave the room if I started playing. His father was the same way. I often wondered if there was something wrong with them, both of them not caring at all about music. Before I met my husband, music was everything to me, and all my friends were musicians, and involved with music one way or another. I was talented, wanted to make it my life."

It's disconcerting to Helen when she sees tears forming in her mother-in-law's eyes as she continues. "I guess you know I got pregnant with Jake when I barely knew his father Carl," Marian says, looking directly at Helen through glassy eyes. "I love my Jake, but I loved my music too. In those days, you gave up everything for family, and women couldn't just go off on their own with a baby. It's still like that in some ways, as you know. My parents were so angry I had no choice. Carl and I were soon married, and I barely knew him. I didn't know he had this thing about music. I found out much later there's a name for it, I can't remember now what it is. But it's a neurological condition involving a person's incapacity to enjoy listening to music. He had that condition, and it was like trying to mix oil and water when it came to him and my music. I eventually gave in, lost all my contacts and music friends, only playing when I had time to myself. He would even complain about the space the piano was taking up."

Helen walks over to the bed, takes Marian's hands in her own, and says, "I'm so sorry, I didn't know."

"How could you? I never told a soul, and by the time Jake brought you back from that horrible commune, years had passed. Sad thing is, Jake has it too. He feels no appreciation for music; couldn't care less, and says it's a waste of time. Must be hereditary. Music was my life, and I ended up with someone whose brain was wired so differently than mine. Always made me feel like I was being punished for getting pregnant. By the time Carl died, I hardly played at all, even for myself."

"Oh, Marian, I'm so sorry. That does explain a lot, though. Just this morning, after I told Jake I had the piano tuned at your request, he got annoyed; and he hates when I put on my radio, especially to the classical station. But oh, you should hear how rich the piano sounds now, even just playing scales!" Here Helen stops, not wanting to divulge too much about actually playing, and she certainly doesn't want to tell her mother-in-law what's happened the last couple of days, even if she did know how to explain it.

"Why didn't you ever learn to play?" Marian asks after a long silence.

"My parents didn't have any money because they drank it all. They didn't want to be bothered, and I was so young when I ran away, it was the farthest thing from my mind."

"You poor dear, so sad," Marian sighs, suddenly looking exhausted.

Helen takes a deep breath, thinking it's now or never, and says, "Well, now that the piano is tuned, I think I should learn how to play it, don't you?"

They look at each other, trying to imagine what the other is really thinking, when Marian says, "Yes, dear, I do. Jake won't like it, though, and I don't want to get involved in your marital problems."

Helen forges on. "When he comes tomorrow, can you please mention to him you think I should take lessons? Ask him to do it for you. Tell him it will make you happy that someone is using your beloved piano. Tell him I'll only play when he's not there, and it won't interfere with my duties. And Marian, to be honest, and I don't want to say anything bad about Jake, especially to his mother... but he's not home very much, if you know what I mean."

Marian looks up sharply from her bed, looking even more shrunken than usual. Grasping the corner of her blanket tightly, she sighs and says, "Like father, like son in more ways than one, then."

After agreeing to help Helen, they end up discussing in depth how Marian should broach the subject, what she should say, and how she promises to stick to her guns. This is the longest the two of them have ever spoken, and they're thoroughly enjoying being co-conspirators. When Helen asks how she can find a good teacher, Marian tells her about the masterful teacher she once had, who passed some years ago. She remembers, though, that his son is still teaching, and that's who Helen needs to contact. With a newfound camaraderie between them, they hug, and Helen thanks her profusely. Now she has a plan, and she can't wait to get started. She knows it will all work out; she can feel it.

#

Brenda has meditated twice since the sensation that came over her in the coffee shop. Both times she felt Vincent, but in an obscure way, where he was always just out of reach. She knew there was something she needed to know, and found it extremely frustrating to not have a handle on it. Finishing a batch of sunglasses, she puts them aside, and goes to the kitchen to make some coffee. Thinking maybe the last thing she needs is more caffeine, she reaches for some herbal tea instead. The dried tea inside the tin reminds her of the dried mushrooms from so long ago that started this whole thing. *What if we had never taken the mushrooms and spent the night in the desert? How would things have turned out differently? Probably doesn't help anything to imagine the road not taken, now does it?* she asks herself.

After drinking her tea, she wanders back to her studio, and spreads some brushstrokes on a new canvas. She feels her muse at work with her, and they create a vision of what it looks like to see Vincent when she meditates. Brenda thinks anyone who sees it would perceive it as a gray, misty mess of light and shadow. But to her, it makes her feel, as much as *see*, what it's like to communicate with him. She sets her brushes aside for finishing touches later, thinking it'll be interesting to see its effect on others when it's done. Some might see what she's trying to convey; others will see nothing but paint on canvas.

Feeling suddenly tired, Brenda closes her eyes and settles in her favorite chair, allowing herself to drift off into sleep. She starts dreaming and sees herself playing piano, marveling at how well she knows how to play, trying to remember the name of the song she's playing. Vincent appears beside her, and bends down to play along. She's unable to turn to see him, but knows it's him, and she's delighted he's playing along. Watching his hands moving with hers along the keys gives her such an immeasurable pleasure. When the song is finished, he leans close and whispers in her ear: "This one knows. Let her find you."

Brenda wakes slowly, not wanting to be pulled from the dream. She holds onto the feeling of playing piano with Vincent in that dream world where nothing is impossible, where everything is significant. She reaches for a pen and writes down what he said, words she knows she'll ponder until they reveal their meanings.

CHAPTER 37

Helen has to keep herself from running through the parking lot after her visit with Marian, forcing herself to slow down in case anyone's watching. Once in the car, she puts her sunglasses on and heads home. Her conversation with Marian keeps spinning around in her head, and she's literally keeping her fingers crossed that Jake will agree to her taking piano lessons. Even if he doesn't, at least she can say she tried asking before doing it anyway. Just in case, she starts thinking about how she's going to pay for it, then laughs, because she's the one who does the books.

Ollie greets her at the door, a little annoyed at how long she'd been gone, signaling that he needs to go out. She lets him out the back door, and rummages around trying to find the phone book. Marian gave her the name of the master teacher who taught her, but couldn't remember his son's name. Good thing he had a son and not a daughter, Helen thinks; a *she* would be more difficult to find if she were married. She finds the last name Westland, but is surprised at how many of them there are. Going down the list, looking for male first names, she then notices an advertisement for Piano Fusion by Nathan Westland. Viewing the ad, she gets goosebumps, and knows this *has* to be her future teacher.

With shaking hands, she calls the number listed, hearing it ring several times before going to an answering machine. She doesn't want to leave a message and risk having him call back when Jake's home, so she hangs up. Trying to decide if she should ring back right away or wait, she decides instead to call again in an hour, and goes about getting her way-behind-schedule chores done. While going over the books, she takes extra care in noting how she can hide the expense of the lessons, but it still doesn't feel right to her to have to go behind Jake's back. She decides before calling again to go outside for a walk with the sunglasses on. Even though she's not a superstitious person, she attaches what she thinks of as *good luck* to the sunglasses, and starts calling them Lucky Strike, from how she felt the first time she got the strong flash and stream of light from them. Ever since Ollie found them, she's had amazing occurrences happening in her life, with no explanation of where they came from. Her mind still can't wrap itself around how the sunglasses could have anything to do with what's been happening to her, but she knows that somehow, they're responsible. The article she hasn't had a chance to read comes to mind, and she thinks of the photo of the woman with the sunglasses on. Helen knows she's part of this too, and makes a mental reminder to read the article.

Calling the number again for Piano Fusion, she starts to think she'll have to leave a message when a breathless male voice answers, saying, "Nathan Westland speaking."

"Uh, hello," she stammers. "I'm trying to reach the son of the piano master Stephan Westland. Is that who I'm speaking with?"

"Yes, Stephan was my father, how can I help you?" Nathan asks.

Helen goes on to explain about her mother-in-law, how she studied under Nathan's father, and that's how she got his name. She then goes on to tell him she'd like to meet with him in person, because something extraordinary has happened and it would be best if she could show him, rather than try to explain it. Helen also expresses the need for some discretion, and that she needs to meet with him as soon as possible.

Nathan's intrigued by the little she's told him, and tells her he can meet her at noon tomorrow, since he's already booked the rest of the day. She agrees to meet him at his studio, gets directions, and thanks him profusely. After they hang up, she goes to what she now thinks of as *her* piano, wanting to try various drills, so she'll have a basis of what to tell Nathan tomorrow.

After an hour of trying to play a song from memory, and then playing along to any classical piano from the radio, she finds it hasn't changed from her previous attempts. When she tries to play from memory, she wishes she had something to guide her; then she could easily do it, she thinks. When she hears the music, even complicated pieces, she can smoothly play with no mistakes or hesitation, feeling the notes start from her ears right through to her fingers. Helen loses track of the time, and suddenly realizes she'd better start dinner. With a feeling of resentment, she leaves her piano to prepare dinner for someone whom she's never sure will come home, and who rarely appreciates it. *I feel like a servant around here,* she thinks as she starts pulling what she needs from the refrigerator. *An unpaid servant at that.*

After tossing and turning all night, Helen's up at the crack of dawn, unable to lie in bed any longer. With coffee in hand, she goes to her desk where she keeps the books, and takes care of the paperwork she'd missed yesterday. She's almost done when Jake comes in and asks what she's doing. She makes up a few accounting things he wouldn't understand anyway, and he finally leaves her alone. At least the accountant said she did a good job, and as long as there aren't any glaring discrepancies and they show a profit, Jake is happy. She learned to do the bookkeeping by trial and error, and takes pride in her work, even though she considers it another chore, not something she especially enjoys. *I should charge Jake by the hour*, she thinks. *He would owe me a fortune.* This thought makes it easier for her to accept that she'd probably have to take the money for her piano lessons without Jake's knowledge. She'll know later today after his visit with his mother. Fingers crossed.

After Jake leaves, Helen rushes around to get everything done. She decides she'll also go to the market after meeting with Nathan Westland, since she'll be close to town anyway. Based on the directions he gave her, it should only take about twenty minutes to get there, and that's easy enough to manage timewise. She then wonders if Jake ever checks the mileage on her car, hoping he doesn't, because if all goes according to plan, she'll be driving to take lessons as often as she can. For the first time in a long time, she's glad Jake is often gone and doesn't pay much attention to her, and hopes it continues. Her thoughts then turn to him visiting Marian, causing an anxious feeling to settle in. She says a prayer their plan doesn't backfire.

Finally, it's time to meet Nathan, and her feeling of apprehension grows. Over and over in her head she practices what she wants to tell him about what's happened to her recently, how she's now able to play piano, but only under certain circumstances. When she pulls up to his house with what looks like an attached studio, she takes a deep breath, muttering, "Here goes nothing," and gets out of the car. As she's walking up the path to the studio part where there's a small sign, the door opens and Nathan beckons her in. They make their introductions, shaking hands, and she gets a good feeling from him right away as he leads her to a small office at the back of his studio.

Helen knows she can't reveal the full truth of how she thinks she came to be able to play piano, and waits for him to ask her a few questions before she proceeds with her story. When Nathan realizes Helen's never taken a formal lesson and doesn't know how to read music, he's quite intrigued as to how she's able to play. Skirting any questions about any details she doesn't want to divulge, she finally asks if they can sit at the piano, so she can show him what she can do. Looking at his watch, he says he has no more than a half hour, then seats her at the piano, while he stands next to her.

She asks him if it's okay if she plays *You Are My Sunshine* for him, and he nods. Since she's practiced it a few times over the last couple of days, she plays it through without any mistakes, although her playing is nothing special. She explains to him she can play it partly because she knows the tune, but had to try several times to get it right, and it helps if she hums along. She reminds him she just started being able to do this within the past week, telling him she started to fool around with the piano after she got it tuned for her mother-in-law. He still finds it interesting but is not especially impressed, as there are people who can pick up piano rather quickly under certain circumstances.

Helen then asks him if he has a radio or recording of some classical piano they can use—maybe something he uses when he's working with his more advanced students. Nathan looks at her oddly, then goes to his office, coming back with a tape recorder that he places on a nearby table. He tells her he uses this as a teaching tool so his students can hear the real version vs. what their playing sounds like in comparison. She asks him to play a classical piece of his choosing, and positions herself in front of the piano, hands slightly hovering over the keys. The rich sounds of one of Beethoven's Piano Sonatas starts playing, and Helen listens intently. It takes her about ten seconds before she starts playing along, and her playing is magnificent.

Nathan is beside himself as he listens to her playing along with the recording, matching it note for note, astonished by what he's hearing. He watches her hands move smoothly, familiarly, lovingly along the keys with an accomplished style, unlike anything he's ever seen before. He's fascinated as he listens and watches her play, mesmerized, until he can finally break away from his trance as she plays the last note. After he turns off the recorder, neither of them say anything for a very long time. Breaking the silence, all he can say is, "That may be the most remarkable thing I have ever witnessed in all my years of teaching, playing, or being involved in music."

"Is that a good thing?" Helen asks jokingly.

They both start laughing, with neither of them able to stop until the tears are streaming down their faces. Then they look at each other and start laughing again. After they pull themselves together, Nathan says, "Okay, let's get serious here. This really is an amazing phenomenon, unlike anything I've ever seen. First off, how did this happen? Did you hit your head, have a car accident, or anything like that? I've heard of this happening, where people have some kind of jolt or something, maybe end up in a coma, wake up, and are able to become an accomplished musician or mathematician or something they previously knew nothing about. Did something like that happen to you?"

Nathan notices a barely perceptible look cross Helen's face before she answers, and he watches her closely. "No, not really," she says. "Like I told you, I had the piano tuned for my mother-in-law, who used to be quite an accomplished player. She's in a home now, but asked me to do it in case she could play it again someday. We both knew it was very unlikely she would ever be well enough to play again, but I went along with it to make her happy. After the piano tuner left, I started fooling around with it, and the radio was on, tuned to my favorite classical station." She says most of this not looking directly at Nathan, and he knows there's more she's not telling him, but he doesn't press it.

"I have another song I'd like you to play. Do you know *Rhapsody in Blue*, by George Gershwin?" he asks.

Helen nods, and he asks her if she can play it.

"I'm sorry, I don't know it well enough to just play it." she says apologetically. "Do you have it on your recorder?"

"Yes, I do. Hold on while I find it," he says while running through the recorder. "Ah, here it is. Okay, ready?" he asks as the notes come through.

Helen listens, nods, and begins to play along with the recorder. Once again, her style is impeccable, and she plays completely engaged, dazzling him with her style. After the music ends, Nathan asks her to come into his office so he can review his schedule, and see where he can fit her in. "I'm sorry to rush you, but I have a student coming in shortly. I want to get you on the calendar as soon as possible, if that works for you. What I've seen and heard today is beyond amazing; and as I told you, I've never experienced anything like it. You're one in a million, with the makings of a world-class pianist. I won't lie to you, though. Where or how you got your talent is odd, and I'm guessing there's more to the story. As long as you can hear the music, you can play it, yet you can't read music, never learned how. Am I right?"

Helen nods and he continues, “It’s like things are backwards, and we have to start you off as a novice, first teach you how to read music. I think once you master that, the rest will go easily. Your ability to play by ear is not only phenomenal, it’s the *way* you can play that makes it even more so. Your style when you play, even if it’s by ear, is that of a seasoned professional, someone who’s played for years and years. Certainly long enough to develop that kind of style. It’s fascinating, beyond amazing, and I very much look forward to helping you develop this remarkable talent.”

Buzzing with excitement, Helen’s smile says it all as he hands her a card with his information, as well as the time and date of her first formal lesson. Glancing at the card, she’s satisfied to see it’s for the day after tomorrow, in the middle of the day. He sees her looking at the card with a slight frown, and asks if there’s a problem with it. She says it’s fine, just wishing it was sooner. They both laugh, and he assures her he’ll try to come up with a regular schedule that’s good for both of them.

Before going home, she rushes to the market and picks up what she needs, content to see that she’s accomplished a great deal in such a short time. On the drive home, she puts on her Lucky Strike sunglasses, and tries to remember the full Gershwin song Nathan had her play, but it’s too complicated. At home, after putting her purchases away, she takes Ollie for a walk and tells him all about Nathan, and how she’s going to become a famous piano player. Ollie just wags, looking at her now and then, enjoying the vibe of her happiness.

With dinner almost ready, she hears Jake’s truck coming up the driveway. She runs to the window and peeks out, hoping to get a feel of how things went during his visit with Marian. Her heart drops as she watches the way he slams the door, and stalks up the walkway. “Shit,” she mutters as she moves from the window and runs into the kitchen, bracing herself for what she hopes is just a passing storm.

CHAPTER 38

"Helen!" Jake calls loudly as he stomps through the front door. "Where are you?"

"I'm in here, in the kitchen."

Jake strides into the kitchen, red-faced, breathing heavily and says, "Who the hell do you think you are, going to my mother behind my back? How dare you try to get an old lady to convince me what's best for my wife or my marriage? What the hell were you thinking?"

Helen looks at him thoughtfully, more prepared for his tirade than she thought she'd be. She's always tried to keep the peace and do what was expected of her, so she understands in a way why Jake is so upset and confused. But this time, it's not going to deter her from speaking her mind, and standing up for herself. With hands on her hips she faces him and says calmly, "After I got the piano tuned, I realized I'd always wanted to learn to play, but was afraid to say anything about it to you, because I knew you'd get mad."

"Damn right I'm mad! You're a foolish idiot. You had no right going to my mother and getting her involved, and now you put ideas into her head, getting her all upset, too," he replies with a raised voice.

While watching his face when he's talking, she almost laughs, thinking of the fire-breathing dragon she saw in the clouds on her walk with Ollie. Jake has gotten himself so worked up over this that it causes Helen to realize how controlling he's been from the time they first met. She was so young, naïve, and always thought he was supposed to know best because he was older, more worldly. But now she sees so clearly this isn't the case. She remembers the vision of her life she saw in the fields that day she got the flash from the sun through the sunglasses, and realizes more than ever, in that very moment, that everything's going to change.

Jake's standing there breathing heavily, waiting for Helen to say something. She's still thinking, knowing the right words will come, and hoping he won't get violent. He's never hit her, but he's changed for the worse from the man she once knew at the commune. "Jake," she says calmly, "I work really hard around here, I do the best I can, I go along with whatever you want, I don't question you. I'm asking for *one* thing I want to do for myself. I don't think it's a lot to ask for. I only mentioned it to your mother because I thought she would like it if I followed in her footsteps, and that the piano would actually get used, not just sit in the corner collecting dust."

"Oh, Little Miss Perfect, is that you? You think you do so much around here, and now you want to go around taking lessons and playing piano?"

"Yes, I want to take lessons. I know I'll be good at it. I'm sorry you don't like music, that you think it's a waste, but I *do* like it. In fact, I love it, and want it in my life."

"Well, I say no, and that's final!" Jake yells as he turns and walks away.

It's on the tip of Helen's tongue to tell him to stick it, and to get someone else to do all the work she does around the farm to keep it going. However, she holds back, knowing now is not the right time to rile him up further. If she had someplace to go, some way of supporting herself, or someone to take her in, she'd leave. For the first time ever, she realizes she'll figure it out, she'll find a way, and make a life for herself. The kind of life she deserves, the kind of life anyone should have, free from a controlling spouse.

The rest of the evening is tense, with both of them staying away from each other in separate rooms, and she's wondering why he's even home tonight. He's been hanging around more than usual, and she thinks maybe he's had a fight with his latest mistress, and that's adding to his bad mood. She's hoping he'll be gone most of the day tomorrow, since she wants to practice on her piano, and she obviously can't do it if he's around.

Helen's relieved when she hears Jake's truck take off early the next morning. She jumps out of bed before Ollie has a chance to wake her, and gets the coffee started. With cup in hand, she mentally plans her day, wondering if she should go see Marian and make sure she's not too upset from Jake's visit. She nixes that idea, thinking it best to leave it alone for a few days, so as not to upset her further. She's still not sure how she's going to handle Jake when he eventually finds out she went ahead with her lessons, despite his adamant refusal to allow it.

She tries to keep from getting angry at what a jerk he's become, and how she's allowed herself to get into such an imprisoning situation. *He's* the one treating her badly with all his affairs, his disregard of her feelings, his disrespect for her as a person, treating her with a contempt she doesn't deserve. She won't have it anymore, and she's already thrown away that sack of guilt she'd been carrying since she was a child. She's done with all that. Her clarity of thought now helps her realize Jake has his own burden he's been carrying around as well, which is partly responsible for his behavior, but it's no longer her problem. That's for him to figure out; she has more important things to do.

With the radio tuned to her classical station, she starts to play along with Beethoven's *Ode to Joy* with such a feeling of elation, sure she's on the verge of bursting with happiness. She's so grateful for the new life music has breathed into her, and relishes the feeling as she plays. For an hour, Helen gets lost in her playing, and suddenly realizes she has work to do. She's decided to act as though nothing's changed, and will continue to do her chores as expected. She'll also play whenever Jake's not around, and she'll take lessons from Nathan. She'll worry about getting caught later. She's no longer afraid. She's on a mission.

After getting the day's work done, with dinner in the oven, she decides to take a break and wait half an hour to see if Jake will make it home for dinner. She's hoping he won't, but has it ready just in case. She settles in her chair with the magazine she's been wanting to read, with Brenda's picture on the cover. Turning to the page with the article, she begins to read, finding out about the life of the woman with the sunglasses, the artist, whose boyfriend died in a car accident at a very young age. While reading, her eyes start to close, and she remembers she didn't sleep well the night before; plus, all the stress has made her tired. Her last thought before falling asleep is, *I'll just rest my eyes for a minute.*

#

At the same time Helen is drawn into a nap, Brenda's in her studio meditating. She hasn't been able to access Vincent while meditating in several weeks, and her last vision of him was in the dream she had of them playing piano together. She meditates to a place that feels like it's as deep down as the inside of her cells, and she hears music. She can't see anything, Vincent isn't there, but she hears music; someone's playing the piano. She recognizes the song; it's the same one she and Vincent were playing. It's beautiful, filling her with a joy she can't describe. Falling into the notes, she wants to ask the name of it, this beautiful composition, but there's no one to ask, it's just her.

Helen wakes with a start as she realizes someone's shaking her, hard, and Ollie is barking. What's going on, who's there? Oh, it's Jake, and he keeps shaking her.

"Stop!" she says loudly. "Just stop! What are you doing? You're hurting me!"

"I thought you said you have it so hard around here, you work so hard," Jake says mockingly.

"Oh, I didn't hear you come in. I was just resting my eyes for a few minutes and must have fallen asleep."

Jake walks away, and Helen gets up to put dinner on the table. They eat in silence. Helen's lost in her music, thinking about tomorrow's first lesson. Jake's brooding, thinking about the argument he had with his mistress. Helen was right; Jake and his mistress, Janie, have been fighting. She wants Jake to leave Helen, and he wants to keep things the way they are. He'll never admit it to Helen, but he really needs her. He's stopped needing her love, or even her companionship, but he does need her as a partner in running the farm, and he doesn't want to give that up. Until recently they very rarely argued, and she never questioned him about his whereabouts. While he's thinking, *Maybe I should give in and let her take piano lessons,* Helen's thinking, *I'm going to do it anyway.*

#

Brenda slowly pulls herself out of the meditation, gradually allowing herself to become aware of her surroundings. Looking around her studio, she feels relaxed, and enjoys letting her eyes fall on the latest painting she's working on. She starts humming, and realizes it's the song she heard while meditating. It's driving her crazy that she can't remember the name of it, and she finally calls her friend Caroline. She tells her about this song she heard while meditating and asks if she knows what it is. Caroline asks her to hum it, and even though Brenda is not especially musical, she hums it fairly well. Caroline bursts out laughing and says, "That's one of my all-time favorite compositions of Beethoven. His *Ode to Joy*, I think it's Symphony Number 9 or something like that."

"I can't get it out of my head, I love it so much. While meditating, I heard it being played on a piano, and the notes were so rich and melodious, I was vibrating inside. I kind of feel like I still am."

"Wow, that's incredible! Things like that never happen to me when I meditate. I just go somewhere deep and relax. I never have visions or hear music like you do. Now I'm going to be hearing *Ode to Joy* in my head the rest of the day. Thanks, Brenda, can't think of a better song to fill my head with." They both laugh, and promise to get together soon before hanging up.

#

Before getting ready for bed, Helen finally finishes reading the article about Brenda. She continues to look at the cover photo and feels Brenda is someone she'd like to know. *What a difficult time she had losing her boyfriend in the accident. How terrible*, she thinks, *and still she went on to become well-known in the art and fashion world.* Helen has now put together that the sunglasses Ollie found in the field were made by Brenda, and feels a special affinity towards her. She's too tired now to think more about how the sunglasses got in her field, who they belonged to, and why she's the one who ended up with them. There's so much to think about regarding those sunglasses. As she puts the magazine aside and decides to make a cup of tea before bed, she finds herself humming *Ode to Joy*, and laughs when she looks down and sees Ollie is wagging his tail. He likes the song too.

CHAPTER 39

Jake doesn't like the look in Helen's eyes, not at all. She's never stood up to him before, and it makes him nervous. He really doesn't understand her need to take piano lessons, but it's more than that. He realizes this is the first time in their relationship that she's attempted to defy him, and strongly express an interest in something like she has about those damn piano lessons. When he saw the look in her eyes this morning, that look of contempt, he got an odd feeling; and for the first time, he was the one who looked away. He was the one who backed down. The look of defiance said, *You're not going to bully me anymore,* and this scared Jake.

He remembers one of the last things his mother said, when she was rallying for Helen to take the piano lessons. She told him he'd better think of taking a step back and looking at the woman he married, because everyone has a breaking point, a tipping point. Helen was close to that point, she said, and he could lose her.

What mostly gave Marian the courage to speak to her son that way was the realization that Jake was treating Helen like his father had treated her. He blatantly cheated on her, disrespected her, and completely lost sight of her as a person and what she aspired to be, taking away everything of who she was. Marian couldn't ignore this same thing happening to Helen, and that was the driving force for her to speak to her son so sharply. That was also why Jake was so mad after visiting Marian at the home. She'd never spoken to him like that before in his adult life, and he was confused.

As he gets into his truck to drive to Janie's house, he thinks he'd better be nicer to Helen and maybe give in about the piano lessons. He really can't afford to lose her; after all, who would do the accounting and all the other stuff? And what about Janie? What if she won't take him back unless he divorces Helen? Jake doesn't understand why he can't have his cake and eat it too, but he's going to try.

Jake's the last thing on Helen's mind as she and Ollie make their rounds. She's practically dancing with every step, in anticipation of her first piano lesson. She already has her sunglasses on, and finds something is different today in the way everything looks. As usual, the clarity is crisp and sharp, but there seems to be slight motion, a mirage like one sees when the heat of the sun shimmers over asphalt. Blinking several times only makes the shimmering more pronounced as Helen stares at a fixed point in the distance, mesmerized. As she continues to stare, the glimmering waves start to take shape and she sees musical notes and symbols. Although she can't identify them specifically, she knows they're related to music, and they feel familiar to her. Involuntarily she looks away, breaking the vision, then up at the sun where a flash of color gives a quick fleeting burst, disappearing before she can even register that it happened.

For a few more minutes Helen looks around, and everything looks like it always does. Admittedly she's a little spooked, and is laughing nervously like people do when an emotional release is called for, and it bubbles up on its own. Walking back to the house, she tries to put into order all the unusual occurrences since the first time she put on the sunglasses. There's no longer any doubt in her mind that the glasses are responsible for all the changes in her life. That's as far as she can accept; fathoming *how* it's even possible is nowhere near her comprehension.

Helen's heart is beating quickly as she steps in through the door where Nathan's waiting to start their first lesson. He smiles, and she starts to feel more relaxed. Leading her to a side table by the piano, she sees he has several books and papers laid out.

"I've been thinking a lot about your special talent, and doing some research. Basically, you need to learn how to read music, not just play it by ear. This will make the difference between you becoming an extraordinary piano player vs. a good piano player. Admittedly, you already have incredible style and poise in your playing, but you need to learn to play not just according to what you hear, but what you see on the page," Nathan says, pointing to a page of sheet music. "So we'll start with learning the mechanics of music."

Helen looks at the page Nathan was pointing to, picks it up, and says, "This looks familiar. I can identify a few things just from looking at it. But honestly, I'm not sure exactly what each one is, or does. I just kind of know what they're called."

"Is that from lessons you had as child? I thought you never had lessons."

"When I was maybe in third grade, we had a music teacher we saw once a week. I remember singing songs, and then she had us try different instruments. There was a piano, and we all had a chance to try to play it. She talked about notes and things. I don't have any strong memories of it, but I know I didn't have formal lessons," Helen says, trying to remember more.

"Okay, well, looking at this, what can you identify?"

Helen starts naming different parts as she points to them. Nathan quizzes her as she goes along, answering Nathan's question without hesitation, and he's impressed. "Wow, you know more than I thought you would. I'm just so baffled as to how you know this. Are you sure you didn't hit your head or anything? Or maybe there's something you're not telling me? Like you really *have* had lessons and you already knew more than you're letting on?"

Helen knows she can never even try to explain about the sunglasses, so she just shakes her head and says, "One day I woke up, and I knew how to play along with the radio. And now when I see the sheet music, it somehow looks very familiar to me. Maybe I was a pianist in my last life or something?" she says questioningly, with a smile.

Nathan continues to look at her with a puzzled expression, then starts to laugh and says, "Yeah, maybe. Who knows? Okay, let's get to work."

They spend the rest of the hour on music theory, with Helen absorbing the information like a sponge. Nathan's impressed and more than a little unnerved at Helen's ability to take in what he's teaching her, and apply it without any difficulty. When their time is almost up, Nathan gives her several books and sheets of music to go over until their next lesson. He tells Helen they can meet twice a week if that works for her, and she asks if it can be more. Nathan says he'll work on it, but doubts he can fit in more at this time, but will let her know right away if anything opens up.

Helen opens her mouth to speak, but hesitates, and Nathan asks her if she has any questions. "There's something I need to ask you. It's important, but if you have a problem with it, I'll understand," she says slowly, as if the words are finding it difficult to come out.

"Go on, you can ask me anything," he says.

Helen takes a deep breath and says, "My husband doesn't want me to take lessons. I'm doing this behind his back. I don't like doing it this way, but he gives me no choice. He's very controlling and he has no appreciation for music. His mother told me that his father was the same way—it's a condition and that there's a name for it."

"Yes, it's called musical anhedonia. Sorry to hear that. It makes it difficult for you, doesn't it?"

"Well yes, it does. I find myself in this incredibly odd situation. Out of nowhere I can play piano, and know stuff about music I never knew before," Helen says, feeling tears in her eyes. "And I'm married to a man I can't even tell about it, or get any support from. I even have to hide it from him." The tears start to flow, and Helen quickly tries to wipe them away.

"How can I help?" Nathan asks simply, with no tone of judgement.

"Please, if you call for whatever reason and he answers, just hang up. If I'm there and I see that happening, I'll call you back when I can. Also, I want to pay you in cash so there's no paper trail. I do all the books, but every now and then he'll open a bank statement or take a look. It'll be safer if I take it out of my household money."

Nathan nods, not saying anything for a minute. Eventually he says, "How unfortunate for you. It's no trouble to do what you ask. But I have to say, you have bigger issues going on here. If you don't mind my saying so, your marriage doesn't sound like it's doing you any good."

For the next ten minutes Helen reveals more about her past while Nathan listens, just nodding, letting her get it out. Before long she realizes she's talking too much when he sneaks a glance at his watch. Gathering her things, she pays cash for today's lesson and heads for the door. They confirm the time and date of the next lesson, and as she's walking out the door she asks, "Do you have the sheet music for Beethoven's *Ode to Joy*?"

"Why yes, I do."

"May I have it until next time?"

Nathan goes to get the music, and handing it to her, says, "If you can learn to play that from reading it, *not* by ear, I'll give you a free lesson!"

"You're on!" she says, taking the sheet music with a smile. As he watches her get into her car, he has no doubt she'll do it.

When she gets home, she gives a sigh of relief. Helen's glad Jake's truck is gone, and he's not home yet. She rushes inside and finishes the rest of her work in record time, thinking about how much we as humans can do with the right motivation. While completing her chores, she runs the lesson she just had through her mind, visualizing the Staff, Treble, Bass, and Notes on the sheet, and can already see them quite clearly. She's tempted to get the sheet music of *Ode to Joy* out of the trunk of her car where it's hidden, along with all the other books and sheets Nathan gave her, but it's too close to when Jake might be home. Instead, she gets started with dinner while she continually visualizes the notes and keys, and where her hands should be.

Once she finishes dinner preparations, she goes into the living room and dusts the piano for the second time that day. She has trouble keeping away from the piano, and feels the draw stronger than a magnet every time she's near it. After dusting, she pulls out her magazine and gazes again at Brenda's picture. She reads the article again, and starts daydreaming about what it would be like to meet Brenda. Does Brenda know the sunglasses she made can do things for people? *Would she think I'm crazy?* Helen wonders. *Maybe it's not the glasses.* Her musings are interrupted by the sound of Jake coming through the door, and Helen draws herself up and goes to the kitchen to put dinner on the table.

Jake's acting weird, and keeps looking at her as they eat. Helen's looking towards the window and can see him watching her out of the corner of her eye. Finally, Jake clears his throat and says, "I've been thinking."

She turns her head to look at him, waiting to see what he'll say. He takes another bite, stalling, chewing slowly. "I've been thinking," he says again. "About those piano lessons you want. I think maybe it'll be all right if you don't go on about it, and you don't play the dang thing while I'm here."

Trying to show no emotion, even though she's got a mix of elation *and* annoyance going on at the same time, Helen just nods while she gathers her thoughts. She too takes a bite, but has trouble swallowing the food, along with her emotions. She's tempted to tell him she doesn't need his permission and she's already started. Instead she asks, "What made you change your mind?"

"Just consider it a reward for doing the books so good, and you can thank my mother, too. I don't like when she's mad at me."

Helen knows there's more behind it, and suspects it has something to do with his mistress, but she just nods again, mumbles a thanks, and finishes her dinner. Jake, satisfied he's done what he needed to do, gets up from the table and informs Helen he's going out for a while. At that moment, she realizes she won't be staying in this marriage any longer than she has to. There are bigger and better things out there, and she finally knows it's acceptable for her to go after them. More than acceptable; it's her destiny, and her prospects have never been better.

As soon as Jake's truck is out of sight, Helen goes to the trunk of her car and takes out one of the music books and the sheet music for *Ode to Joy*. Sitting at the piano, she surveys the keys and then the sheet music, trying to match the notes with the keys. One note at a time, she reads through the music, playing as she reads. Since she does this slowly the song doesn't really take shape, but she continues to do this for the next hour. Once she gets a feel for it, she starts from the beginning with the Note Values this time, until the song starts to sound like it's supposed to. Part of her wants to cheat and turn on the radio, and play along with whatever composition is on, but she sticks with trying to play from reading the music, and it starts to become second nature.

#

While Helen is practicing, Brenda is in her studio painting. She's discovered she likes to listen to music sometimes while painting, and her latest favorite is a full orchestra version of Beethoven's *Ode to Joy*. She just can't get enough of it, although sometimes it does bring her to tears, and she doesn't paint as well when she can't see. Laughing, she stops to get a tissue, blows her nose, then picks up her brush to continue, still humming, even though the music has stopped.

CHAPTER 40

After several months of lessons with Nathan, Helen has become an accomplished pianist. She's learned to read music as though she's been doing it her entire life, and her style is so poised and graceful that Nathan never tires of watching and listening to her play. She does still play by ear sometimes, depending on where she is and who she's playing for, but she's learned to read music and can play just about any composition put before her. Playing the piano gives her more joy than she's ever imagined, opening so many doors to a more fulfilling life. Her confidence and self-esteem have grown exponentially, and she's even become more beautiful, inside and out.

As she sits in front of the piano, with Nathan taking his usual spot, they start going over a very difficult Chopin piece that even Nathan has difficulty with. After about twenty minutes, Helen asks if they can take a break; Nathan agrees, and asks her what's wrong. Since working so closely for several months they've become friends, and even though Nathan is her teacher, he's also become somewhat of a father figure. When asked, he'll offer guidance in whatever aspect of her life she needs help with. He never pushes his opinions on her, and when he senses something wrong, he tells her he's there if she needs someone to talk to. Oftentimes she does seek his advice, although sometimes she holds back, trying to make decisions on her own.

Although she's told Nathan a lot about her unhappy marriage, she hasn't told him how much more it's deteriorated in the last two months.

Jake doesn't bother to come home more often than not, never telling her when to expect him. Then he'll come waltzing in whenever he wants, offering no explanations, expecting her to make dinner for him, or give him an accounting of the books. If she happens to be playing piano when he comes in, he expects her to stop and pay attention to what he wants. They've been sleeping in separate rooms for a long time now, and Helen's lost all feeling for him. She tells Nathan she wants to leave him, but has no money of her own, except the little she squirrels away each month from the household money. But then she worries about Ollie; she couldn't leave him behind. She feels selfish telling Nathan she also can't leave Marian's piano behind, as it has become her salvation.

Nathan listens intently, nodding in understanding about how she feels. He then tells her things have a way of working out, and he'll help her however he can. Helen thinks he means he'll listen to her troubles, and doesn't realize Nathan's thinking well beyond just listening. He's been mulling over her situation ever since she started to confide in him, and has thought a lot about ways he could help her gain her independence. It's too soon to tell her what he's been working on, and he needs more time to pull together some of the pieces. He's certain Helen's a very special person who's somehow manifested an amazing talent. That, along with her will and determination, are the combination that's sure to get her where she needs to be.

Once they're done with the lesson, Helen thanks him again for listening to her troubles and apologizes for burdening him with them. "Thank *you,* Helen for trusting me with your worries. Now I'm going to ask you for even more trust, in two different ways."

She looks at him with raised eyebrows and asks, "What do you mean? I already trust you with all my heart."

"I know," he says with a smile. "Now, you have to trust in yourself to know what to do. To know that *you* know what's right for you. Believe and trust in that, with all your heart. Next, you must focus your attention and energy on what you *do* want, and trust with all your heart that the Universe will bring it to you."

Helen's listening with tears in her eyes, nodding. "It's hard sometimes, you know?"

"I do," he says. "And the third thing is to trust I'll always have your back."

Teary-eyed, they hug, appreciating how wonderful their friendship is. As Helen opens the door to leave, she turns around and says to Nathan, "Thank you, thank you so much." She then smiles and says, "With all my heart."

Three weeks later, Nathan can barely wait for Helen to show up for her lesson. He's been working behind the scenes and has fantastic news for her. At least, he hopes she thinks it's fantastic. "Ah, there you are. How are you?" he asks with a silly smile on his face.

"I'm good, how are you? And why do you look like the cat that just ate the canary? What are you smiling about?"

"I have good news! I hope you think it's good news, too. Do you remember I told you about a friend of mine who's a mechanical engineer consultant?"

"Yes, I remember you telling me he and his son started their own firm. What about them?"

"They need someone to do their accounting. The daughter was doing the books, but she recently got married and her husband was offered a great new job, but they'll have to relocate. My friend knew this was a possibility, so it's no great surprise. The business is growing and he needs someone at least part-time for now. I told him about you, and he's interested in meeting you."

"Oh, wow, that's great! But does he know I don't have a formal education or training? I doubt he would want to hire me."

“Listen, Helen, I know you’re good, and you’re a hard worker. You practically run your farm singlehandedly, and know more about real-life accounting than any new graduate. Am I right?”

“I like to think so,” she says, a small smile starting to form. “Do you really think he’d hire me? And how will I work for them and still do everything else I do?” Suddenly she’s frowning with the prospect of the decisions she’ll have to make.

Nathan looks at her, not saying anything, waiting for her to toss it around in her head, letting it sink in. She walks over to the piano, sits down, and starts playing *Moonlight Sonata.* The rich sound fills the studio, helping her to relax. When she’s done, with her hands in her lap, she says, “Did he say when he wants to meet with me?”

Nathan tells her his friend wants to meet with her as soon as this afternoon, and that the company’s offices are only ten minutes away. He even offers to drive her. At first, she says she needs more time to think about it, and Nathan simply asks, “Don’t you think it’s time?”

Even though she’s petrified, she nods and says, “Okay, but I’ll drive myself. Don’t you have a student after my lesson?”

Nathan calls his friend and informs him of when Helen will be there, and they have a short lesson. He gives her directions and makes her promise to come back when she’s done, to tell him how it went. He has trouble concentrating with his next pupil, and is glad he’s a good student and doesn’t need a lot of handholding. After the student leaves, he’s mostly done for the day and goes to check his phone messages. There’s a message from the Chamber of Commerce asking if he’d be able to supply them with his best student, to play piano at a cocktail party in two weeks, honoring the arts and entertainment industry in their city. They leave a number for him to call back, and ask if he’ll give them an answer by tomorrow if possible. He immediately thinks of Helen, and feels this would be a perfect venue for her debut. She’s more than ready, and definitely his best student by far. He almost picks up the phone right then, but realizes he must ask Helen first, not just assume she'll want to do it.

At the precise moment Nathan has decided Helen would be the perfect pianist for the cocktail party, his friend is offering Helen a job. She's been honest with him about everything, from her lack of formal education to her circumstances at home. Nathan's friend doesn't divulge that he already knows any of what she's telling him, even though Nathan did tell him some of it. He admires her honesty and has a good feeling about her, but is a little concerned as to how she'll be able to manage her duties at the farm and her work with him. They decide between them it would be best for her to have regular hours, and if she is unable to come in for whatever reason, he'll allow her to make up the time whenever she can, as long as she gets the work completed as needed. The salary he offers her is commensurate with the type and amount of accounting she'd be required to do, and she can hardly believe her good fortune. They shake hands and Helen says she'll be there a week from now, ready to get to work.

She has to keep from running and jumping in the parking lot before she gets to her car, breathless with excitement. She puts the key in the ignition, but sits for a few minutes gathering her thoughts. She knows she's going to have to tell Jake, and he's not going to be happy. *Too bad, so sad*, she laughs to herself, knowing it will all work out somehow. She can't wait to go back to Nathan's to tell him the good news, and has to keep herself from driving too fast.

Pulling up to Nathan's studio, she jumps out of the car and runs up the walk. Barging in, she tells him all about the interview, and how nice his friend was. She's sure she can do the job and that she'll like working there. Her excitement is contagious, and Nathan listens with a big smile on his face. After thanking him profusely, she starts to wind down, and then begins talking about her concerns with Jake and the farm, and how she's going to be able to do it all. They talk about it for a few minutes and come up with a few ideas Helen needs to think about. Nathan insists she think of herself first, and things will fall into place.

Once Helen has settled down and they're both just sitting there with their thoughts, Nathan turns to her and says, "By the way, I got a call from the Chamber of Commerce. They want me to supply them with one of my students, preferably my best student, for a cocktail party they're having in two weeks."

Helen sits up and waits for him to continue. "I was hoping you'd be available to do it," he says quietly, downplaying his excitement.

"Really? Really?" is all Helen can think of to say.

"Does that mean yes, you'll do it?" he asks, laughing.

In answer to his question Helen jumps up, runs over to the piano, and starts playing *Ode to Joy* with an enthusiasm that gives him his answer.

#

One wonders if music can travel faster than the speed of light, considering that at the exact same time Helen starts to play, Caroline and Brenda are walking through the flea market where they first met many years ago. They're browsing and reminiscing about all that's occurred since they first met, when George brought Caroline to Brenda, still in college, where she was selling her hand-painted sunglasses. The music being piped in is classical, and Brenda comments on being surprised it's such a good selection.

"Wait," Brenda says as she takes hold of her friend's arm. "Listen, it's that song, *Ode to Joy*. Isn't it wonderful? It makes me feel so good. Listen."

"Ah yes, come over here by the speaker, we can hear it better." Caroline takes Brenda's hand, and they stand there listening until the next selection comes on.

"Let's find the old space I used to have, and see who has it now," Brenda says as she guides Caroline to where she used to set up.

When they find the space, they see a short, squat man with a fleshy nose and heavy bags under his eyes rearranging a few items on his table. Brenda points, letting Caroline know that used to be her table, and they walk over. The man looks up and eyes them from head to toe, until they both feel self-conscious. He figures they have money from the way they're dressed, and is already thinking of how he can rip them off. He asks if they're looking for anything in particular, and they politely say they're just looking. Caroline picks up what looks like an antique hand mirror and the guy says, "That mirror is over a hundred years old and was made in England. It's worth three hundred dollars, but you can have it for two hundred." He flashes her a yellow-toothed smile.

Caroline's still examining the mirror when the vendor at the next table comes over and says, "Hey Arnie, is that the one that was made in China? Come from the same lot you had twenty of, am I right?" The guy starts laughing and walks back to his table.

Caroline looks at Arnie, puts the hand mirror back on the table, takes Brenda's arm, and they walk away. She nods a thank you at the vendor who warned them, and when they're out of earshot she says to Brenda, "What a horrible little man."

CHAPTER 41

Helen feels sorry that she hasn't been visiting Marian as much as she should have. After her big blow-up with Jake about her taking piano lessons, and then Jake relenting partly due to what Marian said to him, Helen feels even closer to Marian, and grateful for her friendship. When Helen does visit, they talk about her lessons and how she's progressing, but Helen has always downplayed how well she's doing. She knows Marian won't believe her if she tells her the truth, and would question how she's able to progress so quickly. Helen figures it's best all-around if she attributes her progress to the considerable practice and study she's been doing every day. She's honest with Marian about how her lessons are eating into her chores at the farm, but they never talk about her marriage with Marian's son. Marian knows her son is a disappointment but has trouble saying it out loud, so they both skirt around the subject—or they have up until now.

Today Helen is going to tell Marian about getting the job she'll be starting next week, and also about what she feels her future plans will be. She isn't looking forward to it, but feels she really needs to be honest to this woman, who has been kinder to her than her own mother ever was. Once all the pleasantries are out of the way, Marian tries to sit up a little straighter in her bed and says, "Helen dear, there's something eating at you. You don't need to be afraid to tell me what's really on your mind. In fact, I have a feeling there's a lot we need to talk about." While waiting for Helen to gather her thoughts, Marian looks at her understandingly.

"Oh, Marian, first I need to thank you for all your kindness from the very moment we met. You took us in when we left the commune, and you were the only one who ever cared about how I felt when I lost the baby. I'm sorry if I haven't appreciated you enough, and I feel now I'm going to let you down, and I feel so bad about it."

"You haven't let me down, Helen. You're like a daughter to me, and at times I feel like I've let *you* down. You're still so young, and when Jake first brought you home, you were such a naïve, broken-down little girl. You've grown so much since then, and I'm just sorry Jake hasn't been a better husband to you. You deserve more. God forgive me for saying this, but my son has become a selfish, misguided person that I don't recognize anymore. He's sullen and moody, and when he does bother to come and see me, I find myself wishing he would leave."

Helen just nods, and for the time being doesn't want to add to Marian's misery by saying anything else negative about Jake. Instead, she tells Marian about the new job she'll be starting in a few days, and how excited she is to finally be able to get paid for something she knows she'll do well at. She confides she's nervous about it, though, and knows it will take away from her duties at home. Marian listens carefully, nodding and gazing out the window at times. When Helen stops for a minute, waiting for her mother-in-law to say something, neither of them are looking at each other. Helen's heart is beating quickly, and she's hesitant to reveal more.

"You're going to leave him, aren't you?" Marian asks in her matter-of-fact way.

Helen's surprised by her directness, and looks over to see that Marian has tears in her eyes. "Yes, as soon as I can manage it," she says, feeling her own tears start to form. "It really is best for everyone. Jake doesn't love me, and I think he loves someone else anyway."

"Heaven help her, whoever she is," Marian mutters.

"I don't love him either," Helen continues. "I do care about the farm. It's the only home I ever really cared about. But I'm lonely there, and Jake only keeps me around to do the books and keep things running. He takes advantage and thinks I'll never be able to leave, so he can continue to use me. But now I have a job, and I'll be able to save some money and get a place of my own. It'll take a while, though. At least I'll have the piano to play and Ollie to keep me company while I'm still there."

Now both of them are crying, and Helen goes over to sit beside Marian on the bed. She reaches down and gently hugs her, feeling how frail and tiny she is. Sitting up, she says, "I have a lot to work out, and I'm terrified of failing and closing off my options. But please know, whatever happens, I will always come to see you, and I will always care about you. I feel better having told you. I didn't want to spring it on you."

Marian laughs, wiping her eyes, and tells Helen she's doing exactly what she wishes she had done, and that she'll help Helen in whatever way she can. They talk more about what her next steps should be, and it's decided Helen needs to tell Jake about the job first. There's no doubt she'll no longer be able to do everything around the farm as she has been; it's just humanly impossible. She needs to discuss everything with Jake, to start there. Marian makes Helen promise she won't back down, that she'll continue on with taking the job, and her piano lessons, no matter what Jake says. It's a start, and in the meantime, Marian promises to think about some possible solutions. Kissing Marian on the cheek, Helen leaves, feeling a weight has been lifted from her. "One step at a time gets you where you're going," she says to herself, as she drives away. "One step at a time."

That evening, for the first time in ages, Helen's hoping Jake will be home at a reasonable hour. She's rehearsed over and over in her mind how she's going to tell him she's taken a job that will be starting in a few days, and that nothing he says is going to deter her from taking it. She knows Jake's weaknesses, and will use everything she can to ensure she comes out of it the victor. She keeps Ollie by her side for courage and security, and waits.

At last Helen hears Jake's truck, and braces herself. He walks in and heads for the kitchen, where she sits at the kitchen table. He notices there's no place setting for his dinner, and he looks around to see if there have been any meal preparations. With Ollie still by her side, Helen asks Jake where he's been. She doesn't ask accusingly. She just asks in a conversational tone. He swivels towards her, not sure what to say, because he obviously doesn't want to tell her the truth, and she's never questioned him before.

He eventually finds his voice and says, "None of your business." He turns away from her, opens the refrigerator and starts rummaging around.

"The reason I ask," says Helen, still in the same conversational tone, "Is that you'll be needed much more around here now. So you'll have to start managing your time better."

"What are you talking about? I can be here whenever I damn well please."

"That goes two ways then, doesn't it? Well, good, because I will also only be around when I damn well please. I got a job, and I'll be working five days a week. Then of course I have my piano lessons, so that leaves little time for most of the things I do around here. If any of it matters, I suppose you'll have to do it yourself."

Jake's staring at her with his mouth hanging open. His eyes are darting around the room, looking everywhere except at her. He's dumbfounded, and can't believe this is happening to him.

Taking advantage of his confusion, Helen goes on to say, "I'll still do the accounting for the farm, for now. But you'll have to figure out the rest. When you've had time to think it over, we can sit down and discuss it." She then gets up from the table, and with Ollie following, goes to the living room to practice at the piano. Her heart is beating double-time and she can't believe what she just did. As scared as she was, she never let it show, and she can't believe she pulled it off unscathed. With shaking hands, she starts to play, hoping Jake isn't going to come in ready to do battle. She plays with all her heart and feels the stress falling away, until she's no longer shaking, just lost in the music.

Ollie lets her know he needs to go out, and she lets him out the back door. Looking around, she sees that Jake's truck is gone, and she breathes a sigh of relief. On a whim, she grabs her sunglasses and follows Ollie out the back door. The moon is brilliantly full, and the fields are bathed in a bewitching glow of luminous moonlight and shadow. The stars fill the sky in that miraculous way they do that makes you feel you can almost touch them, fill your pockets with them. Helen feels so content in this moment, so optimistic and grateful to be alive.

The moon looks bigger and fuller than she's ever seen it before, and the illusion makes her realize things are not always as they seem. Her logical mind tells her the moon doesn't get bigger overnight, but she can't help feeling it *is* bigger, just for her, at this very moment. Putting her sunglasses on, she looks fixedly at the larger-than-life moon, and marvels at how well she can see the craters and textures from so far away. She remembers someone at the commune telling her that if it weren't for the moon there would be no people on earth, and this makes her marvel even more. Through the sunglasses she sees well beyond light and shadow; she sees life and infinity, promise and hope. She knows she's been given an amazing gift, and vows to be worthy of it.

Taking the glasses off, she calls Ollie and they go back inside. Helen starts playing again, and thinks about which pieces she should play at the Chamber of Commerce cocktail party. Mentally she goes over a combination of well-known classical combinations and more modern pieces. She'll ask Nathan to help her come up with a definitive list, and also ask if he'll recommend some sheet music to bring, in case some selections are requested she doesn't know by heart. She really has no idea what to expect, as she's never been to a cocktail party, then remembers Marian telling her she'll need an elegant dress for her debut. Tomorrow she'll have to shop for a dress, and also some more clothes for work. So much to do; how wonderful is that?

Even though she told Jake she'd be doing less around the farm, Helen's still up at the crack of dawn, making her rounds with Ollie. This is one thing she's going to miss, and wants to savor it as long as it lasts. She can't help thinking of all the things that'll be involved with her leaving, and she looks down at Ollie, wondering what he'll think if they leave the farm. She worries he'll be alone a lot more once she starts work, and mentally adds it to her list of things she needs to work out.

Finishing as much as she can before her piano lesson, she arrives breathless and a few minutes late. She apologizes for being late as Nathan asks her if everything is all right. She informs him everything is better than all right, and tells him about her confrontation with Jake. She can tell he's really proud of her, but also that he's worried. He asks if there's any chance that Jake might get violent, and Helen shakes her head, telling him Jake's a bully, and backed down easier than expected.

Nathan nods, hoping she's right. "By the way…" he says dragging it out.

"Oh boy, here we go. Whenever you say, 'by the way,' I know you're up to something," she laughs. "Okay, out with it."

"Stay here," he says as he leaves the room. She can hear him rummaging around and waits impatiently. Finally, he comes back with a black dress on a hanger. He holds it out to her and says, "Do you think it will fit?"

"Is it for me? Where did you get it? Oh my God, it has sequins around the neck and the sleeves. It's beautiful!"

"Do you think it will fit?" Nathan asks again, ignoring her questions. "Why don't you try it on first?"

Helen grabs the hanger and heads into the powder room to try it on. Amazingly it fits perfectly, and immediately transforms her into an elegantly dressed, beautiful young woman. The mirror in the powder room over the sink only allows her to see how she looks from the waist up, but it's enough to know the dress is exactly what she needs.

She shyly comes out of the powder room to show Nathan, and he claps his hands with delight. "I knew it!" he says. "You're the same size as my daughter-in-law. I should say she *was* the same size as you before she got pregnant, and now, some of her old clothes don't fit her anymore after having the twins. She was going through her closet to see what she could no longer wear, and we thought you could use it. It's perfect for you. You can wear it for your debut."

Helen hugs him with tears in her eyes. She can't thank him enough, and knows this destiny train she's on is the most magnificent ride she'll ever have in her entire life.

CHAPTER 42

The night before the party, Helen has trouble sleeping. Her mind won't stop long enough for her to get any real sleep, and she gets up feeling groggy, in need of some strong coffee. She's so excited about the cocktail party this evening, but also very nervous, afraid she'll feel far out of her element. Her comfort zone definitely doesn't include rubbing shoulders with well-to-do artists and entertainers, and she has to keep reminding herself what Nathan said about them. He told her they're just people like you and me, they're simply better known, but that doesn't make them any different or any better. She's really glad he'll be there to support her. "Hey, I'm just a regular guy, and I'll be there," he'd told her.

Nathan is so much more than a regular guy, but she knew what he was trying to tell her. She knows she'll play well and will practice the pieces she's decided on again this afternoon. Nathan likes her selections, and feels this exposure will help her tremendously, in more ways than one.

After making her rounds with Ollie and catching up on the paperwork for the farm, she can't help trying on the dress that Nathan gave her. Looking at herself in the mirror, she realizes she needs to do something with her hair, and will also need some makeup. Fortunately, she has good skin and a few cosmetics to work with, but she needs some ideas. She grabs her favorite fashion magazine and gazes at Brenda's cover photo before trying to find some eye-makeup tips. She wonders what Brenda's eyes look like behind those sunglasses, and tries to find another photo. There are a few, but none are closeups, so she has to try and copy from one of the ads. Deciding to go with the *less is more* look, since she's not used to wearing makeup, she goes with some eyeliner, mascara, blush, and a light pink lipstick. Now the hair. Going through the magazine again, she sees hair pulled up, back, short, long and various colors, but nothing like her hair, which is long, wavy, and the color of straw. Maybe if she pulls some of it back so it's out of her face in a nice clip, then leaves the rest down, it'll look more elegant than just loose. For a half hour she fools around with different looks, and finally gets it right with a half swept-up look that goes well with the shape of her face. She puts her dress, makeup, hair tools, and magazine aside and goes to practice for an hour.

After practicing, she finishes some chores, and is starting to feel really tired from not getting a good night's sleep. She doesn't want to go to the cocktail party in a sleep-deprived state, and decides a nap before getting ready will do her good. She sets the alarm so as not to oversleep, giving herself plenty of time to get ready. Settling down for a rest, she falls asleep immediately and starts dreaming. In her dream Jake's chasing her, telling her she needs to come home and get to work. She runs and runs until finally, out of breath, she stops, and finds herself at the zoo. The animals are so soft and friendly, not minding when she pets them. The biggest of bears is leaning against her, holding a kitten against his chest. The kitten is sleeping and the bear starts talking to Helen. He tells her she was chosen to have her abilities because she was able to see and hear the *Universal Mind.*

"It is a gift you've earned from before you were here; it goes full circle." She ponders what the bear said and looks down at the kitten, who stretches and yawns, still snuggled in the bear's arm. She looks back up to the bear, and he has her sunglasses on, and she's sitting at the piano playing a song she's never heard. *Beep, beep, beep, beep.* Ugh, what is that sound? She gradually wakes up and slaps at the alarm clock, trying to hold onto the dream, trying to remember it.

#

Unbeknownst to Helen, while she's dreaming, Brenda is meditating. Brenda hasn't seen or felt Vincent the last several times she's meditated, and hopes this time will be different. She has a feeling, has had it for weeks now, that she's on the brink of something. She laughs to herself, hoping it's not the brink of destruction, and that it's something significant. She knows there will always be that void in the deepest part of her being since Vincent died, but she's slowly been feeling the hole filling in, and not being so painful. She finds that at times she even feels joyful, especially when she creates what she feels is a masterpiece, or when she hears certain music, especially piano and cello. Brenda knows that when she meditates with appreciation of all that is good in her life, grateful for every breath, she can go deeper and has a better chance of seeing Vincent.

While Helen dreams, Brenda meditates, and Vincent appears. He beckons her to the piano where he's playing, and invites her to sit. He plays beautifully, but doesn't invite her to play along. Instead he tells her, "Another's gift will be revealed to you, and the circle will continue." The music goes on, Vincent fades, and Brenda drifts in warmth she doesn't want to leave.

Feeling especially refreshed from her meditation, Brenda writes down in her journal what Vincent said, knowing she'll be pondering it for the rest of the day. She knows from previous sessions that the meaning will reveal itself eventually. She starts thinking about the cocktail party she'll be attending this evening, and goes to her closet, pulling out various dresses she feels would be appropriate. Brenda's looking forward to the event, mainly because she'll see several of her friends and fellow artists, and it's always enjoyable to catch up with them. She has to admit, she does like dressing up and drinking champagne on occasion, especially with people whose company she enjoys. George and Caroline will be picking her up, and she's glad they'll be going together. She considers them, especially Caroline, to be her closest friends, and doesn't know what she would do without them. In high spirits, she chooses a dress and accessories to go with it, and heads to the shower to start getting ready.

#

Nathan and his wife pick up Helen a half-hour early so they can get her situated before the official event begins. She's a nervous wreck and tries not to show it, but Nathan knows and calmly talks with her as he drives. His wife Anne knows all about Helen, even though they've only met a few times, and she understands why Nathan has taken her under his wing. She tells Helen she looks beautiful, and not to worry—as soon as she feels nervous or starts thinking too much, to just play, and that will calm her down. Anne has heard her play and knows how talented Helen is, and has no doubt, just like her husband, that Helen will be a big hit.

Siting in the back seat, Helen tries to breathe deeply and just think about the music she'll be playing. She almost pinches herself to make sure she's not dreaming.

The venue is the most upscale hotel in town. Nathan helps his wife and Helen out of the car, and leaves it with the valet. Helen has to remember not to gape as she looks around the overly bright lobby, with its marble floors and crystal chandeliers. One flight up and they're escorted into the ballroom where the event will take place. The host brings them over to the piano, and Nathan's delighted when he sees it's a Steinway baby grand. The host tells them it's been donated for the evening by Mrs. Forrester of Forrester & Co., the premier piano store in the area. Helen looks at the piano, and is so overwhelmed she feels she might burst into tears.

Nathan and Anne both see Helen's anxious state as they lead her to the bench and help her get seated. Anne lets go of her hand and Nathan indicates he wants Helen to move over. He then takes a seat next to her and says, "Let's do a duet to get warmed up. Do you want to do the Mozart we practiced yesterday?"

Helen nods, and right before they begin Anne leans down and whispers in Nathan's ear, loud enough for Helen to hear, "You just want to get your hands on this Steinway, you can't fool me." They all laugh, and then Helen and Nathan begin to play *Eine Kleine Nachtmusik*. The glorious sound fills the almost empty ballroom to the rafters. The host and staff setting up before the crowds arrive all stop what they're doing and listen, feeling it to be almost sacrilegious to do anything else while this transcendent playing is going on. When they're finished, Nathan and Helen smile and hug, while those around them give resounding applause. Anne has tears in her eyes and says, "I think you're ready." Helen and Nathan just smile, trying to hold back their own tears.

While Helen gets her sheet music ready, Nathan finds a place to store the extra music he's brought along. Reviewing her list of selections one more time, Helen begins with *Rhapsody in Blue* as the cavernous room starts to fill up. At first, she keeps her head down, just focusing on her playing, but as the noise level grows, she starts looking around and is surprised when several people standing or walking close by smile and nod, looking directly at her with appreciation for her playing. This gives her confidence, and smiling back, she continues to play with all her heart.

Brenda, Caroline, and George are walking through the lobby of the hotel at the precise moment Helen starts to play. As they look around, walking slowly to take in the beauty of the lobby, they move slightly aside to allow three people heading towards them plenty of room to get by. The three people are Marlene, Preacher, and Donna, who are coming from meeting with the events director to confirm Preacher's next set of motivational conferences. Brenda and Marlene make eye contact, and Brenda gets a disconcerting feeling, then looks away. Marlene keeps staring and almost bumps into George, who's walking slightly ahead. She looks up at George, mumbling an apology, then looks directly at Brenda again, and says, "I'm sorry." Brenda just looks at her and shrugs, not recognizing her as the woman who stole Vincent's sunglasses out of her purse. As they all walk on, Caroline turns around to see Marlene still staring. "Do you know her?" she asks Brenda.

"No, I don't think so," Brenda replies. "That was really weird though, wasn't it? She said she was sorry, and when I first saw her, I felt strange, but

I don't know why." They both turn around to look again, but Marlene and the others are gone.

Once in the ballroom, Brenda's immediately drawn to the piano music and stops to listen, before she gravitates towards the middle of the crowd. George is looking around for a waiter with a tray of champagne, finally spots one, and motions him over. With champagne flutes in hand, they join a group of people they know, sipping their champagne and getting immersed in the warm feeling of an elegant party. The three of them tend to stay together the first hour or so, then George is pulled aside by some of his movie people, and then it's just Brenda and Caroline.

Several people come over to congratulate Brenda on her magazine exposure and latest art show, while others come to oh and ahh over Caroline's latest trends, which are making big news in the fashion industry. Some say arts and entertainment people that have *made it* are stuck up, egotistical, and arrogant. But when looking around, Brenda feels she's in her element, and that this particular group of people tends to be pretty down to Earth; just talented people who've gotten over the hurdle of making it. She expresses this thought to Caroline, who nods, and they clink glasses in agreement.

They're both by the piano now, and talk about how talented the young woman is who's playing these amazing classical pieces. The composition Helen was playing ends and she looks around, stretches her neck, then starts to play *Ode to Joy*. Brenda's head whips up and she feels such a happiness spread through her as she listens. Those around her stop their conversations or lower their voices, while others start to sway, and the room feels mesmerized under the spell of Helen's playing. When the piece is finished, she gracefully lowers her hands to her lap and takes a deep breath. Caroline excuses herself to use the lady's room, and Brenda heads towards the piano, hoping to catch Helen before she starts another song.

When Helen sees Brenda standing there, she smiles with recognition, somewhat awestruck by actually seeing in person the woman from the magazine standing in front of her. Brenda smiles back, saying, "Your piano playing's superb; you bring every piece alive, and your selections couldn't be better. I've been enjoying you all night long. *Ode to Joy,* I think, is my all- time favorite. Whenever I hear it, I'm brought to tears. Good thing I'm wearing waterproof mascara," she laughs.

Helen laughs too, then says, "*Ode to Joy* is my favorite too. It's impossible really to choose a favorite, there're so many wonderful compositions, and I'm still learning them all."

"For a young woman, you play like you've been doing it since you were born," Brenda tells her. "You truly are an inspiration to listen to."

Helen, feeling suddenly shy, thanks her and says she still has a lot to learn. The two women start talking like old friends, when Nathan comes over with a glass of champagne for Helen. She takes it gratefully and sips after introducing Brenda to Nathan.

"So, you're Helen's teacher? I've so enjoyed listening to her play this evening."

"Isn't she wonderful?" Nathan asks with a smile. "And her playing has nothing to do with having such a great teacher."

They all laugh, and Helen gives him a little nudge, saying, "He's an incredible teacher. I can't thank him enough for all he's done for me, truly."

There's more light banter before Nathan's pulled away by Anne, and it's just Brenda and Helen. They're both appreciating the feeling of meeting someone they have an instant connection with, finding it very uplifting to meet someone they instantly like. Helen eventually mentions Brenda's cover photo with the sunglasses, then goes on to say laughingly, "My dog Ollie actually found a pair of your sunglasses by the edge of our cornfield at the farm. I still have them, the prism painting is beautiful, and there are two sets of initials inside, not just yours."

Brenda stills, feeling an odd mixture of foreboding and disclosure wash over her. "Oh, really?" she asks, suddenly feeling like she's speaking outside of herself. "When was this?"

Helen too feels like this is a pivotal moment and begins telling Brenda about the farm, how Ollie found them half-buried, and then how she saw Brenda's photo on the cover of the magazine, and knew they were a pair she and Vincent had made after reading the article. She holds back from saying more, but gives Brenda a look that tells her there's more, so much more.

Brenda leans in so closely, Helen can smell the champagne on her breath, and putting her hand on Helen's wrist, she asks, "Has your life changed since you found the sunglasses?"

Anyone else would think this was an odd question, maybe even a silly question, but Helen leans back, meets her eyes, and says, "You have no idea."

"Oh, but I do," Brenda answers shaking and nodding her head at the same time.

In the moment it takes for both of them to catch their breath and start to absorb what's happening, Carter's mother Judith comes over, not realizing her timing broke up an amazing occurrence. Judith lightly holds Brenda's arm and says, "Oh, there you are. I've been trying to catch up with you all evening. I was hoping I could meet you at the Gallery tomorrow morning to pick up my painting. I'm so excited, and know exactly where I'm going to put it. My son Carter is coming with me—he wants to meet the artist I've been raving so much about."

Brenda politely holds up a finger to Judith, motioning to give her a minute. She turns to Helen and says, "Do you know where the art gallery is on the corner of 10th and Mason?"

Helen shakes her head, then says, "No, but I'm sure I can find it."

"Please, can you meet me there at noon tomorrow, so we can have lunch?" Then, bending down close, she whispers, "We need to talk."

Helen nods and gives her a shaky smile. "I look forward to it."

As Judith leads Brenda away to continue their conversation, Helen starts playing again. Brenda turns around, and the two women look at each other and nod as if they have the biggest secret in the world between them, because they do.

CHAPTER 43

On the drive home, Nathan and Anne rave about Helen's playing and about how many people mentioned it, and were impressed by it. Helen really appreciates their sounding like the proud parents she never had, and even though she's smiling, she can't stop thinking about the conversation she had with Brenda, and what she'll find out when they meet tomorrow. Her thoughts are all jumbled, and she's torn between being elated and feeling frightened. It's impossible to feel both of these emotions at once, and the effect is just making her more anxious. She knows she's done nothing wrong, yet the look on Brenda's face seemed like maybe she had. Although Brenda seemed happy too… so maybe she's feeling the same mixed-up emotions as well. Around and around her thoughts go, until she becomes aware that Nathan is speaking to her.

"You're awfully quiet back there," he says. "Everything okay?"

"Oh, sorry. Guess I'm just a little tired. It's been some evening. I'm sure I'll remember it the rest of my life." Little do Nathan or Anne know how true this statement is as they nod and start chatting again about how wonderfully Helen performed this evening.

Helen's heart sinks when she sees Jake's truck in the driveway. Nathan asks if he should walk her to her door, and Helen tells him she'll be fine. Anne tells her to call if she needs anything, and Helen uses her key to unlock a front door that's hardly ever locked. She and Nathan exchange a look as she goes inside, locking the door behind her.

Jake's been waiting for her and asks, "Where the hell have you been, all dressed up like that?"

With a big sigh, Helen explains to him about the event and how she played almost the entire evening. He listens with raised eyebrows, looking surprised, as though he's having trouble understanding it all. "I saw my mother today, and she told me you were going to play at the big fancy hotel tonight. I thought she was exaggerating," he says, scratching his head. "You know what I think? I think you've turned into some kind of a witch, or you sold your soul to the devil!"

"What? What are you talking about?" Helen asks, really baffled by what he's saying.

"Well, one day out of the blue you talk about taking piano lessons, and then a few months later you're like some kind of genius or something. That's just not normal, and I don't like it."

"Oh, I see," Helen says slowly. "I can see in a way why you might think that. But I guess I was always meant to play, and I learned quickly. There's nothing weird about that."

"My mother said you're going to leave and become a famous piano player," he blurts out.

"Jake, I'm really tired, and don't feel now is the time to talk about this. We do have some things to talk about. You and I both know there's someone else you'd rather be with, that our relationship has been over for quite some time now, so we'll talk about it later and figure it out. Not now, I'm just too tired." With that, she takes off her shoes and heads off to bed, with even more confusing thoughts than before.

#

Shortly after Helen leaves, Brenda's being driven home by George and Caroline. They're talking about this particular evening's event as being one of the best of its kind they've ever attended. Brenda mentions the piano player, and they all agree her playing was part of what made the evening so special. Caroline then says she saw Brenda talking with the piano player and she asks if she knows her. When Brenda says it was the first time they met, Caroline is surprised, and says that the way they were talking, she was sure they knew each other. Brenda just shakes her head and changes the subject. She too is feeling anxious, like Helen is, but hers is a more sophisticated anxiety. She's lived with the knowledge and history of the sunglasses for years now, and is accustomed to the vast variety of emotions they evoke. She's hoping she can add relief to the spectrum of emotions that have surrounded her since the creation of the glasses—relief in being able to share the story with perhaps the only other person who would believe it, who already knows about the power they have, or at least part of it.

The next morning, after a fitful sleep filled with fragmented dreams, Helen's doing her rounds with Ollie. She was glad to see Jake's truck gone when she got up, giving her more time to think. She's already decided to go see Marian this morning, knowing she'll want to hear all about how the event went. She also wants to find out what she and Jake talked about, and where he came up with thinking she's a witch. Ollie's walking more closely to her than usual, and she wonders if he senses what's going on. Looking down at him, she starts teasing him, telling him it's all his fault for finding the sunglasses. He looks up at her with sad eyes, and she bends down to give him a hug, telling him it will all work out. For the rest of the walk, she puts the sunglasses on, and thinks about how she'll clean and polish them before she leaves to meet Brenda at noon.

Marian is pleased to see her and listens intently to every detail Helen gives her about the cocktail party. She makes Helen give her a blow-by-blow description, complete with every piece and composition she played. After she winds down about the event, Helen asks her what she and Jake talked about, and tells her what Jake said about her being a witch. Marian acts a little embarrassed when Helen says this, and looks away.

"Oh dear," Marian says looking everywhere but at Helen. "All I said was it was as though someone put a spell on you, and all of a sudden you could play piano. That's all I said, and you know how Jake twists things around."

"Well, that was a weird thing to say, don't you think?" Helen asks.

"It's just that I played piano, and it took me years to play as well as you can play. Years and years before I could play for an event like you did last night. I know what it takes to be a piano player. It's hard to understand how you got so good so quickly," Marian says, crossing her arms.

"Oh, I don't know how I do it. Maybe I'm a prodigy or something. But I'm sure as hell not a witch. I've been working really hard at it ever since I learned I had a talent for it."

"I didn't actually say you were a witch. Jake said that. He was all upset at how things were going at home. I asked him if he loved the mistress he has, and I thought his eyes were going to bug out of his head," Marian snorts, and almost laughs.

"What did he say?"

"He turned all red and said Janie, that's her name, was a good woman. I told him that may be so, but he has a good woman at home who needs to be tended to. He just shook his head. The man's confused."

They're both glad to get more out in the open, and Helen shares that she will definitely be leaving once she sees how her job works out and she's able to save some money. She tells Helen she's thought a lot about what to do and feels it's best for everyone if she leaves, but she has to take Ollie with her, and she wants to buy the piano from Marian if she'll let her. Marian just waves her off. Helen's not sure what that means, and decides to address it later.

"To be honest, the only thing besides Ollie and the piano I'm concerned about is who's going to do the books for the farm. We have an accountant, but Jake needs someone who can handle it real-time, to keep the books in order, to manage the money, and make sure he maintains profitability. He can get someone to do a lot of the other things I do; in fact, he can do them himself if he's going to be home more. But he would probably have to hire someone part-time to do the books, someone he trusts."

"Why don't you do it?" Marian asks. "You could still keep up with it in a few hours, maybe two or three times a week. Have Jake pay you, like an employee."

"No, that wouldn't work," Helen says dismissively.

The two women discuss the idea further, and Helen finally agrees that maybe it *could* work. She'll discuss it with Jake; that now, she wants to start getting paid for keeping the books. She'll explain to Jake how this will allow them to see how much time it actually takes per week, and also help her to save more towards getting an apartment. She bears no ill will towards Jake, and she'll tell him so. Maybe they can work this out peacefully. Realizing the time, Helen tells Marian she needs to go, and thanks her for her understanding and support. As she's heading out the door, Marian tells her not to worry about the piano, and waves her out.

During the time she spent with Marian, she hardly thought at all about Brenda, but now that she's on her way to meet her, she's starting to get nervous all over again. She checks the time, then looks at her directions, and figures she'll actually get there a few minutes early. That's good; it will give her a chance to find the place, a good parking spot, and to gather her thoughts. Driving through town, she spots the Gallery and circles the block, looking for a parking space. To her surprise, she finds one easily. Turning off the ignition. she takes several deep breaths, checks her reflection in the rear-view mirror, and takes out the sunglasses. She previously cleaned and polished them to a shine, and now she examines them closely, taking in every detail, appreciating their familiarity. They feel warm in her hand, purposeful, and she realizes how much she loves them. Putting them on one last time before going in to meet Brenda, she feels almost as though the glasses are loving her back, as if they know the intensity of her appreciation. She kisses the frames and puts them back in her purse, then gets out of her car.

Walking slowly towards the Gallery, she notices the other shops in the area and considers coming back sometime, when she's not on a mission, as she's never been in this part of town to shop. Looking towards the doorway, she sees a middle-aged, well-dressed woman with a young man coming out of the Gallery. The young man is carefully carrying a wrapped painting. The woman looks familiar, and Helen realizes she's the woman who interrupted the conversation she was having with Brenda at the piano last night.

Almost upon them, Judith looks up and says, "Oh, hello, good to see you again. I'm Judith—do you remember me from last night?"

"Yes, hello. Nice to see you. Looks like you've bought a painting. Is it one of Brenda's?"

"Yes! I'm so excited—the painting is fantastic, and I know just where I'm going to hang it," Judith answers.

Carter gently lowers the painting to lean on his leg, and puts his free hand out. "Hi, I'm the dutiful son Carter."

Helen takes his hand, introducing herself, while Judith apologizes for her bad manners in not introducing them. Carter isn't listening to his mother's babbling; he's too focused on the beautiful young woman in front of him. "My mother raved about your playing last night," he says, smiling.

"Oh yes," Judith says. "I'm so glad we ran into you. I wanted to give you my card and get your information, unless you'd rather I go through Nathan. I'd like to have you play at other events coming up if you're available. Some of them are for charity, but there are others that would be glad to pay for someone of your caliber."

Helen takes her card, and blushes when she sees Carter still staring at her. "Going through Nathan would be fine. Thank you, that would be great," she says, smiling. "I have an appointment now with Brenda, though, so I need to get going. Thanks again, and I'll look forward to hearing from you." Carter is still smiling at her, and she nods to him before going through the door.

Brenda's by the door waiting for her, and when Helen approaches, she takes both of her hands, then pulls her into a hug. Helen's a little taken aback by this but doesn't resist, and finds the embrace to be warm and loving. After they exchange pleasantries, talk about where they're going for lunch, and dance around every subject except what they really need to talk about, Brenda asks, "Do you know Judith and her son Carter?"

"Why no, I don't. I mean, well, now I sort of do. I remember Judith from last night, and she just asked me if I'd be interested in playing at more events. Of course I'm interested, and she gave me her card. I've never met her son Carter before, though he seems like a nice guy."

Brenda lowers her voice and says, "The most extraordinary thing just happened, and I'm still trying to process it. Judith brought Carter because he wanted to meet me. As it turns out, he bought a pair of my sunglasses at a flea market a couple of years ago, and he really liked them, considered them a prized possession. He knew I hand-painted them, as his mother had purchased a custom pair a few years prior to that, and he wanted to meet me, tell me a story about the sunglasses. He lost them when he was skydiving! They came off while he was on a skydive and he had to save someone who passed out. He doesn't remember exactly when they came off, but he told me the whole story. He saved one of the other jumper's lives during that skydive, and even afterwards, when he hit the ground, after falling through a tree. What makes it even more fascinating is, he knew how to keep the guy alive while they were waiting for help. He did things someone without medical training wouldn't know how to do. He saved the guy's life!"

"That's remarkable," Helen says. "Did you ask him what the sunglasses looked like?" she asks anxiously.

"He said they had a miniature prism painted on them and two sets of initials on the inside of the temple piece," Brenda replies, watching Helen closely for her reaction.

Helen gasps and turns pale. “Did you ask him what you asked me last night? Did you ask him if his life had changed since he bought them at the flea market?”

“I didn’t have to. His story already gave me the answer.”

Helen reaches into her bag and pulls out the sunglasses. With shaking hands, she holds them up. Now it’s Brenda’s turn to gasp as she reaches out to take them.

CHAPTER 44

Brenda can't believe she's holding Vincent's sunglasses again. They feel electric in her hands, and she bursts into tears. Helen's alarmed at her reaction, and reaches out to hug her. Brenda awkwardly holds the sunglasses to her chest as she lets Helen hold her, apologizing through her tears, trying to get a handle on her emotions.

"It's okay, it's okay," Helen says patting her back. "Here, let me get you a glass of water."

Brenda shakes her head, finally able to speak. "Let me just freshen up in the restroom here and then we can go to lunch." Helen nods, letting her go, and stands there looking around. After a few minutes, she realizes Brenda may be a while, so she starts wandering around the Gallery. More than half of the paintings on display are Brenda's, and Helen's fascinated by what she sees. Mesmerized, she stands in front of a desert painting, feeling as though she's there, inside the painting, when Brenda touches her arm, letting her know she's back.

Helen jumps a little and Brenda smiles, telling her she didn't mean to startle her. "Oh, no problem. I was just immersed in your painting here. It's really wonderful. Hard to describe—so lifelike, yet otherworldly, making it almost more than three-dimensional. Does that make sense?"

Brenda laughs and says, "That pretty much sums it up."

They decide to walk to a cafe that's only four blocks away. Neither woman speaks as they walk in companionable silence, each lost in her own thoughts. Once seated in the back, they peruse the menu, making small talk. Once they've ordered and gotten their drinks, Brenda takes the sunglasses out of her purse and says, "Helen, you start. Please tell me everything that's happened since your dog found these sunglasses. Then I'll tell you from the beginning an amazing story that will help *you* make sense of everything that's happened to you. Please understand that what I reveal to you I've never told another soul, and we must promise each other that what's said here today will never be revealed to another. I also have to tell you what an amazing relief this is for me. Once you hear my story, you'll understand that, too."

Helen looks at her with eyes as wide as saucers, listening carefully to every word. She can't believe this is happening, and yet she always knew there was so much more to everything that occurred this past year. Nodding, she takes a deep breath and begins. "It's hard to just start with the exact time when Ollie found the glasses, because so much about me from before the sunglasses has been affected. Do you know what I mean?"

"Yes, of course. That's the way it works. Cause and effect; for every action there is an equal and opposite reaction. I understand. So just tell it however you want to." Brenda waits patiently for Helen to gather her thoughts.

She tells Brenda first about being born prematurely, her childhood, and the guilt she grew up with. Then about the commune, her best friend dying after being taken advantage of by the leader, then her getting pregnant and leaving with Jake. Through tears, she talks about losing the baby, and then moves on to her lonely life on the farm. When she gets to the day that Ollie found the sunglasses, her whole demeanor changes, and Brenda can hear the hopefulness that crept into her life from that moment on.

"Things actually started to look differently from the moment I first put them on. I could literally see more clearly, besides being able to *feel* more clearly. Like how I was used to seeing my life from within was all blurry, but with the glasses, things started coming into focus. Then one time

I had them on while driving, and trees and cars started to change shape and got enormous. That scared me, and I took them off right away. My vision cleared after a couple of minutes, but I thought maybe I was having a stroke or something. But I was fine. It was like everything shifted, and I was being taken along on the ride."

She goes on to tell Brenda about how she loved listening to the radio, especially classical music, but had to do it when Jake wasn't around because he disliked music. She explained about the musical anhedonia that his mother had told her about, and that his father had it too. She told her about Jake's mother and that her piano is in their living room, and she promised her she'd get it tuned. "I don't know why I promised her to get it tuned that day. I knew she would never be able to leave the home and play it, and I didn't know how to play then. I guess I felt it would make her happy. Well, that day, after I got back from seeing her, I was walking the farm with Ollie and I had the sunglasses on. The first couple of times it happened I just got kind of a feeling like a little *blip*, but this time it was more like a BAM. It felt like something was streaming into my eyes, right into my brain. I think I went into a trance or something, because I started to see my whole life flash before me, and I was watching it all unfold, just like a movie. That's when everything really started to change."

Brenda's listening intently and nodding at certain points, like she understands exactly what Helen is explaining. She doesn't interrupt until the server brings their food and has left. "When you got the big BAM, as you called it, is that when you attributed what was happening to the sunglasses?"

"Not really. At first, I thought I was losing my mind, but then I saw the magazine with your picture on the cover and the sunglasses you had on. For some reason I felt connected to you, even though I didn't know you. I kept wearing the sunglasses outside and looking around, trying to make it happen again, but it didn't. The real change was after the piano tuner came to tune Marian's piano. I told you I love listening to classical music, and I had the radio on after the tuner left. The piano was still open, and I had played some scales he had me do to make sure I was satisfied. I can't remember which composition was playing, but I started listening closely, really intently, and all of sudden my hands were on the keys and I started playing along. Some force was working through my hands, but I felt it was coming from me as well. It's hard to explain."

Brenda nods knowingly and says, "Something similar happened with my painting. I understand exactly what you mean. Go on, please continue."

"So I started playing when Jake wasn't around, and realized I could play by ear, but could barely play the simplest song if I wasn't hearing it. I realized I needed some help with it and wanted to start taking piano lessons, but knew Jake wouldn't go along with it. I had another one of those *blip* things later when I was walking with Ollie, but nothing like the one that put me in a trance. I knew I was on the brink of something incredible, and that it was unheard of to be able to one day just be able to play piano when I couldn't before. And it wasn't just simple songs I could play. It was complicated pieces, as long as I could play by ear. Your cover photo kept coming to mind, and several times I started to read the article, but never finished it until much later."

Helen goes on to tell her about going to see Marian at the home, telling her about getting the piano tuned, and how delighted she was; then finally convincing Jake, with Marian's help, to take piano lessons. Sadly, she tells about how her marriage deteriorated even more as her independence grew. But her face lights up when she talks about her first meeting with Nathan, and how quickly he assessed her talent, realizing it was somewhat of a miracle, but knowing she needed to learn to read music in order to develop it further. She said Nathan was puzzled and almost suspicious that she wasn't telling him the whole story of her sudden talent, but he didn't press further.

By now their food is cold and the two women sit looking at each other, breathing deeply, letting it sink in.

Brenda reaches across the table, takes Helen's hand, and says, "I'm beyond thrilled we found each other. I can't find the words to express how important this is to me. No one would believe us except for Vincent. I think this is what he wanted, and that it's making him very happy."

"Oh, I'm not sure I understand. I thought Vincent died several years ago, when he was at the height of his career. I'm sorry," Helen says with a look of confusion.

"I think maybe it's my turn to tell you more of our story, and then my story after Vincent died. From reading the article, you have an idea of the events of my life, but not the life of the sunglasses and their cause and effect."

Brenda tells Helen how she and Vincent met in college, she an art student and Vincent a year ahead of her, studying optical engineering. She backtracks a little, telling Helen a little about her childhood and never truly feeling loved by her parents. She then goes on to tell her about how they decided to celebrate Vincent's graduation, and their new summer jobs, by taking a road trip and spending the night in the desert. "It was Vincent's idea; it sounded like a fun idea, and we wanted to celebrate. We were so happy, and everything was going our way. Besides getting a job at the art gallery, I was also selling hand-painted sunglasses at the flea market. I think the article talked about that. Anyway, when we got to the camping area, we set up our tent, and then Vincent took out some psilocybin mushrooms. Do you know what they are?"

Helen nods and says, "I think they're like a drug the Indians took, right?"

"Yes, a hallucinogen. There's a lot to it. I remember being hesitant to take it, but we ended up spending the night in the desert high on these mushrooms. It was really incredible how everything looked, and I'll never forget the alternate reality they took us to." She stops for a breath and to see Helen's reaction, but Helen just nods, so Brenda continues. "That night I felt like I did an emotional purging, and afterwards my painting was different, more… *something*. It's hard to describe, but after that night I became a true artist. For Vincent it was different; he actually made a connection with some kind of higher source. I don't know how else to describe it short of calling it

God. Vincent called it the *Universal Mind*. He was given information, real, tangible information in the image of formulas, that he was able to write down. These formulas went on to be the basis of his work, his creations that made a difference in the world, his award-winning achievements."

"Wow. That's incredible, but I'm confused. Did he have sunglasses with him when this happened?" Helen asks.

"No, Vincent was an optical engineer. He didn't create the sunglasses until much later. He wanted to recreate what happened in the desert when we were on the mushrooms. He felt he could do it through optics, specific light, filtering. He wanted to be able to experience accessing the *Universal Mind* at will, and to perhaps allow others this gift. I can understand, in a way, his wanting to do this, but he got obsessed with it. It made me uncomfortable and gave me a feeling we shouldn't be trying to alter fate, or control destiny, or dabble in something we weren't meant to. I didn't realize until much later how intensely he was working on it. Then, finally, he succeeded, but didn't tell me about it right away. Instead, he brought home a beautiful pair of sunglasses in a sturdy frame, and specially designed lenses. By then I was well established in my sunglasses business, with me painting and initialing the finished product, and Vincent making the lenses to order. He told me about this new pair he made for himself, and asked me to do a miniature painting of a prism, with a spectrum of colored light, and to put *both* of our initials on the inside frame. I thought it was a great idea, and I did the painting; and when it was dry, I tried them on in front of the mirror, to see how they looked. The sunlight from outside bounced off the mirror directly into my eyes, and I got that BAM thing you talked about."

"Oh my God, is the pair Ollie found the same sunglasses?"

"Yes," Brenda says. "Incredible as it sounds, it's the same pair, the ones he made for himself that I painted, not knowing what they were capable of. That same afternoon, before I could talk with Vincent about what happened, I was inspired to do a painting like I'd never done before. It was dark and awful, and hurt to look at it. But when I finished, I felt like a new person. All my pain and suffering from my childhood, all the hurt I had bottled up for years, was splashed on that canvas, like a spread of poisonous vomit. That was my first experience with the way the sunglasses affected me. After that, my painting evolved quickly to masterful status, and I still had bouts of emotional purging.

"As far as Vincent went, he continued to try accessing the *Universal Mind* through the glasses, and I honestly don't know how much he was able to, or how much more he learned. I do know he went on to make breakthroughs and discoveries in his field that were happening faster than his colleagues could keep up with. We were happy; our relationship was good. We were both doing work that we loved, that we thought was making a difference." Here Brenda's voice changes, and she says, starting to break down, "But then he died." The tears start flowing, and she tries to stifle her sobs. Helen gets up and sits next to her, putting her arm around her. The server walks by, knowing enough not to bother them now. She asks if everything is all right, if she can bring them anything. Helen shakes her head no, and asks that she clear their plates and bring them some coffee.

Once they get their coffee, Helen tells Brenda it's okay if she doesn't want to continue, but Brenda indicates that she does. "As you can imagine, I was a wreck. My friends are the ones who got me through it. My work and my friends. I continued to make the sunglasses, with a colleague of Vincent's doing the lenses. I continued painting, and was pleased to see my work was still good, almost as good as it was before Vincent died. I was also still using the sunglasses every chance I got, trying to access the *Universal Mind,* trying to see if I could use them to see Vincent again. Amazingly, I still was getting *blips* now and then; these helped to keep me going as well. Then I started having dreams after I would get a *blip,* and Vincent would be there talking with me. I also started drinking heavily, and my friends were worried about me."

"One night while I was still a mess, still grieving, still drinking too much, I met my friend Sarah, she was my college roommate, for a drink. She was in town and we always got together whenever we could. As soon as I got there, I started slamming down the drinks. I remember her telling me to slow down, and the worried look on her face. When she had to leave, she made the bartender promise to put me in a taxi to get home. I can't remember much after she left, except talking to a woman at the bar, before I got into the cab. The next morning, I was so hungover I didn't realize the sunglasses were gone until later. I don't know if they fell out, or I lost them, or they were stolen. I just don't know. All I know is that they were gone, and I was devastated. I fell into a funk. They were all I had left of Vincent, and now that was gone too."

"Oh, that's terrible," Helen says with tears in her eyes. "No one should have to endure something like that, and then not be able to tell anyone what happened. It's amazing you didn't lose your mind."

"I almost did," Brenda continues. "But my friends Sarah and Caroline saved me. They insisted I take a yoga and meditation class with them. The first time I meditated deeply I saw Vincent again. I can tell by the way you're looking at me that's hard to believe. But it's true. I still see him sometimes when I meditate. Vincent gives me messages; he even told me about you."

"Really? What did he say?"

"His messages are cryptic, but he did tell me, he said, 'This one knows. She'll find you.' And even before you, I knew somehow when the sunglasses changed hands. I would get a feeling, a shift in the energy around me. I think that's what I felt when you discovered you could play piano. Sometimes Vincent will give me a message, telling me something's happening. But I never knew who or where or how many times the glasses have affected someone's life. Until now, that is."

The two women sit spellbound with the knowledge of all that's been revealed, finally, silent and out of words for now. The cafe has long since emptied out from the lunch crowd, and their server is sitting a few tables over counting her tips. Brenda realizes she's probably waiting for them to leave before she can go home, so she signals for the check. They thank her for allowing them to sit for so long, and Brenda hands her a very generous tip.

Once outside, they're not sure what to do with themselves. Helen speaks first, telling Brenda this has probably been one of the most enlightening days of her life. Brenda nods in agreement and reaches out to give Helen a long embrace. They exchange information and promise to be in touch soon. They have so much more to talk about.

Driving home, Helen is deep in thought, going over their conversation piece by piece, trying to digest it all. Brenda too is deep in thought, but also feeling elated and relieved to, at last, have someone else know and understand about her life, about the sunglasses. She then realizes she has them in her purse and almost thinks to put them on. But it's getting dark out, almost civil twilight. She then thinks maybe she should give them back to Helen. At that precise moment, Helen wishes she'd had a chance to wear the sunglasses one last time.

CHAPTER 45

Both Brenda and Helen have a lot to think about after their revealing talk at lunch. If anyone else had been privy to their conversation they would have thought they were nuts, or maybe from another planet. This is what Helen's thinking two days later on her rounds with Ollie. She's talking out loud to him, telling him the entire story, and he appears to be listening. But only intermittently, getting distracted by the usual stuff dogs get distracted by when walking outdoors. Some of what Brenda told her, if she thinks logically, seems impossible. Then again, a lot of what's happened to her seems impossible. She watches Ollie, who accepts everything around him without question, as though everything is as it should be, and she decides this is probably the best way for her to look at things too. *Sometimes the animals really do know more than us,* she laughs to herself. Ollie turns around to look at her as though he agrees, and she bursts out laughing. What a wonderful life this is.

#

The same time Helen's coming to these inspiring conclusions, Brenda's looking at the sunglasses and missing Vincent terribly. She thought for sure that once she got the glasses back, she'd be able to access the *Universal Mind* and Vincent almost at will. Instead, the exact opposite has happened. She's worn the sunglasses almost nonstop since she got them back, and nothing happens except for the clarity of vision they've always provided. She finds it interesting she can wear them indoors, and even while she's painting, but she hasn't gotten even a *blip*, not even in direct sun or light bouncing off the mirror. What's worse is that she hasn't been able to see Vincent in her dreams or summon him during meditation. Examining the glasses closely, she thinks maybe she should give them back to Helen; maybe that's why she's no longer seeing Vincent. They never actually discussed which of them should keep the sunglasses, yet Brenda definitely got the feeling Helen wanted her to have them, especially after hearing her story. *Or maybe I just assumed that's what she thinks; I never even asked her.* She reaches for the phone to call Helen, to ask if she wants to meet again. They still have a lot to talk about, and Brenda really likes her. She feels a connection with Helen, and knows they're building what will be a long- lasting friendship.

#

Helen's just come inside when she hears the phone ringing. She already knows it's Brenda calling, and gets a warm feeling as she picks up the phone. They both say how they've been thinking of each other and agree to meet on the weekend, since Helen has a lot to do before she starts her new job the following week. Brenda's disappointed, as she was hoping they would be able to meet sooner, but doesn't express it. She just agrees and they hang up, both looking forward to their next encounter. *Maybe now,* Brenda thinks, *maybe now I should meditate and see what happens.*

#

Both women are busy the next couple of days, but never too busy to stop thinking about each other, the sunglasses, and all that's transpired. The difference is that Helen's been happier and has stopped feeling as though she *needs* the glasses. Brenda seems happy enough, relatively speaking, but has become obsessed with reaching Vincent. Even though she's sure he somehow knows she has the glasses back, she's craving a message, some kind of confirmation. Before her last yoga class, she heard two women talking, and one seemed to be giving advice to the other. The only thing she remembers about the conversation she overheard was the one woman saying, "Don't push the river." She's heard this expression previously, and thinks about it a lot during the class. While driving home with the sunglasses on, it comes to her what it really means, and she thinks maybe the message is for her.

At last it's the weekend, and time for the two women to meet in the town park. It seemed like a good idea to spend time together outdoors, and it's about equidistant for both of them. The morning starts out sunny, but by noon some clouds are accumulating. Rain isn't in the forecast, but it's always hard to predict this time of year. Helen offered to bring some sandwiches and drinks, and they meet by the picnic tables in the center of the park. It's such a beautiful area, full of trees and several paths for walking. Some of the tables are shaded by trees and others are out in the sunlight.

Their embrace upon seeing each other is long and heartfelt. There's already a strong sense of camaraderie, even though they hardly know each other on the surface; yet the depth of their connection is indescribable. The sunglasses aren't brought up by either of them; instead they speak about their personal lives, their concerns, and their creative endeavors. Helen's delighted that Judith contacted Nathan for another upcoming event, and she's actually going to be paid for this one. She proudly tells Brenda that Nathan said there will come a time when the student surpasses the teacher. She shyly says this won't happen any time soon, and laughs. Brenda talks about how she sold two more paintings, and the Gallery is asking for more. She's not sure, but thinks there's something in the air. They both laugh at that comment knowingly, and thoroughly enjoy their time together.

As time tends to do, it goes too quickly, and Helen has another place she needs to be. Brenda takes the sunglasses out and hands them to Helen. "Oh, thank you. I just wanted to hold them again," she says. "I just wanted to feel them one more time." She puts them on, looks around, takes them off, and gives them a big kiss. This makes both of them laugh until the tears are rolling down their faces. Between breaths, Helen says, "That's not the first time that I've kissed them, you know!" and this starts a new wave of laughter that goes on until their sides ache. Finally, they stop laughing, and Brenda hiccups. This makes them chuckle, then they grow silent.

"I can't thank you enough for everything," Helen says with tears in her eyes. "I wish I had known Vincent. I hope somehow, he knows how much my life's changed because of him." She hands the sunglasses back to Brenda and thanks here again.

Brenda takes the glasses and says, "Do you feel you're meant to keep them? Please tell me the truth."

Helen looks up, surprised and says, "No. From the minute you asked me at the cocktail party if my life had changed since Ollie found the glasses, I knew they were yours. After thinking about it for a few days now, I feel I was meant to have them, but that they were sort of on loan. Do you know what I mean? A life-changing gift."

Brenda looks down at the glasses in her hand and nods thoughtfully. Instead of answering, she hugs Helen tightly and says, "I'm so very grateful our paths have crossed. I'm sure now we'll be walking our paths together a lot more. Please call and tell me how your new job goes, and the other stuff you're dealing with."

Helen gathers up her things, gives Brenda one more hug, and hurries off to where her car is parked. Brenda needs to put more thought into some emotions she's feeling unsettled about, and decides to walk along the treelined path before heading home. She realizes it's been years since she's walked this path, and finds herself feeling calmer, as her thoughts settle more easily and become less confusing. She stops frequently to look around, enjoying the sound of the rustling trees and chirping birds. She's not sure how much time has passed when she notices it's become quite overcast, and she can see through the trees how the clouds have grown dark and heavy. It becomes very quiet, and she notices the birds have stopped chirping, and now the treetops are swaying back and forth.

Brenda starts to hurry back to her car, hoping to get there before the rain starts, when she realizes how far she's walked. She's going as quickly as she can, and curses the impractical shoes she's worn, when a roll of thunder rumbles closer than she feels comfortable with. For the first time she realizes she's alone on this path, and she's not sure how much farther she needs to go. Again, there's a lightning bolt shooting down, a huge flash right in front of her face, and a simultaneous earth-shaking boom of thunder. Oh, the pain! Like being hit on her head with a mallet! Then she's melting from the inside out, stinging with a thousand needles as the shock goes through her body. Paralyzed, she's thrown to the ground; her shoes fly off, the sunglasses airborne as they're loosened from her grip.

#

While Brenda lies unconscious on the ground, Jerry and David are watching the lightening in awe, congratulating themselves for delaying their run until the clouds cleared. They usually run together on weekend mornings, but were delayed due to helping a friend move into a new apartment. The move took longer than they expected, and when they finally got back to Jerry's house, the clouds started accumulating quickly, and with the wind picking up, they decided to wait until the squall passed.

Getting impatient, Jerry points out the break in the clouds, and they watch as the sky turns bright blue, the clouds disperse, and the sun glimmers with that after-storm radiance. "Let's go," Jerry says as they lace up their running shoes. "This is the perfect time, and we still have a couple hours until dark."

"I'm right behind you," David says as they take off down the steps. They run companionably for the mile it takes to get to the park. Jerry veers off, racing ahead, and David follows him down the tree-lined path, savoring the freshness in the air. Once on the path, it's cooler, not as bright, and they start to set a comfortable pace. They don't speak, enjoying getting into the zone until they're almost on automatic. David sees it first as they come around the bend. "What's that up ahead?" he asks as they get closer.

"Don't know," Jerry says. "Ugh! Looks like a person!"

"Jesus! She looks like she's dead. Oh God, turn her over, she's unconscious. Look at her hair—her wrist looks burned. I feel a slight pulse. Jesus, I think she's been hit by lightning. But she's still alive; get back," David says as he starts to give Brenda CPR. In between, he yells at Jerry to go get some help; there's a gas station at the edge of the park. Jerry takes off running faster than he ever has in his life, as David continues giving CPR.

"Don't die on me, I know you're in there," he says quietly over and over again. "Don't die on me. I know you're in there. You're going to make it. Come on, breathe, keep breathing." He stops to feel her pulse, and refuses to believe there isn't one when he doesn't feel it any longer. "Please, please don't give up."

Brenda's watching the frantic young man from above, feeling sorry he's so distraught. She sees herself lying there and realizes she doesn't hurt anymore. She gazes curiously, enjoying the floating sensation, when a voice tells her to go back. She must go back, *it's not time to leave yet, you have much to do*. She's not sure she wants to go back to her body, but she obeys.

David keeps up with the CPR, stopping periodically to feel her pulse. She doesn't wake up and he's becoming frantic, a surge of panic almost bringing him to tears. "You can wake up now," he tells her, "you're good now, I know you can hear me." He takes his shirt off and puts it under her head and continues the CPR, hoping an ambulance will arrive soon. He hears a slight intake of breath, and feels her pulse again. With renewed faith, he continues the CPR, talking continuously, as much for himself as for her.

Finally, he hears the sirens in the distance, and almost shouts with relief when he sees the lights, and the ambulance careening over the grass towards the path. The ambulance can't get through the trees, but he sees Jerry jump out and lead two attendants towards where he and Brenda are on the ground. They have a stretcher, and one of the attendants pushes David aside to see Brenda's condition. "She's breathing, still has a pulse, but it's really faint," he tells the other rescue worker.

"I've been giving her CPR," David says. "I hope that was the right thing to do."

“Perfect thing, buddy,” he nods towards David. “Hey, Kevin, get that stretcher over here.”

With Brenda being attended to, the ambulance takes off. Jerry and David look at each other and blow out a big sigh. “Man, I hope she’s all right. She was really gone, really out. Thank God we got here when we did. That was awesome the way you gave her CPR,” Jerry says.

“I had to take a course before my lifeguard job that summer when we were still in college. I honestly never thought I would have to use it. I felt like I lost her there for a minute. I’m feeling a little shaky—the adrenaline, you know?”

“Yeah, man. Let’s go back to my house. Then we can call the hospital and see how she’s doing.”

“Okay,” David says as he starts to follow Jerry. Out of the corner of his eye, he sees something wedged up again the tree closest to the path. He bends down to see what it is. Huh, it’s a pair of sunglasses. He picks them up, sticks them in his running pants without really looking at them, and takes off after Jerry, feeling that strange feeling one gets after a traumatic experience.

CHAPTER 46

Helen found out from Nathan, who found out from Judith. That woman seems to know what's going on even before the news vans show up. Caroline also found out from Judith, who then told Sarah, who then told Brenda's parents. Brenda's lightning strike also made the papers, and David, the jogger who gave her CPR until the ambulance arrived, is being called a hero. His running mate is a secondary hero for running, literally, for help. Now, if only Brenda would regain consciousness.

She's been checked from head to toe, and her condition has been upgraded from fair to good. Her heart was weak but has since regained almost normal functionality, still being carefully monitored. All of her vital signs appear to be good, although they have no way of knowing how long her heart may have stopped, and how it will affect her brain function. The doctors know she's in there; they're almost certain she can hear what's going on around her. They just don't know how she's interpreting what's going on around her, and they don't know when she'll wake up. They're optimistic, but not willing to make any predictions.

Brenda's parents are coming out of her room, where Helen is waiting for her turn to sit with Brenda. She feels funny knowing so much about them from what Brenda's told her, and has to keep herself from staring. They know nothing about Helen; they don't even know she exists, so she looks away and waits for them to pass. Brenda's mother glances at Helen and dismisses her quickly. Then goes back to talking with her husband. "You would think after three days she would wake up, wouldn't you? I feel silly talking to her, babbling on when I don't think she can hear me. How long do you think we're expected to stay here?" Brenda's father doesn't answer, barely shrugs as she continues talking as though Brenda being in a coma is an inconvenience.

Poor Brenda, Helen thinks as she pushes past them, closing the door behind her. *Brenda's parents would get along great with mine. They would have a lot in common and not even know it*, she thinks grimly. "Hey, beautiful," Helen says brightly when she sees Brenda. "I've brought you something I know you'll like. I wanted to bring it yesterday, but had to put more music on it. I borrowed this recorder from Nathan; he has amazing pieces recorded he uses for teaching, and the sound is surprisingly good. We're going to start with your favorite. Here, listen."

Ode to Joy begins to play, and Helen watches Brenda closely. The only movement is her breathing, but somehow Helen knows Brenda can hear it. She reaches for Brenda's hand and asks her if she can give a squeeze or any little sign to let her know she can hear her, hear the music. But she doesn't; she just continues breathing steadily. Helen kisses her on the forehead when the piece ends, then turns the volume down so she can talk.

"So, I'm sure you want to know what's going on at the farm, and I have a lot of interesting news. But first, I have to tell you that everyone is rooting for you; you have so much to come back to, and we all love you. But you know that already, right?" Helen hears the catch in her voice and swallows hard, trying to make her voice sound normal, upbeat.

She tells Brenda that so far, she really likes her job, and her boss is really nice. He's been so flexible in working with her on the schedule, and told her he likes how she's been organizing the office. When she's there she works really hard, and finds she knows a lot of what needs to be done. When she has questions she asks, and she's been stopping at the library to get books on accounting. She's thinking about going back to school part-time.

Taking a breath, she talks about how her music is progressing, and that Marian said she could have the piano. Helen also tells Brenda she's been to the Gallery, and another of her paintings has been sold, and they're waiting for her to wake up before allowing the purchaser to take it. On and on she talks, often holding Brenda's hand, until a nurse comes in and tells her she needs to leave; Brenda needs a break.

I can hear you, I'm in here. I'm stuck, I can't move, but I can feel you. I heard the music. Please come back, don't go, Brenda thinks as she hears the door close. *This is so strange. How did I get stuck in here?* Brenda's agitated, but there are no visible outward signs of her agitation. She wishes Helen knew she could feel her holding her hand. *How can I tell anyone about this strange world I'm in? I don't think I like it in here; I want to get out, please.*

That evening, Brenda has a period of calm when no one is in her room. No nurses, no visitors, and everything is quiet except for the low beeping of machines. Out of nothingness, Vincent materializes and walks slowly towards Brenda. He's wearing a flowing blue robe and is smiling. Brenda wonders how he got in here, into this strange world she's inhabiting, when no one else seems to be able to get in. He embraces her, and it feels like she's being slowly lowered into a warm bath of the perfect temperature. He finally speaks, telling her she'll be able to leave soon, to return to the life she knew before she got struck by lightning. He tells her she's almost ready; all she needs to know is that she must do it on her own. Everything thereafter will be better.

Caroline and George are visiting Brenda now, and they're on either side of her, holding her hands. Brenda knows they're there and hears their voices, but she's not really listening to what they're saying. The word *sunglasses* comes to mind, and *painting,* but she's somewhere else today, and is tired of trying to get out. It takes such great effort, and she doesn't have the energy. She can't move, and wonders if she's in a straitjacket. Others come and speak with her, and she remembers Sarah telling her she loves her. *I love you too, Sarah. Can you help me with this straitjacket, please?* The rest of the day goes by timelessly. She feels her favorite nurse, the only one who ever tells her exactly what she's doing and why, come in and attend to her.

Once again, when the quiet period of calm descends, Vincent arrives, and he's carrying a black canvas bag. *You should be ready to leave soon,* he tells her. *But before you go you must put all the hurt, fear, and all that's holding you back into this sack. You will leave all of that behind; you must go back without it. You still have work to do, beauty to create. Others are waiting for you. I'll help you when you're ready.* With that he's gone, and Brenda's confused, still feeling trapped.

Brenda's focus gradually becomes less obscured, and she looks at the bag Vincent left behind. His words begin to make sense, and she tries to bend down to pick up the sack. Her body is stiff, but she feels if she could bend, she could reach it, and she tries again.

At the precise moment Brenda's hand reaches the bag in the world she now occupies, her favorite nurse is by her bedside, checking her vitals. For a split second, the nurse thinks she sees Brenda's hand twitch, ever so slightly. She waits and watches, but there's no other movement. She starts speaking with Brenda, asking her if she moved her hand, if she's ready to wake up. Encouraging her, telling her they're all there waiting for her.

Brenda hears her but doesn't concentrate on the words; she's too fixated on the uplifting sensation caused by the release of the blackness Vincent told her to discard. The bag fills quickly, then comes close to overflowing, and Brenda looks around, wondering what to do if it overflows and she can't close the bag. Eventually, the contents settle, and she reaches to close the bag; it takes more effort than she thinks she's capable of, but she finally does it. Vincent materializes and starts hauling it away. *Don't worry,* he tells her. *I'll always be with you.* With that, he's gone again and Brenda waits, knowing she can't leave yet.

The nurse now has confirmation that Brenda may be starting to wake up, as she definitely saw hand movement at the exact time Brenda was filling the bag with all that was holding her back. She runs to find a doctor and they stand vigil, waiting for more movement or for something else to happen. After waiting a while, with the doctor coming and going, and the nurse remaining stationary, nothing's happened. Eventually the doctor says, "Well, we'll just have to wait and see." The nurse finishes her shift and goes home.

The sun rises, the hospital buzzes with activity, and Brenda drifts in and out of awareness. She senses visitors come and go from her room, hears voices and footsteps. The difference today is that she doesn't feel panic or fear; she just is, waiting in her patient state of is-ness. As before, when the quiet period descends, Vincent materializes in his flowing blue robe, and this time he's wearing boots. "Are you almost ready to go?" he asks Brenda. She nods, and he tells her to put her shoes on. She hesitates, trying to move her head as if looking around. "We don't have our sunglasses; I need them," she tells him. Vincent shakes his head, and tells her it's fine to let the sunglasses go. "They're not for you anymore. Let them go." Brenda trusts Vincent, and nods her acquiescence. She bends as if to find her shoes, and the last thing she hears him say is, "There *is* another pair."

Brenda's favorite nurse is beside herself. Brenda's moving her head, really moving her head. She's mumbling as if trying to speak, and now her feet are moving. She runs to get a doctor and they continue to watch and speak to Brenda as she slowly opens her eyes. She appears to be agitated and confused at first, but by now there're several medical staff attending to her. Brenda's given the best care the hospital has to offer, and without further resistance, surrenders herself to that care, gradually letting it sink in that it will all be better now.

#

It's over a week before Brenda is fully aware of what had happened to her, and where she is at the moment. She's put through a battery of tests, and the doctors are amazed at how well she's recovering. They're able to confirm that they've found no signs of any brain damage, and she has full use of her arms and legs, although she's still weak and starting to undergo physical therapy. Amazingly, her heart shows no permanent damage, although they continue to carefully monitor her.

Brenda still has so many visitors, and today Helen's excitedly telling her about the two- family house she'll be renting half of. One of Nathan's students is living in the two-family house and his father, who occupied the other half, has recently passed away. The son inherited the house and wants to continue living there, but needs to rent out the other part. It's perfect for Helen, and the son loves dogs, and gave his blessing for having Ollie there too.

"And here's the best part," Helen says excitedly. "He plays piano, as does his wife, so now we'll be known as the *piano house* of the block! They really like that I play piano too. I've just been so fortunate the way everything is working out, and I have *you* to thank."

Brenda just smiles and shakes her head. Then Helen moves her chair closer to her bed and asks softly, "Did you have the sunglasses with you, you know, when it happened?"

"I don't know. I don't think so, I'm not sure, I don't know," Brenda says. "Caroline brought my car home, and my purse was in the car. She brought it over and the glasses weren't there. I think they're gone." She thinks of telling Helen what Vincent said about letting the sunglasses go, but for some reason she holds back. Even though Helen's really the only person she can tell about communicating with Vincent while in the coma, she keeps it to herself. She suddenly remembers him saying there was another pair, but she's not sure if she's remembering correctly.

Helen sees an odd expression on Brenda's face and doesn't want to upset her, so she doesn't press it. She thinks that if they're gone, maybe it's for the best. She bends over and gives Brenda a hug, telling her how glad everyone is that she's recovering. "You'll be out of here soon, and I can't wait. You can come over for dinner once I'm settled in, and you can meet Ollie."

Brenda's dozing when she hears a tapping on the partially closed door to her room. She opens her eyes to see a young man poking his head in. "May I come in?" he asks.

Brenda doesn't recognize him, and hopes it's not someone from the press. She doesn't say anything, trying to size him up, when he says, "I'm David, I'm the one that gave you CPR."

"Oh, yes! Yes, please come in. I'm so glad you're here. I've been wanting to thank you."

David comes in, feeling suddenly shy as he puts the small paper bag he has with him by her bedside, and sits down. "I'm so happy to see how well you're doing. Last time I saw you, well, you gave us quite a fright. Now, when I think of it, I feel it was some kind of divine intervention that led me and my friend Jerry—that we were sent there to find you. I never saw Jerry run so fast in all the years we've been running together," he laughs. "We're just so glad it wasn't your time, that we were there to help."

"I haven't told anyone this, but I was outside of my body. I watched you giving me CPR. You were so diligent. But I was told to come back," Brenda says through the tears that are now making it difficult to speak. "Thank you again. I hope you know how grateful I am."

Now David is having trouble holding back his emotions, his eyes glassy, on the verge of tears himself. "I think being there, and doing what we did, is the best thing I've ever done in my life. Thank you for coming back. I think I would have been really pissed if you'd given up," he laughs, trying to add some levity. Brenda laughs too, and they continue to talk for over an hour, with her asking him all kinds of questions about his life, trying to get to know him. She doesn't give him a chance to ask about herself, and he respects that. When it's time for him to leave, he takes Brenda's hand and promises to stay in touch. He then notices the paper bag he'd brought and temporarily forgotten about.

Picking it up, he hands it to her and says, "You must've dropped these when you got struck. I found them by the path, up against a tree. When I showed them to my wife, she knew right away what they were, and who you were. She said she read an article about you and saw your photo on the cover of the magazine."

Brenda takes the bag and pulls out Vincent's sunglasses. She looks at them lovingly, then hands them to David, saying, "Here, you keep them. Give them to your wife as a thank you for saving my life."

"Oh, I know they're worth a lot of money," he says. "Are you sure?"

Brenda smiles, and nods as David says, "Thank you so much! Felicity will love these!"

THE END

ACKNOWLEDGMENTS

I would first like to thank my editor extraordinaire, Floyd Largent, who made this book whole; never doubting the essence of the story. His skill and guidance provided to this novice writer, along with his enthusiasm, encouragement and support, were invaluable. He's my hero.

To my Mom, an avid reader from my earliest memories. Thank you for always having books around, the encouragement to read them, and showing me the infinite worlds, they bring us to.

Every one of us has it in them to be a dirt bag or a saint, a genius or a ne'er do well. Thank you to everyone in my life who has shown me this in the best and worst lights. This has provided much inspiration for the best stories. Last but not least, to my assistant muse and partner in everything, John. For being my biggest fan, for brain storming no matter when or where, for love, for laughter, for always having my back.